DATE DUE

		PRINTED IN U.S.A.

THE LAND OF STEADY HABITS

THE LAND

of

STEADY
HABITS

A Novel

TED THOMPSON

Little, Brown and Company

New York Boston London

Little, Brown and Company
Hachette Book Group
237 Park Avenue, New York, NY 10017
littlebrown.com

First Edition: March 2014

Little, Brown and Company is a division of Hachette Book Group, Inc. The Little, Brown name and logo are trademarks of Hachette Book Group, Inc.

The publisher is not responsible for websites (or their content) that are not owned by the publisher.

The Hachette Speakers Bureau provides a wide range of authors for speaking events. To find out more, go to hachettespeakersbureau.com or call (866) 376-6591.

ISBN 978-0-316-18656-8
LCCN 2013954891

10 9 8 7 6 5 4 3 2 1

RRD-C

Book designed by Marie Mundaca

Printed in the United States of America

For Kip and Delia

PART ONE

1

One of the great advantages of Anders's divorce—besides, of course, the end of the squabbling and the sudden guiltless thrill of freedom—was that he no longer had to attend the Ashbys' holiday party. Their party, like all of the parties he'd attended in his marriage, was his wife's domain, and he was relieved to no longer have to show up only to be a disappointment to her friends. In fact, the Ashbys' holiday party had become a sort of emblem of obligation to Anders, a reminder, at the end of his marriage, of the kind of man he'd become, when at last year's party, after three quick whiskeys and a squabble with Helene about their grown children, he'd turned and announced to the room that they hadn't had sex in five months, and, even though he was over sixty, *it wasn't because of his penis either.*

The amazing thing, though, was that after all that, after it was clearly his decision to end the marriage; after he'd left what her friends saw as a perfect woman for a life in a condominium, retired, pretty much alone; after he'd openly scorned them and was sure she'd revealed all of his dirtiest secrets to them over brunch, a card arrived from the Ashbys, as if with the season, inviting him once again to their holiday party.

They held it every year in the week after Thanksgiving to get a jump on the season and, he'd always thought, to claim it as their own. It was the only invitation he'd received, so he brought it inside, set it on his small breakfast table, and ate dinner across from it, staring at the familiar handwriting, the Santa Claus stamp, trying to decide if it was a peace offering or if they'd simply forgotten to take him off their list. Divorce, he'd learned early on, was not so much from your spouse but from all of the things you'd forged as a couple—the home, the parental authority, the good credit, the friends. He pictured Helene in her elegant party clothes holding forth in the Ashbys' kitchen—a brave single woman in a chenille scarf who, after a year of injustice, maintained the dignified poise of a survivor. She would be an honored guest there, a woman who'd spent her career helping adults learn to read and was now forced to face the season alone.

The invitation was stiff and glossy—a photo of the Ashbys in front of their tree. *It's That Time of Year* was all it said, as though if you were receiving this, you had been for twenty years, which, Anders realized, was about right—twenty years of enduring this soiree, and still, after he'd thumbed his nose at the lot of them, after he'd announced to Helene, in the heated mania of a bedtime fight, that the stench of Mitchell Ashby's cigars made him wish he'd been born without a *face*, he'd been invited. He placed the card on his mantel, the Ashbys beaming down at him in cable knits, and settled below them onto the couch.

There was also the issue of the other piece of mail that came that day, a product of that final meeting with the lawyers, when Helene had shown up with a firing squad of attorneys and asked him, without warning, if she could keep the house, and in a moment of regrettable pride, though it was half his net worth and carried a disastrous second mortgage, he'd told her of course she could. Or, as his attorney reminded him, he'd *implied* she could, after she'd implied in front of all those men and women of the law that he'd been anything but a man of responsibility. What he'd actually done was put his palms on the table, lean toward Helene and her posse of lawyers in rimless spectacles, and say, "The *house?* All you want's the goddamn *house?*"

The trouble was that he had planned to use the money from the house to pay for his early retirement. He could afford the house or he could afford to retire, but he couldn't afford both. This put him in the uncomfortable position of having to admit to Helene what had become her biggest grievance: that he had chosen himself over everyone else, that he had thrown them all under the bus. Which wasn't true. Which, if you considered the college educations of their grown sons and the house he had mortgaged up to his eye sockets and the extravagant kitchen she had insisted on building *after* their children were gone, all of which he had paid for, all of which he had worked his rump off to provide for *them*—his family, his brood, his paramount responsibility—was downright insane. He had done everything they asked of him, and he had done it for them. What else in the world could she possibly want?

Well, the house, as it turned out. So now the letters were piling up, ominous things with yellow forwarding stickers over the address windows and language that was quite explicit: he had until the end of the year before the bank brought in a judge. It was a situation that could be cleared up with a single phone call to Helene, an opportunity, really, to come clean and admit he'd bluffed—the right thing if ever there was a right thing—if

5

he could just find the moment when she wasn't so fragile and he could stomach her disappointment in him, when it didn't feel like a single piece of bad news might be enough to send her away for good.

What it all meant, at least in terms of the Ashbys' holiday party, was that he should probably have a shirt cleaned.

◆

As it was his first party as a single man, it surprised him how cordial he could be, how confident, crunching alone up the Ashbys' wide, candlelit path; nodding at some acquaintances as they passed him; removing his coat and hanging it on the rack and turning to a room of rosy faces, their chatter rising over Harry Connick Jr., voices familiar; making his way across the living room, past the mantel full of teepeed cards, his eyes falling across their handsome photographs — a golden retriever, some newlyweds, a ten-year-old in a soccer uniform.

Before he could get to the bar, Lydia Hickman had spotted him and was motioning eagerly to have Anders join her. Lydia had been an intimate member of his wife's support system during the divorce — a coffee-getter who had been through two divorces herself and who, Anders always imagined, had strong opinions about the incompatibility of men and women. She was standing with four others, some of whom Anders had met before but couldn't recall where.

"So how have you *been?*" said Lydia, her eyes wide.

Anders glanced around the circle of faces. He was the first of his peers to retire, and he could feel he was being tested. The truth was he had proceeded as planned — selling his un-needed furniture, buying a condo and a decent TV, repainting, getting his green square of lawn ready for spring. The truth was he enjoyed his time alone, his three mugs of coffee during his morning shows, his lengthy shower, the long daytime hours of walks and mail and raking. "I'm getting involved with charity," he said.

"Wonderful," said Lydia. They waited for him to continue but he had a moment of self-awareness and couldn't.

"Which one?" someone asked.

"Disease," he said. "Cancer."

Lydia nodded gravely and a strange silence fell over them. That word had a tidy way of ending conversations.

"So what do you do?" said a man. He wore French cuffs and a tie with a muscular Windsor. Anders could feel him angling for familiar cocktail banter, the sort of sniffing of butts that he had sworn off with his retirement.

"He's *retired*," said Lydia.

"Oh," the man said. "Lucky dog."

"From Springer Financial," she said.

"Oh," said the man. "You left Springer? I mean, you're still young. Aren't you?"

Lydia, intrigued, turned to hear his answer to this one.

"Am I young?" said Anders.

"Yeah," he said. "I mean, it's early, isn't it?"

This was the topic his older son had coached him to avoid, the one he'd sat Anders down in the weeks immediately following the divorce and, as if in an intervention, begged him not to broach in public. "Even if everything you're saying is true," Tommy had said, "you can't rant. It makes people uncomfortable. You seem…"

"*Crazy?* Is that the word you're looking for?"

"Assholey."

7

But the tirades came out of him, like the lie about the charity had, in ways that at first seemed appropriate. They had asked him about his retirement, his career, his decisions, hadn't they? They wanted to know why he had turned his back on a life that was so similar to theirs. And so out it came: the reddening of his face and the raised volume of his voice, the mounting extremity of his language.

"The guys at the top are crooks," he was saying to Lydia and her inquisitive friend. "They're not in it for the client, they're in it for themselves. And let me tell you something, Paul, they *have* to be. That's become the industry—save yourself, outsmart the other guy, don't worry about the consequences. That's the corporate ethos and if it doesn't make you sick, you might want to think about having your head examined. Because it's not just the banks, it's everything, Paul, it's a system of monstrous greed—and for *what?* More toys? Bigger houses? Trips to the goddamn Caribbean?"

It wasn't really him, Helene had said after a similar outburst at last year's party; it was like a child throwing a *tantrum.* If he actually listened to himself, he wouldn't be able to follow it. First the problem was the banks, then the lawyers, then their town, then every single person who lived there. Nothing was spared. It was all scorched earth. "I just don't understand where it's all coming from," she had said. "It's all so *extreme.*"

"I'm not going to hide how I feel."

"Anders, you hide your feelings about as well as an infant."

"So I should just be like Mitchell, is that it, buy myself a giant boat and join that conversation about bilge pumps?"

She shook her head. "I don't understand why you're so unhappy. I mean, look at yourself—what could you possibly want?"

This, of course, was exactly it—even when he'd calmed down and could think with a clear head, he had no real answer. The question was more like, What did *she* want? They had two boys with impressive degrees, and grandkids who went horse-back riding. His bonus last year was more than he'd made in his first decade at work. Were they supposed to become one of those couples who travel all the time and send Christmas cards of themselves on camelback or, worse, buy a condo in Charleston and fill it with art? It must be terrible, she'd said that night in bed, to do everything right, to play the game so by the book and still find yourself unhappy. Maybe he should talk to a professional to figure out where this was coming from. Maybe all this anger was just rooted in the fact that he was confused.

"Confused? What could that even mean—*confused?* Confused about *what?*"

"Honey, it's a nice way of saying 'fucked up.'"

When he finished talking, he was out of breath, and Lydia Hickman was staring into her wine. It was a moment Anders knew well, so he also knew his audience would split off in different directions—for the bathroom, the bar, another more urgent conversation—and as they did, he stood alone, drinkless, listening to the shrill cheeriness around him and searching for a way to quietly escape.

Which was when he saw Monster, the Ashbys' bushy golden retriever, curled on the back deck. There was his excuse—go out, pet Monster, and slip away to his car. He found his parka on the rack and grinned mildly at anyone who caught his eye as he made his way through the sliding glass door and into the icy evening air. When he'd closed the door behind him, he heard giggles from beneath the deck and an urgent whisper: "Guys,

9

guys, someone's here," followed by a waft of reefer so potent it nearly made his eyes water.

Anders leaned over the railing to see the shadow of three prep-schoolers with shaggy and terrible hair. They reminded him immediately of Preston, his younger son, whom they had sent away to St. Paul's for the individualized attention but who had come home each Thanksgiving and June taller, more unkempt, more broodingly silent, his face a puffy red mess. It wasn't until his senior year, when the school discovered a four-foot bong in his room and tossed him, and Helene insisted they check him into a rehab facility against his will and search his entire room for clues—reading his old love letters from camp, his yearbook inscriptions, and finding only one unopened box of aging condoms—that Anders realized his failing as a father: it wasn't that he couldn't provide, for he gave his boys everything; it was that he knew nothing of them, nothing of their internal lives, and though he was their sole male role model, doling out advice each week over the phone, he had never even attempted to ask.

The boys held their hands behind their backs and pretended to be cool.

"Yo," said one of the boys from the shadows. "What's going on?"

"Just getting some fresh air. It's warm in there." They all nodded as if Anders had said something very wise. "What are you guys smoking?"

They froze. One toed the gravel.

"Relax, I'm not going to tell."

"Seriously?" said the tall one in the middle. "Because if you're one of my dad's friends who he sent to narc on me, then you can go back and tell him he's really predictable and sad because we were just looking at the constellations."

"Charlie?"

There was a pause. "Who is that?"

"It's Anders."

The boy stepped forward from the shadows, squinting. "Christ."

"Look, don't worry. I'm not one of your dad's friends, first of all, and second of all…" He couldn't think of a *second of all.* The first was true, and he had surprised himself with it: What else did the kid need to know? "Anyway," said Anders. "Enjoy your constellations."

"Wait, dude," said Charlie. "Come down here for a second."

Anders went down the stairs and onto the dark packed dirt beneath the deck. The boys were taller than he'd thought, all of them meeting his eye.

"You know me, but that's Arnie and that's Gorbachev," he said, fiddling with something that looked like a small, deflated basketball. "So what d'you mean, you're not friends?"

"I'm not. I mean, I was. And my wife is. Ex-wife, sorry. She's their friend. I can't stand them. Really, I find your parents unbearable."

Charlie let out a laugh and went back to the thing in his hands—a mini-pumpkin, it turned out. After a moment he glanced up again. "Seriously?"

Helene had met Sophie Ashby in a prenatal fitness class, five strangers in the shallow end at the Y doing a workout so low impact, she called it "manatee hour." When the babies came and Helene found herself with two tyrants in diapers and the demands of a career, it was Sophie who, according to Helene, kept her from losing her mind. They started a playgroup, trading off tantrum duty and daytime PBS, and by pre-K, carpool drop-off became a respite of coffee and chitchat, and on Fridays a splash of wine, with Sophie indulging in two drags of a cigarette before stubbing it out in a potted plant while the kids ran rampant and Helene savored the thirty minutes that she was responsible only for her shiraz.

By the time Charlie came along, thirteen years after his sister, Samantha, the children of the playgroup had retreated behind the closed doors of their bedrooms, and all the hand-me-downs had long ago trickled to Nicaragua. Although everything about Charlie's birth appeared to be an accident, he was, in fact, a miracle of progesterone and planning, a little bundle of joy born to a woman of forty-four and into her circle of love-starved friends. He was passed around for babysits and his bassinet was given a space at the table during dinner parties, where he was as quiet and pleasant-smelling as a candle. When Samantha became Sam and buzzed her hair and had a bar jammed through the soft skin under her lower lip, Charlie was in the Cub Scouts with an adorable little neckerchief. And when Sam moved out to Seattle—always too poor or too busy to fly home; likely a lesbian; even more likely a vegan; her only regular communication with her family the poorly copied issues of a magazine she'd created, a jumble of cartoons and words that bled right off the page that neither Mitchell nor Sophie could make any sense of—Charlie would sit on the sofa in the living room and regale dinner guests with an impersonation of his gym teacher, his legs crossed exactly like his dad's.

To say he was spoiled wasn't quite right—he was simply given everything: a Gameboy he bowed his head to at the restaurant table, and sneakers with wheels embedded in the heels. And when those things failed to please him, his parents capitulated and bought him a box turtle that they knew would live forever and that he used to set loose at inopportune times so that, at least once, a dinner guest was sent shrieking from the bathroom.

"You know how to rip one of these?" he said, holding up the pumpkin. There was a Bic pen jammed into the side of it and a trough hollowed out that he'd filled with pot.

"I don't even know what that is."

"This," he said, "is resourceful."

Curiously enough, the last time Anders had participated in this ritual was several years ago on a vacation he and Helene had taken with Charlie's parents. Not four hours into their stay in a Costa Rican villa, Mitchell Ashby had produced rolling papers and a dime bag to go along with the afternoon tea. The vacation, it seemed, gave him permission to revert to the habits he'd formed in prep school, habits he'd had to give up with their firstborn. Anders had felt as helpless then, when he was asked to roll the thing and spilled most of the delicate leaves on the glass countertop, as he did now, with the contraption held in front of his face and his new friends staring at him with calm expectancy.

It was hard to describe the efficiency of what followed—the hurricane of drug that entered his lungs and the brutal eruption of coughing that ensued—but by the time he'd pulled himself together, the boys had all cracked wide, knowing grins.

"How's the party upstairs?" Charlie asked, blowing a hit casually out of the corner of his mouth. "Real rager?"

Anders liked Charlie. He was a smart kid. He was hilarious.

"How're you feeling, Anders?"

"I feel great. Joyful. And sad. So sad. Jesus, sadder than I've ever felt before."

"Yeah," said Charlie.

"This grass is serious," said Anders.

"Nah," he said. "That's the PCP."

They all nodded, somber themselves.

"Wait, what?" Anders said. Charlie blinked at him with yellow, rheumy eyes. "We just smoked PCP?"

Charlie shrugged. "We don't technically know what it is. It's more of a blend."

Anders wasn't even sure exactly what PCP was, though he knew it was serious and likely addictive, which made him more distraught, seeing himself for a moment spending Christmas at the men's shelter, waiting in line with his cafeteria tray for a processed-turkey dinner served to him, sympathetically, by Helene's community-minded friends. "I have to get back to the party."

"Have at it," said Charlie.

Reaching the top of the deck stairs, Anders realized why he had come—it wasn't, of course, to interact with these people, but to see Helene, to talk privately with her about the party, about his isolation, to come clean with his lie about the house and tell her about the stupid thing he'd just done. Looking through the sliding glass door, he surveyed the party, the clumps of people and their muted conversations, all men without suit coats and women in wool; searching for Helene, whom he found, standing tall and proud with a glass of red.

He was startled by a knock on the glass and Mitchell Ashby's face, hands cupped around his eyes, on the other side. He rumbled the door open and smacked a hand on Anders's shoulder. "What're you doing out here, buddy?"

"Getting some fresh air."

He held Anders's elbow and lowered his voice. "Well, I am so happy to see you," he said. "It's been a big year." He sighed. "A big year. But it wouldn't have been the same without you."

"Thanks."

"So, listen, I was actually looking for my son. He disappeared earlier and that's cause for worry." He grinned at Anders, who was watching Mitchell's constricting pupils. Pupils, he suddenly realized, were remarkable.

"He was supposed to be in his room studying. Kid failed three of his exams, *three* of them, so I had to make some calls to the school." He shook his head. "Phases," he said. "Right now he's entering one I call 'brain-dead.'"

Anders was watching Helene over Mitchell's shoulder. She had gathered a crowd, probably telling a joke. She told great jokes.

"I mean, it's a different world." Mitchell held a lit cigar with a curled index finger, as if it were the trigger of a gun. He spit something from the tip of his tongue. "They got the Internet, and they got amphetamines, and even though it kills me that I can't do anything about it, I tell him he has to be *careful.*"

Anders heard a door click shut beneath them. Charlie had been listening the entire time.

"Did you hear about that kid who sucked down all that ecstasy and leaped from his dorm window in a loincloth? I mean, this is *real.* And since I can't be up there every waking second, when he's home I have to lay down the law. It's a real battle, a real battle."

Mitchell shook his head and stared at the deck flooring.

"I mean, Christ—what am I talking about? You know better than anyone. After age ten, they're all pathological liars. They'll bankrupt us. When Samantha was at Smith, you know what they were charging? And for what? The pleasure of teaching her to hate everything I stand for?" He puffed on his cigar. "How did you get through it? Seriously, with yours. Was there

15

a program—did they drag him into the woods or something? I mean, I look back on what you guys went through and I'm astounded." He shook his head. "But it worked out, that's what matters, am I right? It worked out."

Anders stared at him.

"Anyway," Mitchell said finally. "The more important question is, How are you?"

"Excuse me," Anders said, the words coming to him like a blessing as he stepped around Mitchell for the house.

It was somewhere into his third stride that he thought he saw what he'd hoped he wouldn't and what, even a few hours before, he'd thought was hugely improbable, when he'd put on his first dry-cleaned shirt in six months and slapped some spicy stuff on his neck and had a moment of panic that Helene might have a date with her. Inside, she was chatting politely with a stranger, nodding and smiling, the fingers of her right hand interlaced with the fingers of the man next to her, Anders's mother's emerald ring protruding from that mess of fingers like a piece of costume jewelry.

Earlier that week, they'd had lunch in the back of a health-food store, behind aisles of puffed wheat and earth-scented vitamins, where you could sit at a thick country table and talk beneath the fluttering of Chopin for hours. It was there that Anders had first wanted to express his regret, where he'd wanted to tell her about the hours of CNBC he now watched, or about how much he looked forward to the mail, or about how he was thrilled the other morning to wake up and discover he had run out of cranberry juice, which meant he could make a trip to the store, which meant his morning had purpose. He'd wanted to tell her this, and about how terrified he was that he'd made the wrong decision, that the life he'd had before—the one that he'd rejected so vehemently; the one that he'd rushed to get out of after he'd decided it was them, his family, his children, his wife, who were making him so miserable; that it was *their* problem, not his, and if he could just get himself alone, away from all their demands and his absurd sense of duty, then he could be okay—*that* life, he'd wanted to tell her, was in fact the one for him.

But when he asked her, out of courtesy, how she was, she lit up around a mouthful of tuna salad and told him how happy she was, how at first she didn't think she'd ever get through it but now the divorce and the lawyers and the moving trucks and the boxes of anniversary gifts all seemed so far away, and she thought she finally got it, that Anders may have been right all along, that the divorce was what was best for both of them. He'd thought about asking her then if she'd met someone, but all of this had come at him so quickly and so unexpectedly that all he could do was force a smile, finish his old-time seltzer, and tell her how happy he was for her.

Now it all made sense. He'd expected his wife to eventually take in an unmarried guy, just as she'd collected other wounded birds her whole life—sad divorcées and AA spiritualists and incessant complainers with fibromyalgia. He knew her well enough to realize that. But still he needed to talk to her. He needed to get it straight, the whole story—how long it'd been going on, how serious it was, if there was any chance she loved this guy. He pushed through, into the hot party.

"Excuse me," he found himself saying to the man's back. It was higher than Anders's, and meaty. No one seemed to hear him. "*Excuse* me," he said again.

In the way that familiar faces are often too close to place, he knew the man who turned around, though it took him a pro-tracted moment to place him.

"Donny?"

"Holy cow," the man said, holding out a huge hand for An-ders to shake. "Look who it is."

"I don't get it" was all he could manage, though it came out more hurt than he'd intended it to and sent them both into a solemn, awkward silence.

"Anders," said Helene. "Let's get a refill."

She went to the bar, stirred some bourbon with ice, came back, handed it to him, and settled into an empty sofa. "Sit," she said.

Donny leaned on the arm beside her, leaving Anders the rest of the couch. The three of them faced forward, staring at the matte screen of a television. Helene turned to him and sighed. "Go ahead and ask," she said. "Get it out."

"How long?" was all Anders could think to say.

"A few months."

"Months," he said, cataloging everything he could remem-ber—there was Emma's horse show and OSU-Michigan and Thanksgiving, Jesus, Thanksgiving. Had Donny been there, at his dinner table, while Anders was all the way down in DC eating from a TV tray in his nephew's suspiciously damp Georgetown apartment? Had Donny met the grandchildren? Had the *grandchildren* known?

He turned to Donny. It was startling how much of Donny had settled into his belly, all that upper body now a pillow for his big team ring.

"You live here now?"

Donny glanced at Helene. "I'm looking for a place."

"Moving!" said Anders.

"Donny was just transferred to the city."

"How about that. And you're still married?"

"I was never married."

"That's right. You just sleep with married people."

Helene turned so her face was only a few inches from Anders's. Whatever he'd smoked was a serious narcotic. He felt as though he were drooling down his chin. "Please," she said. "Don't."

He took a slug of his drink. "Don't *what.*"

Helene shook her head in a way that Anders knew meant she was leaving the party, and he'd be the one to stay to the very end, drinking awkwardly with her friends. She lowered her voice. "Look around you," she said. "Do you notice the people here?"

The rest of the room seemed somehow very far away.

"They're too polite to say it, Anders, but they're wondering why you're here."

"I was invited," he said.

Her face fell into an expression of pity.

"*Everyone's* invited."

Even though he suddenly knew that was absolutely true, and even though he felt his dike of composure beginning to give way to a tide of humiliation, he didn't say anything.

"What?" she said. "You think this is *funny?*"

He shook his head, but it was too late. He was laughing and wasn't going to be able to stop.

She leaned in very close. "You were the one who wanted space," she whispered. He nodded vigorously, as if to say, *I know, I know,* but she was already off. "I am so through with this crap, Anders, I am *done.* It's not my job to babysit you anymore." She shook her head. "Why would you come here?" she

19

said. "You're not welcome. These people are not your friends. I mean, you were the one who wanted out, so for God fucking sake, get *out*."

He knew it would hurt like hell tomorrow morning when he reconstructed her words as best he could in his head, listening to the exact way she'd enunciated *welcome*, as in, "You're not wel-comb," trying to figure out if what she was saying was that he had no right to be mad or that he had no right to be there at all—trying to determine if his desire to hold her squirming against his chest as he had the night her mother died was during or after their little talk—and he knew he looked like a crazy person, giggling as someone scolded him, his eyes red, his drink mostly gone, and there was nothing he could imagine that would sober him at this point, until Mitchell Ashby came through the living room dragging Charlie by his armpits across the hardwood floors, yelling angrily for an ambulance. Charlie's face was gray, his neck slack beneath his bushy head. Within seconds some doctors had gathered and pulled him out of the room with most of the party following, and it seemed a few seconds later the living room was filled with the eerie flashes of emergency vehicles, the scratchy voices on their radios cutting through the house like the Morse code of an urgent message.

The two other boys stood in the kitchen doorway on the opposite side of the room, watching with their mouths open. Helene got up and ran to see if she could help, and before long, as Charlie was being slid into the fat back of the ambulance, Helene had her hand on Sophie Ashby, who, with her broom-handle arms and blow-dried hair, looked to Anders more like a scarecrow than ever. After the ambulance had pulled away and the truck idling had disappeared, along with the party's hosts, some grabbed their coats as if to leave and then milled around the foyer, suddenly uncomfortable with abandoning a house that had just been plunged into distress before their very eyes. A team of helpers had started cleaning up, making quick trips to the kitchen garbage with fists of soiled napkins and plastic cups bloodied with wine, and soon the foyer guests joined them, their own fur coats open and purses hanging off them as they cleaned and cleaned the room, until finally someone opened the stereo cabinet and politely killed the music.

2

To hear her tell it, and she often did, it was a miracle that Anders and Helene had ever met in college, much less fallen in love, because, as a scholarship kid besieged with scholarship duties — dish scraping and book filing and towel folding — Anders spent every moment he wasn't wearing an apron sequestered in a bubble of academic determination. Though he liked the halo of hard work her story put over him — especially later, when they would be, say, sitting with people around a wicker table at a beach home on the Cape and he could feel the others pause to consider, for the briefest moment, how much of any of this they had honestly earned — it wasn't completely true. Not that Helene had invented it. The facts, in her abridged version, were right. It was just that a few important details had been omitted, details he'd never discussed with Helene but that, like all unspoken things, contained the real truth — namely, that he wasn't actually a scholarship kid, at least not in the way she'd implied, and also that he'd known who she was from the moment he'd arrived on campus.

He first saw her perched on a high stool and wearing a name tag that was filled from edge to edge with bright block letters. As the Info Girl, her primary job was to greet visitors, most of whom had just made the unpleasant trek up to coastal Maine in the off-season, and hand them brochures with glossy collages of lobster boats and seminar rooms and the quad at the height of autumn. She smiled at just about every single person on campus, including an endless stream of lonely men—fellow students, yes, but also kitchen staff, grounds crew, assistant coaches of most major sports—who hung around the info desk with a regularity even Anders noticed, trying, it seemed, to exhaust her unusually deep wells of patience. She was polite to them and she was beautiful, elevated on her stool in the middle of the middle of campus, all of which meant Anders, who had found himself staring at her in the mayhem of registration and had told his roommate that she was "sirenic," went well out of his way to avoid her.

He had chosen Bowdoin, a speck of a college on the scribble of the Maine coast, because they had given him full work-study regardless of the fact that his father, a judge in Fayetteville, North Carolina, could have bought his way onto the trustees' table during the school's annual lobster bake. Instead, Anders had saved for even his bus ticket and had shown up on campus that first August astounded by the tall evergreens and the ancient chapel and the peninsulas that ran for miles into the Atlantic on nothing but pine needles.

They'd placed him on a floor of hockey players, guys from Nashua, New Hampshire, and Tewksbury, Massachusetts, and Digby, Nova Scotia; guys like his roommate, who kept a tin of dip in the pocket of his shirt and whose accent was thick as a fish-stick commercial and who worked summers tarring cracks on the state highways—guys who generally seemed more in need of aid than a southern kid who'd slept on sheets that'd been ironed by a domestic employee. But he'd submitted his financial aid as an independent, no mention of parents, and his name miraculously had been on the list at the work-study meeting, so he was able to pass, on the dish line or the grounds crew, as another kid working his way through school.

Because the truth was, he did need the money. His father, Judge Portis Hill, was a stern man who, after his first two sons had so disappointed him by becoming physicians, would tolerate only one kind of life for his youngest, what he referred to as "a calling to the law," which was a fancy way of saying a life exactly like his. By the time he was thirteen, Anders was so tired of hearing about the importance of American jurisprudence that he intentionally flunked the entrance exams of every major prep school in the South—one of them so spectacularly that the headmaster had called Judge Hill with concerns that his boy was retarded.

These stunts, as his father called them, soon became the stuff of legend in Fayetteville, where the clerks in every store knew Anders's full name, a development that forced Judge Hill to respond in the only way he knew how—by making more rules. If Anders was going to smile to his face and then turn around and humiliate his family by pretending to be a retard, then there would be no imperfect grades, no athletics, no movies, no dances, no long walks home, no locked bathroom doors, no unclean plates, no blue jeans or comic books or music of any kind. It was all an attempt, of course, to force Anders back to whatever prep school would still take him, but neither he nor his father would budge. If he hadn't been mandated to sit on the stiff living-room furniture with his schoolwork in front of him every moment the old man was home, and if he hadn't been banned from whittling rabbits, nice basswood figures he'd spent hours on in his room, he likely would have relented eventually and headed off to meet his fate at Wood-berry Forest. But instead, he ran away.

He didn't get far—his friend Spencer's room on the other side of the state highway—but after the night he spent tossing on Spencer's chilly floor, everything changed. Judge Hill, at his wife's urging, decided to disengage from his youngest entirely. For Anders, there was surprisingly little difference between his father engaged and his father disengaged, except that now during meals his father would reach across him for the salt and talk right over him and leave the table cluttered with dishes for Anders to bus. But that wasn't so bad, because Anders no longer had to do anything for school, it turned out, so long as he didn't ask his father for so much as a pencil. So when the time finally came, he applied to college without speaking a word to his parents, writing away to schools as far north as he could find and accepting an offer from one whose name they wouldn't know how to pronounce.

And so began the project of remaking himself. This meant working—for the college, yes, but also at a pancake house in town, where he picked up dishwashing shifts, and at an inn out in Harpswell, where he spent the weekends changing the linens and running the graveyard shift—all of which were time-consuming and menial but soon became a compulsion for him, necessary, as though the harder he worked on jobs that, as a judge's son, he should never have had to take, the farther away all of the expectations of that life became. His days stretched for eighteen and twenty hours, during which he shoveled walkways or laid sod or sprayed scalding-hot water on dishes that were glued with syrup, and while he made enough money to eat, he had little to say to his classmates, much less to the only daughter of an orthopedic surgeon from Wellesley, Massachusetts, who was already surrounded by men.

That is, until he got back to his dorm one night and she was sitting on his sofa. She was wearing old sweatpants and a green track T-shirt that was worn down to its final gauzy threads. Her hair was loose and she was hugging her knees, which had a can of beer held between them. Normally his manners would have compelled him to introduce himself, but he had been working at the inn since Friday night and now that it was technically Sunday morning, he had the energy only to walk past her, pull off his boots, and collapse into the chair at his desk.

"Are you asleep?" she asked eventually.

He shook his head, but it wasn't until he heard the sound of the toilet flushing that he opened his eyes.

"Are you here with Donny?"

"Um"—she glanced around as though checking to see who was listening—"it's not official or anything."

Anders slumped back in his chair. "He didn't tell me."

"I'm Helene."

"I know."

She smiled. "You're reading my favorite book." She gestured to a paperback edition of *Middlemarch* on his desk, easily the fattest book he'd been assigned.

"I didn't actually read that."

She drained the rest of her beer. "Where are you from?"

"Because I haven't read *Middlemarch*?"

"Because I'm trying to be polite."

Anders smiled. "North Carolina."

"Long way from home. You miss it?"

"God, no," he said. It was the first time anyone had suggested such a thing. "I hate it there."

She blinked a few times with a warm sort of smile, as though he'd just confessed something deeply intimate. "When people say things like that they're usually just talking about their parents."

Anders raised his eyebrows. "You should start charging for this."

"Funny," she said without seeming amused. "That's exactly what Donny said."

"Roommates," said Anders and they both nodded.

The door opened and Donny was standing there in a Bowdoin Hockey sweatshirt. Helene stood up. "Good night, southern boy. Dream of tobacco fields."

"I told you," he said after they'd shut the bedroom door. "I hate that place."

When she came by the next day to bring Donny his sweatshirt, she asked Anders how he was doing with a kind little grimace, as though there were some sort of ailment he were battling, an ailment that, as the semester wore on and his work piled up, seemed to grow inside of him. He had classmates and dorm mates and coworkers—indeed, he was surrounded by people all day—yet none of it felt real. Late at night he would wake up convinced he was tucked into his ironed sheets and listening to the pulse of cicada through the screens. It took a moment to recognize the hiss of the steam radiators and the stink of Donny's practice socks drying on the irons, and to remember, in a terrible moment, that he was alone in the North. It was Helene, his roommate's new girl, who had seen it before she even knew him and who had, when he took a detour by the info desk later that week to say hello, suggested he stop working so much, take a day off, and go skiing or something.

"I don't ski," he said.

"Oh, it's not hard," she said. "I could teach you in fifteen minutes."

It was finals week and the campus was clearing out, and Donny, he knew, would be on a bus back to Nashua by Thursday. "How's Friday morning?" he said.

The drive to Sunday River was about two hours on narrow country roads that wound up into the sparse interior of the state, where even the barns seemed abandoned for winter and the motto Vacationland was only a cruel reminder of the lives on the other side of Route 1. He brought along his wool hat and his copy of *Middlemarch*, which he was actually enjoying, but everything else down to the long underwear had been borrowed. He spent the morning trying to snowplow at Helene's instructions and the afternoon trying to mask his frustration every time his skis popped off and he ended up Supermanned in the middle of Easy Street. Learning to ski, it turned out, was an activity better done in private, and it was hard to pretend that crashing was a hoot after he could no longer bend his knee. Helene of course was a beautiful skier, which he finally saw in full form as she carved off down the hill, looking for a medic who could retrieve Anders with a sled.

The knee wasn't anything as serious as the daughter of an orthopedic surgeon might fear, but it did require that he limp to the car and put his arm around her neck while she eased him into the front seat. The real problem—the ailment that, it turned out, had actually been growing inside him during the three sleepless months he had been in the North—started with a tickle in the throat that, after he'd spent an entire day face-planting in the snow, became a violent cough that seemed to be kicking at his chest from the inside. By the time they made it back, he was burning up, and she put her hand on his fore-head and his cheek and told him that she felt terrible, that the whole skiing thing was all her stupid idea, and could she at least make him a cup of tea, which she did while he curled up on her dorm-room couch. "There," she said as he blew on the steaming mug and took a sip. "Does that feel better?" He stayed three days.

He knew all the laws regarding roommates and girls, but in his defense, he did have pneumonia and the flu at the same time, and he did stay confined to the couch, almost entirely unconscious, and when Helene did finally kiss him, it was only on the forehead during the height of a fever so he was never entirely sure if he'd dreamed it. All of which Anders would gladly relay to Donny, even though Donny had told him noth-ing about his pursuit of Helene, had in fact kept it all quite hidden in a way Anders found thoroughly shady. But regard-less, he remained in her room instead of returning to his own, a detail that was hard to explain, as was her staying awake at night to read to him from *Middlemarch*.

He woke at dawn after the third night, the sky lightening from navy to white and a blade of pink light burning the eaves across the quad. He cracked open the window, and the coastal air washed over him, a mix of salt and smoke and spruce. In a few hours she would be up to check his temperature and put a cool rag on his forehead and look at him with a squint of sympathy that was so imbued with affection it made him grin like an idiot. It turned out his fever was back up to 103. He needed more care, she told him, from a doctor, and he needed a real bed. The dorms would be closing soon and she had to get home for her own holiday in Wellesley, so it was understandable, at least rationally, that during his subsequent

29

sleep, she called his house in Fayetteville and spoke to his father.

He would pay to hear a recording of that telephone conversation, to hear how Helene had introduced herself to his mother, how his mother had responded, how Helene had explained the predicament—that Anders was too sick to ride the bus and certainly too sick for an airplane—and, once his mother went to fetch his father, as he was certain she did, to hear what Judge Hill had said to this strange girl who had his runaway son on her sofa. In her defense, he hadn't yet told her much of anything about his life at home, and so, as most people from functional families do, she'd made the assumption that his parents were worried about where he was.

"You did *what?*" Anders said when he woke up.

"He was very nice. As soon as he heard you were sick, he said he'd be right here."

"Here? He's coming *here?*"

"He said he'll call from the airport in Portland."

"I have to go," said Anders, sitting up and searching around for his things.

"Just relax. He thanked me for calling. He seemed, I don't know, relieved."

Anders shook his head. "You don't understand. This is exactly what he's been waiting for. I'm never coming back here."

"Anders. How would you know if you haven't *spoken* with him?"

"I need you to take me to the bus station."

She shook her head. "Your dad's already on his way."

"How could you *do* this to me?" Anders said and erupted into a fit of coughing. She kept her arms crossed until he caught his breath.

"Where did you think you were going for the holidays?" she said.

"Nowhere."

She stared at him.

"The YMCA in Bath."

"Oh, Anders."

"I have to work."

She shook her head. "This is a much better plan."

Within hours his duffel was packed and his hair was combed and his father was standing in the middle of his roommate's girlfriend's room, which suddenly seemed cluttered with candles and cheap, unswept rugs. Judge Hill wore the same thing year-round—a cotton sweater between his tie and jacket—and his face remained slack regardless of circumstances, so the only indication of his mood was in the angle of his flocculent eyebrows. He kept cedar blocks in his drawers, so he smelled of wool and wood and a sharp lotion Anders could never identify but that smelled as though his father went to the wet bar each morning in his undershirt and slapped some whiskey on his jaw. He had arrived without a hat or a coat, the toes of his wing tips stained by snow, and, even after a flight, with a crease so firmly ironed in his slacks it seemed sharp enough to cut you.

"These all your things?" his father said.

"Yes, sir."

Judge Hill looked at the duffel and then seemed to take in the rest of the room.

"Can I get you anything?" said Helene. "Some tea, maybe?"

She gestured to a bookshelf, where two mugs she had borrowed from the dining hall sat, discolored from a semester of instant coffee. Beside them were a collection of ceramic animals, squirrels and chipmunks and the like, that she collected and rearranged in different familial scenes that seemed to please her immensely.

Judge Hill stared at the shelf. "Thank you, but I believe we'd better be on our way."

"It's too bad it's such a dreary night," she said. "It's really a beautiful campus."

"I'm sure it is."

"You'll have to come back in the fall. It's spectacular. Have you told him about the lobster bake?"

Anders stared at her.

"It's amazing. The whole school sits at these long tables and everyone has one of those plastic bibs on, even the president, and there's a band—what's it called? The music with the trumpet and the bow ties?"

"Tin pan," said Anders.

"Yeah, it's a school tradition—they have a *tin-pan* band playing this happy oompah music with banjos and—"

"I know what it is," said Judge Hill.

"Right," said Helene. "Well, it's a nice place."

"I'm sure," said his father and looked at her for a long moment. "Thank you for your help," he said, and he turned and left.

When he was gone she gave Anders a shove on the shoulder. "He's so southern!"

Anders rolled his eyes. "He isn't known for his conversation."

"He misses you. You can tell by the way he looks at you."

"Okay."

"*You* can't see it, but it's plain as day."

"I appreciate that."

"Your father loves you," Helene said and Anders kissed her fully on the mouth.

In retrospect, especially that which is afforded by forty years, everything was clear. It would have seemed, through the next two days he and his father spent on I-95, with Anders in a heap in the backseat of the rental car, listening to the insistent rhythm of the road, that he'd completely blown it. He'd misread all the cues—she was an only child with parents who were still married to each other, destined already for one of the helping professions. He thought of the way she spoke to those guys with the stains on their shirts and the bits of toilet paper still stuck to their necks from shaving. It was the same way she spoke to her ceramic squirrel when she thought no one was listening: her attention had nothing to do with the person. He thought again and again about her look of panic and confusion after he'd kissed her, the firmness of her push on his belly as she stepped away. Donny was a six-four defenseman on the hockey squad who, surprisingly, could talk your ear off about the Battle of the Bulge, and what was Anders? Another lonely guy confusing her kindness with interest.

They stopped at a diner in New Jersey, Anders's face hot from sleep and imprinted with the rented Pontiac's upholstery.

"Tell me something," his father said from behind his menu. It was the first time either of them had spoken in hours. "How do you pay for that school?"

"Why?"

"I looked it up. It's expensive."

"I rob banks, Dad."

His father turned a big plastic page.

"Scholarships, mostly."

"They pay for it."

"Yes, sir. Most of it."

"And how did you convince them to do a thing like that?"

33

"Why does it matter?"

"Because I had a conversation recently with Douglas Knight."

"I don't know who that is."

"He's the president of Duke University and he says he'll take your northern credits."

Anders took a deep breath and shook his head. "Not interested."

His father dropped his menu. "Tell me, what is it about Bowdoin that's worth working yourself until you're infirm?"

"It's pronounced 'Boh-din.' "

"Let me explain something to you," his father said abruptly. "You can run around and pretend to be whoever you want. I don't care—you can change your whole name. But one of these days the thing you're going to need more than anything else is a sense of being. A home. And you can't invent that out of thin air. It's already been given to you. It's where you were born, and like it or not, it's who you are."

Anders stared at him. Judge Hill settled back into reading the menu.

"Your appointment with President Knight is in the second week of January."

Anders walked out of the restaurant.

He spent that break sitting with Miss Rose by her ironing station in the basement of his house in North Carolina, watching her make astonishingly swift work of a basket of fitted sheets. She was in her sixties, at least a decade older than either of his parents, and nearly six feet tall, solid, with arthritic knuckles and a stare from behind her bifocals that could stop Anders cold. She would never let him help with any of her work but he enjoyed being around it, as he had as a kid—the hiss and smell of the iron, her radio mumbling—though this time, he did most of the talking, telling Miss Rose about all of his jobs up north and the air that smelled like pine and how they had lobster even at the drive-ins and how his friend Helene had taught him to ski. She listened intently and when he was done, she clicked off her radio.

"It sounds to me like you're headed back there," she said, spraying one of his father's shirts.

"Of course I am."

She peered over the top of her glasses.

"Does your father know that?"

"He will soon. And you're not going to tell him."

She shook her head. "You bet I'm not."

"Oh, come on. He'll live."

Miss Rose opened the collar, sprayed some starch.

"Not him I'm worried about."

She'd been there for the eruption over the exams, when his father had called him a parasite and roared that in his day they'd killed kids for less, that if Anders had been alive then he'd already be dead and buried out back like a mule, and she'd been there for the long years of silence that followed. She knew more about his family than anyone in the world, so she knew what was coming. A few weeks later, his father drove him to Durham, and he found his way out of the back of the admissions building and to the bus station while his father was still idling out front in his Cadillac.

He made it up to Brunswick, still in his rumpled interview suit. The campus was white and quiet, freezer-burned with the sort of air that punched the breath from you and seemed to muffle every sound other than the squeaking of footsteps. He had no coat so he ran to his dorm and when he opened the door, his lips blue and the tips of his ears burning, he saw the room was bathed in candlelight. Donny and Helene had covered a cardboard box with a white sheet and were eating lamb chops on Chinet plates.

"Sorry," Anders said, turning to leave.

"Don't be retarded," said Donny. "Come back. Where would you even go?"

Anders blew into his hands. "I don't know. The union?"

"Jesus, you're shivering," said Donny. "What the hell're you wearing?"

"It's a long story."

"Sit down. Take some food."

"I'm good."

"Jesus, just take some. You look like a bum."

Donny handed him a plate and a plastic cup filled with cabernet from a jug. He and Helene made room for him at their table. After two days of eating from vending machines in bus depots, Anders could feel himself coming back to life.

"Look at him go," said Donny. "Sure doesn't seem like he's dying."

Anders looked at Helene. If she'd told Donny anything, it seemed he'd taken it well.

"So what's up with the suit? You in court or something?"

"Sort of."

"Sort of!" Donny glanced at Helene. "This kid. What does that mean, 'sort of'?"

"I had an appointment with the president of Duke."

Donny was grinning, waiting for it.

"But I blew it off and got on the bus to come here."

"Yes!" he said, clapping his hands. "I love it." Helene wasn't smiling. "You know his dad's a big shot?"

She made a gesture that was neither a yes nor a no.

"Well, he is, and, man—that takes balls." He put his arm around Anders and pulled him in tight. "You made the right decision, buddy. No question. He made the *right* decision, didn't he?"

Helene had gotten up to clean.

Anders would never know what version of the truth Donny had been told, and after a few days it didn't seem to matter. When Anders made it home at night, a walking dead man in two sweaters and a huge hunting jacket from Goodwill, there they'd be—Donny and Helene, with beer and leftovers and a dessert with three plastic forks. So they became a kind of family, or at least Anders thought so, with he and Helene huddled together in the bleachers at all of Donny's games, ringing a cowbell for every goal, and biweekly 1:00 a.m. picnics on the dorm tiles. At first, Anders slept in the second room whenever Helene stayed the night, but it was so often that soon he migrated back to the bedroom, where he became used to the big, still pile of limbs across the room. They had their privacy, he figured, during the many hours he was gone, though he never once opened the door at the wrong time to find them in a full-blown make-out session, or worse, and so a fantasy formed—one that, in retrospect, he supposed he needed—that Donny and Helene were actually as platonic together as children, and so, in this new family, forever separate from the mess he'd escaped down south, everyone was really the same. On Sunday nights they were the only nonsmokers watching the long black-and-white movies that played at the union, and when Helene's underwear accidentally ended up in his laundry, he'd get it into the machine as fast as he could, without looking. One long weekend, when Donny and Helene could have jumped on a bus to South Station, they decided instead to surprise Anders during his shift at the Longfellow Inn, which was when, as is the nature of threesomes, everything came apart.

It was a gloomy Friday in February, and the only other guest was an elderly lady from Beacon Hill, which meant they had the run of the place if they wanted. Donny and Helene sat with Anders behind the desk for a while, asking politely about all his duties, and when that wore thin, he sent them outside to admire the bay. He folded starched napkins and watched, through the old wavy window, as Donny and Helene strolled to the dock to look at the empty moorings bobbing in the inlet. He was happy for them, proud even. At first this unexpected goodwill had stemmed from guilt—one way to absolve himself was to stay as close as possible to the betrayal without ever crossing the line—but now it seemed to have broken through to something else, an appreciation, really, of his two best friends in love. Or maybe not in *love*—that phrase was a little overused when it came to late adolescents, especially within a dormitory whose air was pollinated with hormones—but companions certainly, a pairing of proximity that had happened, so far, to work out. Donny was lucky, and though he didn't seem aware of how lucky, Anders was glad Helene had someone to hold her hand as the sun threw a thousand orange sparkles across the water, and to take her upstairs afterward when she had a *splitting* headache, to be with her in the room till she recovered.

It was inn policy to deliver every guest a silver carafe of decaf in the evening, and since Donny and Helene seemed to have skipped dinner altogether, Anders found what was left of the breakfast scones and teatime cold cuts and prepared a plate for them. No one answered on his first knock so he tried again, harder, and when there was still no answer, he decided to place the tray inside the door so it'd be there if they woke up. Looking back, Anders thought it might have been a subconscious ploy to shame them—for being up here when he was down there; for not having to work, except at breezy campus jobs; for giving him pity rather than admiration for all the work he did and then coming to his place of employment and flaunting their greed for each other—but at the time, the whole spectacle was just embarrassing. A lamp was on, for one, and though the rest was a scramble of skin and sheets, he'd seen enough of their faces to catch not only their panic but also their smiles. They wore grins of embarrassment but probably felt the opposite—the thrill of conspiracy—and what sent him back down the stairs and to the front desk, where he sat with the tray on his lap and the coffee cooling and the cheddar sweating, was the burning subtext of those smiles: that he was excluded from them.

Which made him think. Of course it wasn't Donny he really cared about; Anders admired him mostly for what he'd endured (a drunk for a father and the task of essentially raising his siblings alone) rather than what he was known for (a punishing presence on the ice whose brutality, frankly, Anders found difficult to ring the cowbell for). Donny was a loyal roommate, but mostly he was a gateway to Helene. She was the magnet that kept the two men together, and without her, neither of them would have much to say to each other. So when she came down the stairs a few minutes later, her hair pinned back and a long cotton robe hanging over her nightgown, Anders found it difficult to even look at her.

"Sorry about that," she said, standing on the other side of the desk like a guest with a complaint.

"About what?" He shuffled through some papers and scribbled something in the ledger. When he glanced up, Helene was still there, smiling at him. She came around to the empty stool.

"You really stay awake all night?"

"It's not bad." He pointed to a big thermos of regular coffee. "With all that."

To pass the time during the quietest hours, he'd been whittling a squirrel out of driftwood that he hoped, eventually, would find a home beside her ceramic friends.

"Are you in love with me?" she said.

He looked up from the ledger. It felt like an accusation.

"Of course not."

"Because we love you. We both do, you know that. But we can't have—"

"I said I didn't."

"You kissed me."

He chewed the inside of his lip.

"Did you two have a little conference up there?"

"Donny's not stupid."

"I had a *fever* when that happened, by the way, and I apologized. What do you want me to say?"

"I just want to be clear."

He took a deep breath and managed a smile. "Don't worry about it. I get it. I understand completely."

The squirrel's tail was still a beige block when he tossed it onto the woodpile out back. When Helene stopped coming to their room altogether because of him, and Donny sulked in after practice alone and refused to talk, Anders finally went out to retrieve it. It was buried under a frozen mound of split logs but otherwise unharmed. The wood was still white and fresh where he'd cut into it and it still smelled like the sea and the trees, which was to say like the air he'd come to associate with both Helene and his freedom. He finished the creature with details gleaned from a wildlife encyclopedia—the texture of the fur, the inset ears, the tiny frown of a mouth—and decided to leave the driftwood unpainted. He arranged to meet her for supper in the dining hall and tucked the squirrel in his big wool coat's pocket along with a card he'd made using a long flat strip of birch bark, but the dining staff wouldn't let him in. His ID number, said the woman in chef's pants at the door, was invalid. Inside, he could see Helene sitting alone at a table, waiting for him.

"Look, I'm meeting someone," he said. "If you could just let me tell her—"

"Sir, you're blocking the line."

He yelled for Helene and waved his arms.

"This facility is for enrolled students only."

He left a note in her mailbox afterward explaining it all—how his father had sent a letter and the college had suspended his aid, so he'd taken out the maximum amount of loans so he could finish the semester and was living in a room above the Penobscot Saloon, which stank of cigarettes and sour whiskey and whose jukebox rattled his floor every night until two, but that he'd love to see her, if only to give her something, a thank-you of sorts for the time she'd saved his life. But she didn't write back to that or any of his subsequent notes. Her life must have been much easier, he figured, with him out of the picture. Donny's room was now a single with two beds that could be dragged side-by-side to make a kind of honeymoon suite, and at hockey games she could ring the cowbell with abandon at every concussed opponent, and mostly she could spend time alone with her boyfriend without feeling like she was disappointing anyone. So you can imagine his surprise when she showed up at his door on a warm April night, holding a stack of his letters and the fat, creased spine of his copy of *Middlemarch.*

"Why do you keep sending me these?" she said.

He was packing, putting the few things he'd collected—books, mostly—into old liquor boxes. By the roar downstairs, he could tell it was somewhere in the one o'clock hour.

"Please," he said. "Come in."

His unmade bed was the only place to sit besides a laundry basket filled with books, so they both stood. She had a jacket over her party dress, and her ballet flats were speckled with mud.

"Can I get you anything?" He had a Coke and some saltines on the windowsill.

"Here," she said, holding out the stack. "These are yours."

"I was hoping you'd come by."

"Take them."

"I wanted to say a proper good-bye."

She lowered her arms.

"Where are you going?"

"Home. I'm out of money."

"So, what, like permanently?"

He shrugged and she plopped down on his bed, the book and the letters in her lap.

"There are loans, you know."

He ignored that.

"Can't you just ask your dad?"

Anders laughed.

"But you have a *life* here."

He stopped laughing and looked at her. She had her hands balled in her lap on top of the book, and her toes were pointed together; she blew at a strand of hair that'd fallen across her face. Apparently she'd been drinking.

"I can loan you money," she said all of a sudden.

Anders picked up the book from her lap and dropped it in the basket. "That's ridiculous."

"I have it. It's just sitting there in an account. My grand-mother wanted me to use it for real estate but—"

"Helene."

"Don't leave."

He sighed and sat down on a box.

"How much wine have you had tonight?"

"That's not fair."

"Your lips are purple."

"I'm trying to tell you something serious—"

"Yeah, that you want me to stick around so you can feel pretty and special without ever having to answer a single letter."

"I couldn't!"

Anders squinted at her.

"My *boyfriend*, Donald Fitzsimmons, also known as *Fitzy*, perhaps you've heard of him?"

"Fitzy?"

"It's a nickname. It's kind of new."

"Good, then let's call *Fitzy* to come get you."

"You know, you're a coward."

"What?"

"Why don't you ask me?"

"Ask you *what*?"

"Anders, you've never *asked* me."

He watched her for a moment. When she was angry, her

eyebrows looked as though they had been cinched with a draw-string.

"Wait a second. You made it *very clear*. You wanted no con-fusion."

"I know."

"So don't come in here and start accusing me."

"Just ask me."

"Ask you what? There's nothing to ask!"

She opened one of the letters and started reading. " 'I still think about you, you know—' "

He reached for it. "Don't do that. Please don't do that."

" '—obviously I do, and sometimes I wonder if I'll ever get a chance to—' "

"Helene."

" '—if I'll ever get a chance to speak openly, and because I can only assume you're reading these, I wanted you to know I saw you first. If that means anything. I know it's stupid, and it probably makes me just another sad guy lurking around you, but it's true. I loved you from the moment I saw you. I loved you from that very, very instant.' "

She looked up from the letter. Downstairs, the bar was roar-ing.

"This is really embarrassing."

"You can't go."

Later, in the easy air of the summer that followed and the six semesters of mountainous debt he happily accrued, and much, much later, after he'd long paid that off and finished paying for the educations of their own children, when every bill-free return trip from the mailbox became a private toast to that accomplishment, he would think about the ways that debt and marriage were intertwined, how the taking on of one had

44

meant the taking on of the other, and that once he'd signed his name to the first, there was only one way forward. It was a simplification, he knew, to reduce a marriage to the cold, flat terms of lenders and borrowers, especially considering all that later transpired, but the idea had first occurred to him on the beautiful morning Helene moved into his room above the Penobscot with nothing but a crate of knickknacks and a camping backpack, and persisted through the evening, eight years later, that he and his new bride left Manhattan for Connecticut.

The story he often told of how he and Helene, two youngsters in love with New York, had ended up out there centered on a particular day in 1975. They had been looking at an apartment, a real steal in the newly renovated One Fifth Avenue, a building that was a genuine prewar colossus, with charming brass fixtures and mosaic floors and a fleet of doormen with taxi whistles around their necks. They'd both rushed there on their lunch breaks and, as the story went, fell in love with an enormous two-bedroom whose every window looked onto Washington Square and the tangle of low-lying buildings beyond. Anders placed a bid and made an appointment with the bank for the following morning. But—and he'd lean in while he was telling this part, letting his voice stay very calm—on his way back to work, nagged by doubts about the future of that increasingly dirty city, he stopped for a paper and saw the headline on the *Daily News*: "Ford to City: Drop Dead." So he canceled the meeting at the bank and withdrew the bid and so lost the apartment that was probably worth millions today.

It was a great dinner-party anecdote, and he used it whenever he could, partially because of the perverse pleasure he took in dangling a dream apartment in front of a bunch of ex–New Yorkers, all of whom had been forever infected by the city's real estate mania, but mostly because it provided a plausible coun-ternarrative to his life and asked them to enjoy for a moment what could have been were it not for President Ford: the Anders of Greenwich Village, who raised his children in the belly of the city and was not an interloper but a part of its storied fabric. He relished the brief pause that followed the telling, when he could feel the table considering that vision of his life. *There was another man inside there*, the episode said, *don't jump to conclusions*. And thus, even though Helene had been there too, it became one of the stories that only he told, one that she must have listened to a hundred times, silently verifying it, even though they both knew it was false.

On the real day, in the real New York, it was blustery, bright October, the sort of day where you walked around clutching your jacket over your arm, and the clouds, like giant warships, revealed or removed warmth as they passed on to wherever it was they were headed. Anders took a cab down Park, with the trip's enjoyable whoosh under the Pan Am Building and out the other side, where eventually stone and glass gave way to the sky and he could see, for the first time, the day's magnificent blue. His cabbie had a heavy foot and caught a remarkable string of green lights, accelerating block after block, almost never stopping, which was fine with Anders, who could feel, with the window cracked and his suit coat unbuttoned, the stale air of the office fly from him and with it the remnants of a meeting that had left him unsettled.

It was silly, he knew, to get hung up on it. By any measure, he should have been celebrating. A deal he had sourced and pursued, despite the fact that it was considered around the office to be a total Hail Mary, had actually been approved, and there was a sudden surge of confidence in him among his superiors because of it. The deal was with an outfit called the Athena Property Group, whose executives wanted to turn the farmland at the northern edge of Kansas City into what they called a "neighborhood," a campus platted with five hundred homes that, at least from the window of a regional jet as it descended into KCI, made geometric designs in the land that swirled and fractaled and reminded Anders of an abstract representation of snails.

At the time, it was considered ludicrous to be sniffing around in housing, with interest rates high and inflation even higher (Brad French, his immediate supervisor, had told him he was playing Russian roulette with all the chambers loaded). But he'd stuck with it because, if you looked a little closer, the numbers were good. Despite every national trend, demand in this particular case was clear—Athena had already presold over a hundred plots to families moving up from the city—and so, as far as Springer was concerned, it had a chance to beat the market. Which was why he'd pursued it to begin with, why he'd risked being laughed out of the room, and likely why he'd found himself being considered for a second promotion in so many years.

But the problem with Athena, the thing he was still trying to understand as the cab blew by Union Square, was that if you looked at the larger picture—specifically, the loans those hundred families were getting (almost all, it turned out, from the same thrift in downtown KC called Liberty Federal), not to mention the thin walls and cheap materials of the development—the whole thing became untenable. And it was untenable because, at a time when property values everywhere were evaporating, none of those loans had taken into account the possibility of those values doing anything but rising. It was all optimism, nothing else. He'd never seen a deal where no one on the other end seemed the least bit concerned about risk. He'd never *heard* of a deal like that. And yet when he'd brought it up in the meeting this morning, when he'd cleared his throat and mentioned that he was concerned about what kinds of loans all of these homeowners were getting, he was met with a kind of perplexed silence, a frankly embarrassing moment that was finally broken when Brad French, now the plan's biggest proponent, asked him directly if he was changing his mind.

And what the fresh air coming through the taxi window was washing from him was the nagging sense that even though he'd been the one to source the deal, and he'd been the one to fly out to KC and have steak with Jim Cranby, Athena's cowboy-booted owner, and bring back a stack of financials packed with impressive numbers, he should have looked at Brad French and that whole table of senior vice presidents and said yes, he had, he'd changed his mind. But the reason he was even in the room, the reason that all those people, including his own boss, were letting him speak, was that he already owned this deal—it was his—and so his success and his pending promotion were already tied to its fate. It had even become how he was identified on the twenty-third floor. Because he *was* good at it, he knew that. For all the reasons to move to the financial center of the universe and build a career at a behemoth like Springer, none was as compelling as that. He was already a success. So if some little savings and loan in Middle America was going to lose its shirt, too bad. And though the houses seemed cheap and flimsy and enormously overpriced, it wasn't really his job to regulate such things. Jim Cranby may have worn shiny cowboy boots and two signet rings and he may have spoken with a boot-heel drawl that Anders felt was a little put on, but there was no question he was building houses that people wanted despite the shitty economy, and in that, there was good money to be made.

When the cab arrived at One Fifth Avenue, Helene was standing outside the building, beside its long green awning, in a patch of bright sun. Her face was serene and tilted at the sky as she smiled in her sunglasses. A doorman opened the cab door, and they followed a real estate broker inside, clicking across the tile floor of the lobby, which still smelled of fresh paint. There was something about the broker, Mr. Addelfield, that reminded Anders of his father—it could've been the marionette lines that came down from the corners of his mouth, making him look forever as though he were frowning, or it could have been simply the attention he paid to Helene, who was the only thing in Anders's life his father had ever approved of, but it contributed to the rush that he felt later as they were handed floor plans across Mr. Addelfield's desk and he could see that, at least with his expected salary bump, the building's asking prices were all within reach. It was an astonishing prospect that provoked a squeeze of his knee from Helene with every floor plan, as it suddenly seemed as though they were being shown a diagram of their future.

After Anders signed the bid and felt the approval in Mr. Addelfield's handshake, they decided to blow off work, and they took a walk lengthy enough to get them pleasantly lost in their new neighborhood. They found a café on the warm side of a quiet street and shared a bottle of champagne with their late lunch. Despite trying several times in later years, Anders was never able to find that café again, its canary-yellow facade lost in the haystack of those streets. But he could never forget that afternoon, with the light disappearing behind him and Helene wearing his suit coat, which she'd put on when she felt a chill, her slender frame swallowed in it as though she were playing dress-up in her father's closet.

They were exhausted when they got home to their rental on Seventy-Fourth Street and climbed the bowed stairs whose worn carpet had a sweet odor that combined with the champagne to produce in Anders a brutal headache. Though the apartment was dark and hadn't been adequately dusted in four years, Helene had no problem pushing him through the door and onto the gritty rug, a fall that was as loud as it was jarring but that didn't stop her from unbuckling his belt with the front door still open.

Maybe it was prudish of him to be unable to concentrate on anything but that open door, what with his pants around his ankles and his wife's underwear beside him, but he couldn't. So he waited it out on the filthy rug and was unable to stop his head from smacking again and again against the floor, as though someone were trying to shake him into consciousness.

When it was over, Helene closed the door and curled up beside him, falling asleep to the muted horns of rush hour, while Anders stared at the blank ceiling and felt his heart rumble in his head. The thing about the Athena deal, which he just couldn't get out of his mind, wasn't just that it was a crappy product; it was that all the people who'd bought it—families, like him and Helene—had projected their futures into empty rooms. And as outrageous as it sounded, he couldn't help seeing their new apartment as being possible only because all those families had entered into bad loans—as the product of a deal that hurt almost everyone except the people who created it.

Because that was the truth, wasn't it? No one was benefiting quite as much from this as he was, and therefore, it would be hugely destructive for him to back out of it now, regardless of what everything in his better self was telling him. Were this a normal day, he'd have been getting home about now, and he would've poured himself an Old Charter, stood in their galley kitchen, and talked the whole thing out with Helene, who, he knew, once she'd heard all the details, would have insisted he back out. But it wasn't a normal day, and, lying exposed on the living-room floor, he could still feel Helene's hand squeezing his knee, the flush of pride it brought him, his baptism into the world of One Fifth Avenue. He could still see Helene opening the bedroom closets and beaming at their size, and he couldn't remember a time she'd seemed so happy. No, it was an exceptional day, the sort of day whole careers are built around, and he had enjoyed every second of it, the sudden awareness of how quickly they had gone from being kids to being property owners and the realization that he had done it entirely on his own — college to grad school to *this* — without the support of his family and without bending to the edicts of his father. So why did he find himself with a knot in his chest and a pounding hangover and the feeling that his wife, deeply asleep at his side, was clinging to him with all her might?

It wasn't difficult to maneuver his way out from beneath her arm, pull up his pants, and go down their creaking stairwell into the sober evening air. Their block was quiet and he walked west toward York, past the single-family mansions with giant planters on their stone steps, for once not even bothering to peer into their parlors and wonder what books lined their shelves. Instead, he stared straight ahead and moved at a purposeful pace until he hit Madison, where he caught a roaring downtown bus without bothering to note its number.

He enjoyed the view through its big window, liked looking down on the hats and shopping carts on the sidewalk as the bus crept its way down the longest swath of the island. He hopped off at a dirty corner in Astor Place and wandered down Bowery, which he'd really seen only from the window of a moving cab but whose reputation he was suddenly drawn to—an entire district of deviants and drunks, of those who, his father often reminded him, were separated from the rest of us by only four or five decisions. He headed west to Bleecker, past the boisterous mobs of NYU, past the booming bars made famous ten years earlier by all of those folk musicians, past an elderly drag queen who was tap-dancing to a Dixieland tune playing from a radio at her feet. He was carried along through the smells of falafel and pizza, his jacket slung over his shoulder, enjoying the very casualness of the night air.

He was twenty-eight, soon to be a senior associate at Springer Financial, a man by any calculation, and yet it suddenly terrified him to look at the wall of midtown, which began with One Fifth Avenue, right on the other side of Washington Square, and extended like an impenetrable forest northward from there. This was where he was headed and yet there was a part of him, a growing part of him, that no longer wanted anything to do with it. And it wasn't just Jim Cranby and his cowboy boots, which he'd propped up on the table, right on the white tablecloth, at the end of their meal; or the soy farmers it was easy to see he'd underpaid for their land; or the fact that the land itself would be bulldozed and paved and dredged to make artificial lakes—none of which, he knew, was any of his business. And it wasn't even Brad French, who, after he'd looked at the financials from KC, had called Anders into his office and closed the door and said that he had really hit it with this one, that it wasn't about chasing the small stuff anymore but about creating new models that opened the door to a slew of other deals like it, and so the SVPs wanted him in their meeting to get his input on this and a bunch of other prospects they were already calling Athenas. No, what terrified him, looking north at those high avenue walls, was the sudden certainty that, right or wrong, his decisions were no longer his to make.

He hoofed it back uptown, determined to put a halt to both the deal and the apartment, which would have been unthinkable even a day ago. But now just the thought of unburdening himself, of leaving the whole mess behind, had him running up their rental's steps, convinced of how little any of these concerns would matter once they had settled into a life far from the glassed-in cubes of midtown. When he burst in, Helene was curled on the sofa, rubbing her eyes with a confused squint. He'd woken her up. The apartment was dark except for the soundless flashes from a television in the other room. There was a bottle of wine open on the table next to a plate for him that she'd wrapped in foil. She saw him in the door and smiled.

"Where were you?"

"Just walking," he said, but that sounded more evasive than he'd intended. "Downtown."

She looked at him a moment, waiting for more. "Why?"

Anders wanted to tell her then about the Athena deal, about the way it was structured and about the farmers and about what the land had looked like when he'd driven through it—one brown arid expanse, not a leaf around, that would be rolled with sod and plumbed with sprinkler systems and staked with adolescent trees. He wanted to tell her about the shoddiness of those homes, how in the model you could feel the wind in the closets but that Jim Cranby had rapped his knuckles on a hollow-sounding wall and assured him the homes would pass inspection, which they would, and they would also be filled with families who would spend their lives working to pay the loans off. He wanted to tell her all of it, how he was able to persuade an entire table of bosses to follow him when the truth was that most mornings he felt ridiculous in his suit, like an actor. There was a private part of him that was waiting for this phase of his life to end, this moneymaking, debt-dissolving, self-negating, morally correct phase, so he could get on with the business of actually being himself. He wanted to tell her that he'd read in the paper there was a shortage of fire-tower lookouts in the parks out west and in a moment of whimsy he'd written a letter to the Parks Department in Colorado and that he'd actually heard back—it didn't pay much but families were allowed, even encouraged, and wouldn't that be something, the two of them at the top of a mountain in Colorado?

But looking at her, sitting in the dim light that came through the window, he couldn't. And it wasn't because she wouldn't understand, because she would, and it wasn't because he couldn't bring himself to deprive her of the happiness he'd seen earlier that day. That was too simple. The real truth was that he liked the way he felt when Helene looked at him, the authority she seemed to think he had, and the confidence. He liked the way she saw him in the world. And because there was a part of him that was still a kid in a dishwashing apron, a part of him that was still in awe of the fact that she was his, and because every time she smiled at him, he felt as though he were being showered in light, he couldn't bear to watch her redefine her image of him. Not now; not today.

"Anders?" she said. Her face had softened with concern. "What's going on?"

He looked out the window then, at the lights of the city, crisp and pure as sodium bulbs. "The apartment," he said. "They took another offer."

By the time Jim Cranby sold the last of his five hundred units, Anders had been moved to an office with a door. And while he'd never admitted to the lie, soon Helene was pregnant and talking about a house with a yard; soon she knew all sorts of surprising things about school districts. So despite his fervent belief they were not Connecticut people, despite his distaste for the best-of-both-worlds rationalizing so many of those people did, he found himself riding the train north on Saturdays and nodding along with Helene as she marveled at the charm of all those old houses.

The house they chose was more than charming; it was, as the agent described it, historic. The floorboards were milled by hand and as old as the nation itself. Though the rooms were dim and cozy, the master bedroom had been renovated with higher ceilings and a pair of walk-in closets, so that while the outside retained a tight box of Protestant restraint, the inside had racks for all four seasons of shoes. As the three of them toured the rooms, Helene repeated each of the agent's selling points to Anders as though he weren't standing right there and hearing them himself, and when they were left alone in the bedroom to confer, she launched into a cartwheel before he could say a thing.

After they closed, a graphite-sketched weekday in January, the agent dropped them off at their new home, which was dark and echoey and empty, and they tiptoed through the rooms in silence. By then, the Athena deal had become the model for thirty others just like it—it was a wild, unprecedented success—and Springer had beaten the charge into an industry that a year before had been left for dead. Walking through those rooms in the dying winter light, rooms that were nothing but dust and shadow and Helene and Anders's own projections — of children and holidays, of a nest of warmth and safety — it occurred to him how stupid he'd been to doubt this. All his life he'd been resisting what was expected of him, a habit of reaction followed by a battery of justification. But what was in front of him, in this case his pregnant wife and their empty Georgian colonial, was all that he could ever want.

His sons were born and his father died, replacing the battles of the past with a steady march of paychecks and workweeks, of predawn mornings and pitch-black evenings and stacks of shirts in cardboard boxes. It was a rush to get to the train and a rush to get home; a rush to get into a market and a rush to get out; there were risks in everything, gains and losses in a day's trans- actions in sums that no man could recoup in his entire working life. There were good days and bad, good hours and bad, a responsibility to shareholders and to senior management, to in- vestors and his own family, a ticking clock of quarterly earnings and an expectation from everyone, especially himself, that he would plunge headlong into the roiling seas of the global econ- omy and come back each time a winner.

He'd taken an interest in the credit market, avoiding the junk and the trends and focusing on dusty old bonds that no one ever noticed. It was a quiet market, a string quartet in the midst of the blaring boom boxes of leveraged buyouts, and its stability seemed a failure when everyone around him was getting filthy rich. He created no overnight billionaires and no overnight bankruptcies, and only the codgers on the board who had sur- vived the Depression respected him. Brad French, however, barked at him to get out of the little girls' room, to go big or go home, so he did that too, engineering the buyout of an outfit called Renfro-Pacific, an undervalued paper company that was transitioning from typewriters and shredders to "business solutions," the burgeoning world of financial software that would later be conquered by Bloomberg. And though the deal was a windfall for Springer and again made Anders a darling, it also gave him a belly of stress weight and a susceptibility to relentless bloody noses. He made a habit of riding home in the bar car and mauling a can of beer nuts and then falling asleep before dinner. He spent his weekends battling weeds and doing violence to a hedge of English laurel, working himself into a heap of grassy sweat and then collapsing on the sofa with an aggravated back. At night, he could barely sleep and found solace in bags of chips fried in hydrogenated oils until, when he was thirty-seven, his heart stopped working.

It happened on the train, in the morning. Mention you have tingling in the shoulder and the whole silver beast is halted and you're yanked out and thrown onto a stretcher at the East Norwalk station, your undershirt cut open and a paramedic counting and a train full of bovine stares. *It could happen to you,* he later wished he had shouted, *any goddamn one of you!* But the fact was that it hadn't, at least then; it had happened to him, a man with two boys under ten, a man with so much of his life left.

What happened next wasn't due to the fact that they rushed him to the hospital and shot his veins full of dye, or that they found four plugged arteries, or that they needed to saw through his sternum and open him like a steer, leaving a long glossy seam from his clavicle to his navel. And it wasn't because of the three softest faces in the world waiting for him when he opened his eyes, or the lectures on diet and lifestyle he received from every cardiologist in the county, or the new lease on life that seemed to come standard with a prescription for beta-blockers and the nitroglycerine pill he was to wear on a medic-alert chain around his neck for the rest of his life. All of those things fell under the codified umbrella of near-death experience; all of those things, on the spectrum of trauma, were totally normal.

No, what caused him to buy a new station car and fall in love with new age music—regardless of his kids' moaning, regardless of his wife's ribbing, discs and discs of Yanni and George Winston, of Enya and the smooth sax of later Van Morrison, some merely the sounds of creeks and wind and trees that, if he closed his eyes, could transport him back to the porch of the Longfellow Inn—what sent him west on a two-week trail ride, a group of men on horses with guides that was transformative and life-affirming, regardless of its many similarities to the Billy Crystal comedy that came out a few years later; what made him come home and announce to Helene that they were moving to Alaska and living off the land, that the kids would adapt and she would get used to it, that it was the only option he could come up with that would keep him alive—to which she had told him to calm down and poured him a drink and reminded him gently of the quality schools in their district and the community the kids already had and how quickly twelve years would go by—what prompted all of that was returning to work a week after the staples in his chest were removed and finding it exactly the same.

Later, his shrink told him the name for this, for the tendency to feel isolated rather than connected after a seismic event, the tendency to withdraw rather than reach out in the face of death, but the term never felt totally right. What to call the sensation of unlocking your station car in the sucker punch of a winter morning, worrying about your heart rate and the tender scar down your torso, worrying that someone might make you laugh and you would be torn open by your own muscles, and arriving to an unchanged platform of sleepy men with trench coats and wet hair, yawning up the tracks toward New Haven? What to call the trepidation he felt as he climbed aboard that silver worm and then sat as it crawled its way along the coast, all the while worrying that it might happen again, feeling every beat in his ribs as the train swayed and rocked and finally hissed to a stop in the dark tunnels under Grand Central? What to call being carried along, as always, through the scent of burning railroad brakes and up into the high marble chamber, where the frenetic clicking of heels was suddenly a threat and his careful pace created an eddy of beige coats charging through the eastern exit? And what to call the Springer Building, an ugly tiered structure of mirrored glass that the designers had meant to be stately and imposing but was now squat and gaudy and shining like a fleck of mica in the canyon of Lexington?

And what to call the newly promoted Brad French, who greeted him with a get-well card signed by the assistants and a delicate pat on the shoulder, then asked him if he was up for work and announced that there wasn't really room for halfway, that he really needed everyone to hit the ground running? To say nothing of the work itself—what to call that? He was responsible for millions every week, nearly a billion each year, numbers he had once cited to his father, who early on didn't understand what Anders did. Now he was citing them to himself while in the men's room on the twenty-third floor, staring at the white tiles in front of the urinal and feeling as though the doctors had replaced his heart with a bundle of dynamite. A billion dollars. That was something, wasn't it? It was a way of affecting people and their lives. It was money that went to build pipelines or expand ballparks or revamp zipper production and came back, after all that, profitable. A billion dollars. That was prosperity, wasn't it? That was enough to affect the whole damn world.

Of course, there was no way to be sure. As he left the men's room and headed back to his desk, which was in an office large enough to need a decorator, he wondered what to call the feeling of looking at the trophies the company had awarded him, chunks of frosted glass with his name etched in them that had accumulated along the sills and cluttered the tables and, eventually, filled the big echoey drawer of a filing cabinet. What to call the long ride home during which he shut his eyes and heard the chatter around him with new ears, the hymn of decency, the song of work and home, all that consensus about the importance of children and schools and opportunity? And who could disagree with any of that? It was the very basis of civilization. So what to call the fact that it suddenly made him furious?

Twelve more years wasn't much. Helene was right about that. The previous twelve had gone by relatively quickly. They were a blur, really. And it wasn't as though he were asking himself to sacrifice for nothing—in fact, nothing was *more* important to him in the aftermath than watching his boys from the sidelines and helping them with long division and checking on their tiny sprawled bodies before he slipped off to bed. So why the thickening fog of isolation he felt gathering around him? Why those silent, resentful nights he spent alone with Helene, the awful feeling that his limited time was being wasted on people who didn't appreciate it? Why his purposeful retreat from them into his own head, those long wooded walks, his exaltation of solitude, and his tendency, when with them, to lecture? Why had it gotten to the point, after a few years, that even his family referred to him in the third person, that they talked about him at the dinner table as if he weren't there?

The day that he decided to announce to Helene that he wanted a divorce was also the day that Preston, their younger son, received his degree in social policy from Northwestern. Anders had already consolidated his investments and given Springer his notice, so they were both preparing for a change anyway. "So long as he doesn't start following me around the grocery store," Helene would say to her friends on the phone, as though he weren't sitting right there. She had given up on trying to reach him by then, no longer prodding him to have conversations about his feelings or asking if he'd read the books she'd left for him on his bedside table, books about rage and aging and living in the present, all written by people with different degrees but the same empathetic squint on the covers. The truth was they hadn't spoken much in months, so he understood why she later described what happened on the trip as an ambush and why, to her, all of it, *the whole goddamn phase of life*, had come out of nowhere.

They were staying in downtown Chicago, its early-May air so chilly they wore scarves and windbreakers and clutched themselves as though they might, at any moment, be torn limb from limb. He decided to tell her on their way to dinner, in the back of a cab whose green-and-white exterior made it seem more like a European police vehicle. It hadn't been an ideal time, he knew that now—and if he could do it over, he certainly would—but they had just cradled hot drinks together in the hotel bar, staring out the window at Michigan

Avenue, and Anders had felt for the first time in a while that he could confide in her, trust her with a piece of his internal life. So he told her: he was no longer happy, he was ready for a major change, and the only way he could see himself being happy was if he was alone, away from the job, away from the house, away from her.

The rest of the cab ride was spent explaining the logistics of the whole thing—how long it would take, how expensive, which lawyer he recommended for her, what they would get for the house when they sold it—and as he rattled on, as if making his way through a PowerPoint presentation, Helene sat quietly, watching the salt-stained roads over the driver's shoulder, as though making sure the cabbie at least was following her directions. Anders couldn't tell if she had expected it because she didn't respond at all—she didn't cry, she didn't yell, she didn't exhale in relief—she just stared forward until they made it to their son's celebration dinner, where she marched into the restaurant and greeted everyone with a warm peck on the cheek before sitting down with the wine list and ordering two bottles for the table and starting the meal off with a proud toast to their son.

It wasn't until they had gotten back to the hotel room and she had removed her earrings that she spoke a word to him. "You've always had terrible timing," she said as he was folding down the sheets to get into bed.

To this, he laughed. He had spent eight extra years commuting, marking off days in his mental calendar as his younger child flitted from culinary school to organic farming to whatever you called a clear-eyed determination not to get a college degree, while Helene had defended the enriching nature of his experiences and noted the courage it took to embark on a personal journey, which turned out to be a five-year baccalaureate in the uses of recreational drugs.

"I don't think my timing is the problem."

"You never have any idea what's going on, do you?"

"He's over thirty years old. We finally got him a degree. I'd say *my* timing is fine."

"I think I'm dying," she said as she wiped off her makeup.

"Look, if you're talking about my doing it on the way to dinner, I know. It wasn't ideal."

"I had a weird mammogram last week. That's what I'm talking about."

"I don't even know what that means."

"It means," she said, "you aren't the only one who can die."

That phrase rang through Anders's head for the next few months, as Helene returned for biopsies and consultations, a lumpectomy, and, when that didn't work, a mastectomy, taking the breast clean off and clearing the way for a four-month period of chemo and reconstruction. Whenever Anders was present, the doctors would talk directly to him, as though he, as her husband, were the guiding force behind her decisions. They would explain to him the options, and Anders would nod along, feeling the icy indifference from the other side of the room.

But he *was* there, maybe in part because of her pronouncement in the hotel room, maybe because it was his duty, even though he had started renouncing that duty with paperwork and lawyers at the exact same time. Mostly it was out of guilt, he figured, and some sense that it was a test of his character. Helene could be dramatic and at times a catastrophizer, and if he stayed consistent and supportive, the quiet rock in the treatment room, he could feel okay about sticking to his plan once the whole ordeal was over.

But it didn't end. Cancer spread to lymph nodes, which somehow created a new tumor in the good breast, a tumor that had to be removed in the middle of the chemo treatments for the other one, and still, despite predictions from Helene's friends to the contrary, he stayed. Twelve months he stayed, a full year suspended in the amber of uncertainty, calendar pages filled with appointments and tests and consultations. He was there for the diagnosis, and he was there for the procedure, and when that didn't work and the tumor's ugly cells had been outside the margins, he was there when Helene asked the doctor, frankly and without self-pity, if she was going to die. And when the doctor's response was laden with worry and medical jargon, it was Anders who had squeezed her hand and let her rest her head on his shoulder and who said, as sincerely as he could, that everything was going to be all right.

He could feel, as the second mastectomy approached, that he had become the person she again relied on, and even though he appreciated her trust, it also terrified him. They no longer talked about the divorce, she no longer broke into fits of rage and tears every time he tried to reassure her, she no longer pretended to be asleep with the lights and the television blaring when he climbed into bed at night. They attended all the same parties with all the same people, many of whom seemed to have no idea that anything had changed between them. And, he supposed, it hadn't. They even spoke of the future—vacations, his retirement, the sale of the house—the way that they had in the apartment above the Penobscot Saloon, with a dreamy disregard for any possibility that didn't fit their vision.

What was it then that made him drink too much and cause a scene that year in the middle of the Ashbys' party? What was it that made him skip out of the hospital during her second operation to catch a Will Ferrell movie, only to return three hours later to find his grown sons in the waiting room, both of them looking up from the glowing rectangles in their palms with expressions that said, *What the hell is wrong with you?* What was it, when the three men stepped into that darkened recovery room to find her wrapped in blankets and on a morphine drip, that made him afraid to even touch her? Instead, he had paced around the room, pressing every button on the hospital walls as if to say, *Look, dear, look how fine these facilities are! I told you I'd take good care of you!* What was it that made him continue on like this, flipping the channels on the television, seeing how the toilet adjusted in height, until Helene, her body still sloshing with morphine, gathered the energy to say her first words since having her remaining breast removed: "Don't do that, honey"?

And why couldn't he stop even then? Soon his boys were telling him, "Dad, stop it," but he continued until it was time to leave and he went home exhausted, falling asleep in his loafers, sprawled out on their king-size bed alone. He dreamed of college then, their days above the Penobscot, cooped up in a studio, when all of it—the beater they drove, the cases of Schlitz they served their friends in their dirt-lot backyard while they projected silent films on a neighbor's garage wall, the hours of classes they'd logged, the insurmountable bank loans, the instant coffee, the mended and re-mended elbows of his sweaters—all of it was in the service of their future life, the life that they imagined endlessly in their kitchen and in their sagging twin bed, the fantasy they shared that made adulthood and aging and the long slog of a career and a marriage seem like something worth rushing into.

Even though that fantasy had changed slightly every few weeks, Anders could remember it went something like this: They would live in New York, in a building with a doorman who knew their names and their favorite flavors of ice cream; they wouldn't need to worry about money; they would have a child who would tow a red wheelbarrow through the park; they would take trips in the winter for no reason other than to go ice-skating on a real pond; they would join the PTA, help a friend get elected to office, throw dinners for charity; they'd live overseas for a few years with their children (three of them) so as not to become too regionalized; they'd learn about wine and have the newspaper delivered and spend their Saturdays at Fellini retrospectives in an art house downtown; they would run together along the Hudson and work their way up to a marathon; they would have a king-size bed; they would send their children to camp. All of these were decisions that were made back then, and in his dream, lying fully clothed with a pillow stuffed under his ear, they actually happened.

3

It was an overdose. The culprit was a handful of Klonopin that didn't mix well with whiskey, though the doctors were clear that the small plantation of cannabis the boy had inhaled over the past month hadn't done much to help, to say nothing of that evening's potpourri of chemicals. "Fucking *angel* dust," Anders's son Tommy said. "At his parents' Christmas party."

He was at the top of a ladder, tapping nails into the condominium fascia. "I guess they've got him rigged to tubes and machines," he said, a nail bobbing between his lips. "Mom says Sophie's a wreck." He shook his head. "I mean, can you *imagine?*"

Tommy's kids were inside, parked in front of a DVD. In the eight short years he'd been a father he'd taken quite easily to the high-handed tone of parental astonishment. Anders gave him a string of lights.

"It's not the end of the world," he said. "The kid'll be okay."

Tommy pulled the nail from his mouth. "Tell that to his parents."

Anders's condo was at the back of a gated complex whose units had been designed to resemble a New England village, with gray clapboards and white fences and lawns stiff with chemical fertilizer. In keeping with the spirit, he decorated his living room with prints of Winslow Homer watercolors, moody portraits of rowboats at sunset and women at the shoreline lifting their hems. And while most of the year his condo's exterior was indistinguishable from his neighbors', the Ashbys' party had, if nothing else, reminded him it was the season of lights.

"And you know what's fucked up?" said Tommy. "Turns out there were other people with him."

Anders stopped untangling the strand of lights in his hands. "What do you mean, other people?"

"Kids. There was a whole group of kids over there, smoking God knows what."

"Who told you that?"

"Mom heard it from Sophie."

Anders went back to the lights. "And how would she know?"

"I'd say her son is a pretty good source."

"He told her that?"

"I don't know. I guess."

Anders handed him a plastic reindeer. "These go on the roof."

Tommy had agreed to make room in his day to help Anders decorate, which mostly meant he checked his watch every time Anders gave him something to hang. He took off his puffy coat and dropped it to the ground. He was tall and still lean, like a basketball player from the fifties, with a sculpted Adam's apple and a strong beaky nose. He looked little like either of his parents, and even as a child, with his swirl of wavy hair and big wet eyes, people used to say that he seemed like he was from another era, one of trolley cars and newsies and whitewall tires.

"Mom says the Ashbys are going to sue."

Anders nearly dropped the strand he'd finally untangled.

"Who in God's name would they sue?"

"The school," said Tommy. "Where do you think he got the stuff?"

"The *school* didn't sell it to him."

"But they also didn't prevent it."

"So let me get this straight—they send their child away and then blame his drug use on the fact that no one was there to watch him?"

"Dad," he said. "You're a parent. You understand. It's about protecting their son."

Anders thought of Mitchell then on his back deck, waving around the damp end of his cigar and asking if Anders could recommend a program to drag his kid into the woods. That too was about protection, as was the enormous wing they added to their house (to "give Charlie space"), as was, presumably, the kind of job Mitchell worked (chief counsel for a processed-food conglomerate). His new motor yacht might also qualify as some sort of opportunity for Charlie—marine biology of the sunburned and tipsy.

"He's a good kid," Anders said. "He deserves better."

"Better than Choate?" Tommy called from the roof.

"Better than *us*."

He could feel Tommy's silence, could picture his rooftop headshake. "Everyone's doing the best they can," he said.

When Tommy decided to move back to town, Anders knew it had everything to do with the boy's mother. Amid the ongoing wreck of his parents' late-life divorce, Tommy had taken on the role of responsible adult, mediating and communicating and, unlike his brother (who was apparently so absorbed in being unemployed that he couldn't return a phone call), trying his damnedest to hold them together. And now that he was living in a musty Cape out in Weston, working in market research, with all those digital slides and terrible fonts, all that consumer data (he'd once shown Anders a chart demonstrating the increased heart rate of the average male when presented with a red box of acid-reflux pills as opposed to a green one and then had declared with great pride that they'd cracked it all wide open), Anders knew it was only a matter of time before Tommy gave up on consoling his parents and started to blame them.

"What about Preston?" Tommy said. "You guys sent him away."

"I didn't *sue* anyone, I didn't—" Anders stopped himself. "It's different."

When his boys were teenagers, Anders had learned that all intimate conversations between them would soon putter into a fog of stoicism, and so he always framed discussions within a task so every interaction would have a function—hand me that hammer, a little to the left, stack those over there—and the moments they shared would never dissolve into silence. From the edge of the roof, Tommy was looking down at him with a kind of tenderness that bordered on pity.

"I heard you went to the party, Dad."

"I was invited," he said.

"I was happy to hear you went. I thought it was, I don't know…brave."

Anders handed him a plastic sleigh to haul up to the roof.

"Is that what your mother thinks?"

Tommy took off his hat and rubbed the back of his head. "I just wanted to be sure you were okay."

"I'm great," said Anders, unwinding a long orange extension cord. He could feel Tommy watching him.

"I heard you saw Mom."

"Yep."

"And met her new boyfriend."

The way he pronounced it sounded so official.

"I've known Donny a long time."

"We don't have to talk about it if you don't want, I just thought it was…" Tommy paused with a psychologist's restraint. "Significant."

A silence settled over them, broken only by the hum of an airplane in the bright gray overhead.

"I thought he lived in New Hampshire," Anders said finally.

"He moved."

"Where? Where is he living?"

Unlike his brother, who had essentially made a career of it, Tommy was a terrible liar. From his son's inability to respond, Anders understood what was going on.

"He's living there, isn't he?"

Tommy said nothing. Anders dropped the extension cord into the bin and walked to the driveway with his hands on his hips.

"They're *living* together?"

"It's pretty new," said Tommy. "I don't know how permanent it is."

"Why didn't you tell me?"

"It wasn't my place."

"They're living in my *house*, Tommy," he said and recognized as soon as he'd said it how ludicrous it was.

"It's Mom's house. I mean, technically."

"Technically, I pay for it. Technically, my name is on the deed."

"It's not your house, Dad."

"You know what, never mind. It's no one's house," said Anders and he chucked a pinecone a disappointing distance.

"What does that mean?"

Anders went back to the extension cord.

"Dad."

"Your mother has to move out," he said.

A low ceiling of New England clouds had gathered and Tommy, silhouetted against them, looked like a burglar in his rolled stocking cap.

"What does that mean?"

"It means I can't afford it."

"Since when?"

"Since I no longer work for that *ridiculous* company!"

Tommy was very still.

"You retired without enough money?"

"I retired with plenty of money."

Tommy had inherited his mother's patience and, like her, understood the power of a silence.

Anders sighed. "There were unforeseen circumstances."

"Don't say the economy."

"The economy," he said. "And the fact that your mother wanted to keep the house."

"And you said *yes?*"

"At the time it seemed like the right decision."

Tommy climbed down. He was the sort of long-lashed person who was terrible at concealing his disappointment.

"Does Mom know?"

"I'm handling it."

"She doesn't know? When does she have to move out?"

"I'm handling it."

"Actually, Dad, it's perfectly clear you're not handling it. It's perfectly clear you haven't handled a single thing."

Anders stared at him.

"I just don't get it," said Tommy. "How can somebody who is so good with other people's money be so very bad with his own?"

"Look," said Anders. "She can downsize. That was always the plan."

"The plan," said Tommy, "that you never told anyone."

"Of course I told people."

"Who?" said Tommy, a question that Anders wasn't going to dignify with an answer. His son shook his head. "I should get the kids."

The midday light was low enough to see the TVs of his neighbors flickering with football, and the cars that rolled by had their headlights on. He and Tommy had accomplished a lot—there was Santa and his herd on the roof and another deer made of white lights grazing on the lawn and a choir of air-blown carolers that beeped an assortment of seasonal songs. Ryan and Emma stood with their father in the driveway, the pom-poms of the kids' hats like softballs balancing on their heads, and waited for the lights to come on. Inside, Anders flicked a power strip and watched all three faces break into smiles. When he came back out, he too was enthralled, and as the four of them stood in the glow of the front yard, he could feel he'd created a new tradition.

He helped the kids into the car, and as Tommy started the engine, Anders knocked on his window.

"What do you say we do Christmas Eve over here this year?"

"Dad."

"You bring the kids and Lisa, we can maybe talk Preston into coming back."

"You know Mom has been talking about Christmas Eve since June."

"I didn't know that. Is she having people over?"

"You know her."

"She's doing the whole thing? The turkey?"

"Look, maybe we can stop by the next day."

Anders nodded and looked back at his new place. It suddenly seemed gaudy.

"I want you to know I didn't put her in this situation on purpose," he said.

Tommy looked in the rearview at the kids buckled and silent in their seats. "Wave bye to Grandpa."

"Tommy, I'm going to tell her. I promise. I just need the right moment."

Tommy put the car into reverse and looked up at the condo, his face blinking with the display. "This place," he said.

"What?"

"It just kind of kills me."

That Helene had been camped at Sophie's side in the forty-eight hours since the party was unsurprising, considering her determined washing of every dirty wineglass in that evening's eerie aftermath. He had watched her, in the haze of that night, spray the countertops with 409, bag what remained of the party—all the paper plates and wasted brie—into three Hefty sacks, and turn off the lights, leaving Anders alone on the leather sectional, giggling into his bourbon.

Since then he had faced the wall of her polite voice-mail greeting. It was a recording that had become quite familiar to him in the weeks after his retirement, when Helene had become inexplicably busy, and it turned out that while he was doing everything he could to strip his obligations to zero, she had gone back to work and asked for a promotion. After twenty years of volunteering and grant-writing and deepening opinions about the societal forces that marooned one in seven Americans in illiteracy, she had decided it was a good time to throw herself at something worthwhile. The board unanimously voted her in as director of an organization that had been bleeding money since the Clinton years, and, despite her recent illness (not to mention the nation's near-total economic collapse), she had been told to fix it. It was an eighty-hour-a-week Sisyphean assignment that kept her in a fluorescently drab Bridgeport office till late at night, running numbers and cultivating donors and ignoring the locomotive ringtone of her cell phone.

Anders tried her as he sat in the long train of cars that connected the dangling stoplights of the Post Road. Since Tommy had left, the sun had descended below the ceiling of clouds and now it was throwing orange light across the roofs of stopped cars. Volunteers in aprons were ringing bells outside the supermarket. It was Saturday; the parking lots were full and the trains were empty, the station wagons strapped with mummified trees. Last year, in the midst of Helene's chemo and radiation, Anders had chosen their tree himself, an enormous Douglas fir that had towered over him in the vaulted space of their new kitchen. He decorated it alone from the perch of a metal ladder. It took him forever, and when he was finished, the result was haphazard and sparse, though Helene put on a grand display of how happy it made her. The tree was a symbol of everlasting life, she told him, inhaling the piney air of the room. Thank you, she said. This was just what I needed.

The light turned green and the traffic began to move. His call went straight to her voice mail.

He would have gone to the hospital where she waited with Sophie, regardless of the many lines he might have crossed by doing so, were it not for his appointment with Howard, a weekly occasion that was always disappointing, not only because it cost so much, but also because, on the scale of local high-priced therapists, Howard, Anders was well aware, ranked last. Which was why it was so easy to get a standing appointment, a move his lawyer had strongly urged, because, he said, in these kinds of cases, when there was no other woman and no clear betrayal, when you had to articulate to a judge that love, in this situation, had evaporated like ethanol in a cupped palm, it was easier for everyone involved if it looked as though you were trying.

And so he tried. He made the appointments and he kept them, driving across town to Howard's minimalist office, which was in the basement of his home in what Anders was certain was a converted playroom. It had been recarpeted and adorned with drapes and decorated with Danish Modern furniture that looked sleek and clever but was about as comfortable to sit on as a rock in a cave.

It had been nearly eight months of weekly appointments, and the judge had already ruled, and neither Helene nor her team of lawyers was objecting to the decision, and things seemed settled and done, so Anders couldn't explain, even to himself, why he continued to go. Was it simply for the process of speaking aloud the events of his week to someone he didn't have to worry he was boring, the way he had done with Helene for so many years, expounding in his undergarments on the risks of a recent hire or the preposterous parking situation at the station as she dropped her book in bed to listen? Maybe that was enough to justify the expense. Maybe, in those terms, Howard's ineffectiveness was worth all the money in the world.

"So," Howard said, shaking Anders's hand and gesturing for him to sit. There was already an empty pause as he scribbled something urgent on a legal pad. Anders didn't say a thing. Finally Howard looked up and met his eyes for a moment, a technique Anders was sure he had learned from a book—*Let the client fill the quiet*—but that only left them both tapping their knees in impassable silence.

"Why don't you tell me about your week."

"My week?" said Anders. "I don't know, let's see. I got the condo decorated. That was a big project, and it looks sharp. Festive, I mean. Easily the best place in the complex."

Howard adjusted his glasses—rimless, almost invisible lenses that were held together by fine wire stems, like pipe cleaners stripped of their fuzz. He had heavy, significant wrinkles that hung, hound-like, from his face and that betrayed his first calling as an accountant, a career that must've actually fit his form, unlike all of the delicate modernism he seemed to assume was required for this one.

He nodded. "So it's the holidays," he said. "How's that treating you?"

"Fine," said Anders. "I like the holidays."

"Are you feeling any pressure to start your own traditions?"

In the thirty-some times he'd met with Howard, the therapist had never started off with this many questions and had never written down so little. They had gone whole sessions with Anders just talking about switching from oil to natural gas, a process that took him months of appointments with frustrating specialists, so that he never quite felt settled in his new place, which was otherwise perfect, he'd made known at the time, and three times greener than your average home.

"I'd say the lights are a new tradition," he said. "I also bought some reindeer, and a Santa for the roof. He waves."

Howard nodded. "And, if I may ask, have you been going out at all?"

"Going out?"

"Seeing people, friends?"

"I saw my son today. What does that have to do with anything?"

"I just assumed this week you may have been more social, less alone."

Anders lived alone. Anders had spent the majority of the past year alone. This solitude is what Howard mostly spoke of when he'd glance back at his pad after five or six sessions, his lids nearly closed, and expound on a theory about Anders's crisis of the self, or his project of un-rooting, or, as Howard called it at the end of their first session, tapping his notebook with that weighty pen, having barely heard the tiniest tip of it, with a kind of gall that Anders still couldn't forgive: *self-sabotage in the face of loss.* That Anders returned after that, Howard should have viewed as a miracle, especially because Anders had known Howard for quite some time, and especially because Howard's sons, both of them muscly and dim, had supposedly paddled Preston and then beaned him with raw eggs on his first day of high school, and also especially because Howard's wife had considered running for first selectman and was a fixture in town, beloved by so many, confidante to so many, including, he was sure, an entire satellite of people who loved Helene.

All of this must have been on Anders's face because Howard

capped his pen, made direct eye contact, and with a sigh said, "I was there."

"Where?"

"At the Ashbys'. I was there. I was there." He dropped his head.

"Why didn't you say something?"

"I should've told you. I'm sorry, I—" He sighed and lifted his head again. "I thought it would be more productive if we got there without that information, but I now realize that that was the wrong choice and I apologize."

Howard was often apologizing during therapy.

"You were there?"

"Kathleen and Sophie Ashby are quite close."

"Right," said Anders, remembering, then, Helene holding Sophie's bony elbow in the eerie flash of those lights, remembering the mustard-gray of Charlie Ashby's face.

"So, let's talk about that night," said Howard.

"I decided to go and I went," said Anders, crossing his arms. "I don't see why it's such a big deal. I was invited."

"Why wouldn't you have been?"

"You know why. That party was Helene's."

Howard nodded. "You looked perfectly at ease."

"Oh, come on. I was panicking."

"Why?"

"I was surrounded."

"Is that why you went outside?"

Anders froze. He could see, all of a sudden, how he must have looked standing on the porch with Mitchell and then striding into the party to find his wife with another man.

"One of the reasons," he said.

Howard nodded but wrote none of it down.

"What is it, Howard?" he said, finally. "What is it that you're getting at? Go ahead and ask me."

"I just want to talk about the party. It seems important in the context of everything else we've discussed over the past few months."

"Really? Because it feels to me like you've made up your mind about it. And I'm tired of pussyfooting around. So go ahead, Doc, just come out and tell me what you think. Diagnose me."

"I don't diagnose people," said Howard, calmly.

"Fine. Right. I forgot, you just lie about what you know and then sniff around for gossip."

"I'm not doing that, you know that. But if there's something about that night you'd like to discuss—"

"No, there's nothing. It was a bad night. For everyone. I feel terrible for that kid."

"For Charlie? Why?"

"Because of all the *sanctimony*, Howard. Because of the goddamn headshaking and astonishment, like no one in that room had ever heard of anyone going off to prep school and smoking dope, like they weren't secretly a little thrilled it had all just unfolded right in front of them and that it wasn't *their* kid."

"It was more than dope, from what I heard."

"What does it matter! He can do what he wants, far as I'm concerned. I told him that. I told him that I didn't care if he was smoking crack or whatever the hell because—"

Anders thought for a moment. Because why? Because nothing. Because he did care. Because he always cared, no matter how much he tried to pretend otherwise.

"Look, don't tell me his fine sense of judgment doesn't run in the family; don't tell me that." Anders shook his head.

When it became clear that he was done, Howard removed his glasses and rubbed his baggy eyes.

"You saw the boy doing drugs?"

Anders shrugged. "Yeah."

There was a pause. "I sense that you feel somewhat guilty," he said, putting his glasses back on.

"Maybe, I don't know. The kid would have been doing it anyway."

"But do you feel guilty?" Now Howard was taking notes.

"Of course, of course I do."

"Why?"

"You know why, Howard."

"I'm not so sure that I do."

"Then you really are as bad at this as they say you are."

Howard raised his face, hurt, and Anders's cheeks flushed with rage, then even deeper with regret.

"This makes you very defensive," said Howard.

Anders nodded. "I suppose so."

"You remember that this is confidential, right? This doesn't leave the room."

Howard spoke in a voice Anders had never heard before—assured, calm, warm. He had complete control over the situation and seemed to imbue that playroom with the professionalism of an actual doctor's office.

"Let me just come clean," Howard continued, clicking his pen and slipping it in his pocket, "and tell you what I see. I see someone who's defensive and accusatory, who put himself on the line last week and doesn't want to talk about it because, for some reason, he thinks he's being cornered." He looked down at his notes. "And by that I mean he hasn't even mentioned his ex-wife, or her new boyfriend, who seems—"

"I did drugs with the kid."

Howard glanced up.

"You did?"

"Outside. When I was trying to leave."

"Okay," said Howard, looking back at his notes.

"There's your honesty," said Anders. He'd expected that he'd feel relief when he came clean, that it would alleviate the weight of that night a little bit, but the longer Howard stared at the legal pad in his lap, the more Anders became frozen in dread.

"That's it?" he said. " 'Okay'?"

"No, it's fine, I'm just—" Howard looked up. "What kind?"

"What *kind*? I don't know; it was some boarding-school stuff." Anders shook his head. "Some kind of blend. With PCP."

Howard's face changed. "*PCP?*"

"I thought it was just grass, I didn't know—I mean, Jesus, Howard, I thought I was supposed to be able to tell you anything."

"You can, you can, it's just—" He stared at the pad again. "The boy is hurt," he said finally, as though that were all there was to it, and before Howard could continue, a phone rang on his belt. "I'm sorry," he said. "Excuse me one second." He took the phone and went through the entryway, leaving Anders alone in the white room with its coffee table full of Klee and Mondrian books. He opened one, paged through its little squares, its stark borders, its right angles. Despite all his questionable techniques as a therapist, Howard had never taken a call in the middle of a session, like a Hollywood producer bored with a pitch. This pitch was his life. This wasn't some game—he shouldn't have to impress Howard with anything.

He was paying the guy too much for that. Anders shut the book, replaying the past few minutes of their conversation. He nibbled on his pinkie nail, got up, and looked for Howard in the entryway, but he was gone.

He opened the office door and poked his head outside. Howard wasn't there either. He listened for his deep, runny-nosed voice and heard only the hum of an airplane in the bright gray overhead. So Anders went inside, put on his coat and scarf, and, on his way to the door, grabbed as many coffee-table books as he could carry, which, it turned out, was quite a few, and they were quite heavy—a stack of decorative crap reaching all the way to his chin.

4

Anders would never pay for it—either the session or his stupid books—and that was it for Howard, his last chance, so he'd have to come begging if he wanted any of it back. He hit the highway. All of this had gotten out of hand. The kid was fine, and Anders's involvement—if any—had been a mix-up. An accident. Wrong place at the wrong time, which happened in the world, Howard might like to learn; it was a thing.

He exited at the hospital, a rectangle at the top of a hill that had been newly sided and expanded and outfitted inside with high-tech screens. They had spared nothing on the renovation. Its entrance had a vast buffed floor and tall, leafy plants that rose three stories to a windowed ceiling, and a fountain somewhere trickling ambient noise. He'd walked through this construction zone with Helene many times during those dreamy, confusing months, marveling at the gall it took to undertake a forward-looking project in the atrium of the dying, and seeing it now, shiny and complete, all waterfalls and foliage, he felt as though she were back in treatment and that he should have come with a bundle of daylilies or a box of Krispy Kremes or a bouquet of chocolate-dipped fruit. Every time he was in this building, he could not shake the feeling that something was required of him and that somehow he had already blown it.

Charlie had been moved to the third floor, reached by way of a glass elevator that looked out on the place as though it were an Embassy Suites. Glancing through the atrium windows, Anders could see a parking lot scored with strips of sod and a tiny silent ambulance whirling its lights. It was three o'clock on a December Saturday, prime shopping time, and down by the water, a line of cars crawled along I-95 like engorged insects.

Charlie's door was open. The room was dark except for the glow of a ceiling-mounted TV. There must have been thirty cards in there, some of them attached to balloons, and an entire bedside table loaded with games.

"Charlie?"

He had his knees up on the bed and was drawing furiously in a sketchbook in his lap. "Hang on." He let out a groan of frustration and began erasing. Finally, he looked up. "Oh," he said. "Yeah, my parents aren't here."

"That's good. Is my wife around?"

Charlie stared at him. "I don't see her."

In the odd androgyny of a hospital gown, he looked small. His face was drawn, and in the light from the TV, it was hard to distinguish the shadows under his eyes from half-moons. His forehead was shiny, and his hair, which had grown in angelic ringlets when he was a boy, was now an oblong frizzled bush.

"How are you feeling?"

"Awesome," he said.

"You look okay," Anders said. "The way people were talking, I thought—" He didn't know what he'd thought. That Charlie would be hooked up to machines? He had thought there would be at least one machine.

Charlie went back to the thing in his lap. "Do you have a balloon for me or something?"

"Here," said Anders. Before he'd come in, he had grabbed one of Howard's books, a heavy volume on Paul Klee. In the car it had seemed the newest of the bunch, colorful and strange and hefty, but in the blue light of the TV, you could see, its jacket was scratched and dinged. "I thought you might like this."

"What is it?"

"It's some art."

Charlie took the book and flipped through a few pages of paintings, their tight little shapes creating what looked like patchwork villages—houses, streets, the moon—that were, despite their precise boxes, coming apart at the edges and falling into a jumble.

"This is pretty sweet," he said. Then he flipped to the back, where, Anders hadn't noticed, a manila sleeve was glued, a library slip still in it. Charlie looked up at him. "Did you lift this?"

"I—" There was nothing to say. "Not from a library."

"You brought me a stolen library book?"

"I didn't actually know that."

But Charlie was laughing.

Of course Howard had taken his fine modernist tomes, his props of good taste, from the library.

"I love it, dude. You show up at the hospital to give me a stolen library book."

"Here, I didn't know. Give it back to me."

"No way, man, this is my favorite present by far. By far; I love it."

"It's not—" Anders shook his head. "I'll bring you something real. What can I get you?"

"Nothing, nothing at all."

"Well, listen"—he scribbled his number on the back of one of the old business cards that were pressed in his wallet—"if you need anything, you know."

Charlie looked at the card, its heavy stock and the raised seal of the Springer logo.

"So what happened to you?" Charlie asked.

"What do you mean?"

Charlie flicked at the corners of the card. "Vice president, securities division."

"I retired."

"Why?"

"It's complicated."

"Try me."

"It sucked."

Charlie broke into a huge grin.

"Yeah," he said. "I get that."

"And a bunch of other reasons."

"I have to go to rehab."

"Yeah," said Anders. "That's usually how this goes."

"I'm not even addicted to anything. My parents are just Nazi assholes."

"They're worried."

"They're embarrassed. There's a difference."

"Well, you did a stupid thing."

Charlie looked up, his eyes suddenly hard. "Seriously? I'm getting a lecture from *you?*"

"I'm just saying—"

"No, no, I'm interested, considering you were high as balls."

Anders lowered his voice. "Look," he said. "We both know you tricked me into that."

Charlie's grin came back. "You were hilarious."

"That was dangerous."

"And amazing." He shook his head. "And weird. And so fucked up."

"Listen, I need you to keep that between us."

"I mean, you were like, 'I'm joyful, guys, I feel *joyful.*'"

"Charlie. I'm asking as a favor."

"You're a trip, man." He went back to the notebook in his lap. "Don't worry about it. That's not my style."

Anders stood for a moment, watching the boy work. "I shouldn't have done that," he said finally. "I know you tricked me but—it was wrong. So, I don't know, sorry."

Charlie squinted at him. "Nobody's blaming you, dude."

"Yeah, well." *The boy is hurt,* he kept hearing in Howard's sad bassoon of a voice. *The boy is hurt.* "I hope you get better."

From the elevated platform of his bed, Charlie seemed to acknowledge, with a flick of his head, that so much of what people say when others are sick is for themselves. They get religious and apologetic; they're overcome with the people they believe they should be. He didn't know what he was looking for from the kid—forgiveness? absolution? a confirmation of his total innocence?—but in any case, the boy didn't look up.

"What are you working on?"

"Just a thing."

"Can I see?"

He handed him a sketchbook with a fake leather cover that had peeled down to the cardboard. Inside there were pages of drawings; it was a comic book, some frames no bigger than stamps, others filling a full spread, torn out, and glued over. In the grand tradition of so many comics, the opening image was a view from outer space, the Earth a glowing mass with a tiny pod hurtling away from it.

"Are you making a superhero thing?"

Charlie sighed and rubbed his forehead. "It's a graphic novel."

The following page was a rendering of the inside of the capsule, a huge control panel and a tiny window and, strapped to a table in the back, unable to touch any of it, a little dog covered in sensors.

"It's about Laika."

"That's sweet."

"You know what, man?" said Charlie, reaching for the sketchbook. "Forget it."

"Hang on," said Anders. "This is good."

"You know what the scientist in charge of that project said about it forty years later? He was one of those Soviet guys with a goatee and a lab coat, and he said, 'Nothing that we learned on that mission could justify the loss of that beautiful animal.' "

"Really?"

"Google it. Laika was a stray and the scientists became really close to her. They, like, raised her."

Anders looked back at the page, the dog strapped down to that table. "That's heartbreaking."

"I *know*," he said. "That's why there are a billion books about her. They lied and said she crashed in the ocean but she really burned alive in the atmosphere. But in my book, Laika's still floating out there and Oleg—that's the scientist—is old now and living in post-Soviet Russia, all poor and shit, and one day he turns on the old equipment and hears Laika's heartbeat." Charlie raised his eyebrows. "She's still out there, waiting for him."

Despite being the sort of people who had little interest in the arts, the sort of people who couldn't enter a museum without whispering, *I mean, I could do that,* Sophie and Mitchell had somehow produced two of the most creative kids Anders knew, kids who had built their independence by retreating into the parts of themselves their parents least understood.

"So what happens?"

Charlie shrugged. "That's as far as I've gotten."

"Oh, come on."

"I'm gestating."

"Wouldn't he try to rescue her?"

Charlie smiled. "Maybe. Or, I don't know. Maybe it's not that kind of book."

The door opened then and Sophie came into the room with a tall Starbucks cup and a pair of sunglasses on her head. "Charles Ashby, what did we talk about? You're supposed to be *sleeping.*"

It took her a moment to notice Anders standing on the other side of the door.

"Oh," she said and looked at her watch. "I thought visiting hours were over."

"He brought me a book," said Charlie.

Sophie looked at Anders. "Well, that was sweet," she said, taking her seat beside Charlie's bed. "You didn't have to do that."

Toward the end of Anders's marriage, when things had gotten really bad, Sophie Ashby had written him a letter. It came on her stationery, a nice heavy stock, and in it she told him, with a bluntness that was incongruous with the light loops of her handwriting, that he was losing his wife. She said that she was sorry he was so unhappy, she really was, and that she hoped he'd find a way through it—they all did—but if he couldn't figure out how to buck up (her phrase) and do what was right for his family, it was clear to her he had no idea how to be a man.

Despite the fact that it felt like a ransom note written on a thank-you card, Anders slipped it inside a book he was reading about emerging markets, and soon it had become his bookmark, worn and yellowed, her caustic words peeking out from whatever volume was resting on his bedside table. He carried it with him nearly everywhere he went. It fit nicely in the outside pocket of his laptop case or the inside pocket of his houndstooth blazer, a stiff rectangle in the jacket lining whose corners he absently flicked while he was concentrating deeply on something, like said book on emerging markets, and the distracting blabber of the rest of the world raged on around him.

"He likes my graphic novel."

"Everyone likes your graphic novel," said Sophie.

"You don't even know what it is."

"It's about a dog."

Charlie shook his head. "It's not about a dog."

"Well, how am I supposed to know what it is if you don't let me see it?"

"It's about a stray dog who is launched into space for reasons she could never understand. It's about being exploited by the people who are supposed to protect you."

"That sounds sad."

"It is sad. It's very sad. It's goddamn heartbreaking."

"The Meadows isn't outer space, honey."

"It's worse. It's Arizona."

"I'm finished having this conversation."

Charlie looked back at Anders. "You see what I'm dealing with here?"

"I'm sorry," Sophie said to Anders. "Clearly he needs to rest."

"He came here 'cause he's looking for his wife."

Sophie's face came back to Anders. "Oh," she said, and for the first time it seemed to make sense to her what he was doing there. "She's at home."

"She's decorating," said Charlie. "The house. With her enormous boyfriend."

"Charlie."

"What? He is." He looked at Anders. "He's big."

Anders nodded. "Thanks."

"He lives there now. A lot of conversations about that. About whether things are moving too fast."

"Charlie, you've made your point," said Sophie. She seemed exhausted.

"But I guess he's loaded, so…" He didn't bother to finish the thought.

"He's not loaded," said Anders, and a strange pause settled over them. "He's not. I've known the guy a long time." Sophie's eyes were fixed on the far wall. For once, both Charlie and Sophie were quiet. "Well, I should go."

"Anders," she said as he was leaving. "She'll call you back when she's ready."

Outside, the sun was gone and the streetlamps were on. The cars on I-95 had come to a standstill. He made it into the recesses of the parking lot before he realized he was still holding Charlie's sketchbook. Under the lights in his car, the drawings were impressive, beautiful little silver things that depicted a world of stark light, one in which people did as they were told and there wasn't room for feelings outside the party line. Khrushchev made an appearance, a portly fellow looking not unlike Mr. Monopoly, and so did the ghost of Stalin, whose body was glowing with a radioactive halo. Charlie had stopped in the middle of a flashback to Laika's puppyhood, an alley in a backwater village named Ozerki. At the center of the page was a note about a recent change.

Parents not dead, it said. *Just dickwads.*

5

It had always troubled him that the moment you reached a point in your career where you had the means to improve a house was also the same moment you no longer had a family to live in it. Their town these days was peppered with empty additions, lit up atria waiting for everyone to come back and enjoy them. Theirs was a full-blown expansion, with recessed halogen lighting and a walk-in pantry and a roof that was lofted a full story to let the skylights "breathe." Everyone agreed that it was beautiful, and it was, though the charm that it had for Helene seemed to wear off soon after it was finished, leaving him with an unfortunate loan and a house on the precipice of a collapsing market and no project they could talk about during the long silences of their empty-nest meals.

In hindsight these things were always head-smackingly clear, but at the time he figured they would recoup the money when the house was sold. Call him crazy for assuming that since he and Helene were now childless, she might not mind selling their five-bedroom home, and also for assuming that a housing market that had spent the last hundred years going nowhere but up would continue to do so. He had been wrong on both counts, and given Helene's last-minute demands in the divorce, not to mention his reaction (*The* house? *All you want's the god-damn* house?), it all made his current situation—sitting at a bar in the middle of a workday trying to figure out, for the first time in his life, how to ask a friend for money—seem somewhat suicidally regrettable.

"Her new boyfriend was your college *roommate?*"

"Yep."

"Well." Larry shook his head. "That takes care of that." He touched his glass to Anders's pint. "Here's to the good life."

It was their third drink already, and, not surprising for a Monday, the Master's Sports Bar and Grill was empty. Strings of plastic flags were hanging, left over from the weekend's NFL games, though now all that was on the bar's many screens were muted grids of yelling sportscasters. Larry Eastwood was the last friend Anders had made without Helene. He had big, unfashionable glasses, a face of papery pale skin, a wisp of hair that he combed over his dome, and a loud midwestern voice with an accent that had been formed during his early years on the floor of the Chicago Mercantile Exchange, so his *a*'s were as flat as if they had been squeezed from the tip of a deflating balloon. For all those reasons, not to mention Larry's endless stock of bawdy jokes and his astounding inability to know when to leave a party, Helene couldn't stand him.

But in the world of finance, a culture of risk addicts with three-inch collar clips and guys who shouted their way onto *Fast Money* and into early graves, Larry was one of the rare few who had the humility to know when to quit. He'd been an analyst at Morgan, a real virtuoso, and he'd liquidated everything at the height of the market to concentrate on his tomato garden. It was virtually unheard-of, a guy with his reputation and future throwing in the towel, and during the carnage of '08, which Anders had watched with a mixture of terror and pleasure from his living room, he had often thought of Larry, who'd gotten out at the top with a mountain of cash and had nothing to spend it on but fertilizer.

"You know what? She may have done you a favor."

"How is that?"

"Because I've seen you these past couple of months and you look like shit."

"I appreciate that, Larry."

"I'm serious. You've been walking around with this stricken look on your face like you've made some terrible mistake. But we both know you did the right thing. And now she went ahead and made the decision for you. That was a favor, the best thing she could've done. It's time to move on."

Larry's wife had left him over ten years ago for a man who ran a horse farm on Long Island, and though he still spoke to her on the phone every week, sometimes for hours, he often talked about her in the past tense, as though she had died.

"I followed her to a party."

"You what?"

"I know. It's just that I was invited and I thought—" Anders wasn't sure what he'd thought. He'd thought it would be normal. He'd thought he would be accepted. "Anyway, it was a bad idea."

"This town," Larry said, swirling his Jameson. "This place. It's all 'sanctity of the family' and 'good public schools' and 'what's best for the kids.' You saw the same thing I did. It's a life of work, empty work. And by the time anyone figures that out, they sell their house to the next sucker and leave. You of all people know this. How many conversations have we had about it?"

"Yeah."

"So you got out. Stop beating yourself up over it."

Larry put a hand on Anders's shoulder. "Okay," he said. "I'm drunk. Dinner's on me."

They took Larry's town car down to Howie's, the snack bar by the beach, and ate their cheeseburgers as they sat bundled up at an abandoned picnic table. The wind was blistering and there was no one around except for the occasional dog walker. When they were done, Larry reached into his pocket, took out two miniature bottles of Dewar's, and handed one to Anders. "Like a private fireplace," he said and sucked half of his down in a single swig. The ocean was gray and lazier than it was in the summer, the whole thing thick as joint compound.

They sat for a long time, listening to the soft lapping of the waves.

"I need money, Larry," Anders said. It sounded so crass.

Larry looked at him. He seemed surprised.

"Huh."

"What?"

"I didn't think you'd get caught up in this thing. But I guess everybody got flattened."

"No, it wasn't the market," he said. Larry waited for him to elaborate. "It's for Helene."

Larry reached into his pocket and cracked another bottle.

"I lied to her," Anders said. "I told her she could keep the house, but I can't afford it, not even close."

"How much?" Larry said.

"A lot."

Larry watched the lights from a power plant blink across the water.

"Jesus, Lar, you know I never thought I'd have to ask. But

here I am, and I'm asking." He sighed. "They're going to toss her out on the street!"

Larry nodded. "Of course," he said. "Whatever you need."

Anders took a long scotch-warmed breath. "Thank you," he said, though he felt like collapsing in the sand. "And it goes without saying this is a *loan*—I want to make that clear. You know I'll pay you back for it, every penny, right?"

Larry stood up. "What is it, Monday?"

"I guess."

"Let's have some fun. This is killing me out here."

Anders held up his bottle. "I'm already having plenty of fun."

"No, I mean like real fun. Like forget-your-wife fun. Want to go to a strip club or something?"

"I've had my fill of humiliation for the day."

"Gah!" Larry tossed his empty bottle into the wind. "Come on, I want to show you something."

They went back to Larry's car and he turned on the heat, then pulled out of the beach and drove down the quiet streets, watching the lights blink on inside houses as people finished dinner and watched *Jeopardy!* with their ties off. They cruised down the Post Road, past the boutiques on Main Street and the movie theaters that had been turned into houseware chains. They rolled past the town hall and the newly renovated middle school, with its soccer fields abandoned until spring. By the time they made it to the station, the sun had set and the world was dark.

There was a line of station wagons and luxury SUVs idling by the platform, cars loaded almost exclusively with women and their children, the map lights on as they read magazines in their laps.

He hadn't been here in nearly a year. It felt smaller somehow, and dirtier. The lamps over the platform threw jaundiced light on the few people standing there, domestic workers or affirmative-action prep-schoolers who were headed back to the broken cities up the coast, but otherwise the tracks were empty, a sad industrial stretch that everyone on the platform stared at quietly.

"What're we doing?"

"Wait for it," said Larry.

It was hard to believe how important those tracks had been to him at one time, curving off toward the bright center of the city, the umbilical cord that connected his work with its purpose—a house and a family, a project that the larger world seemed to affirm was as meaningful as you could have. It had gone without saying—the tie and the trench coat and the college names decaled to the back of the station car.

A few moments later the tracks went bright and a silver train blurred into the station. The doors hissed open, spilling dark-coated people onto the platform like a gutted fish. The figures rushed past one another for the exits, then scattered, half of them speed-walking to their cars in the outer lot, half searching, chins up, for their rides, drivers who were waiting for them politely, white tails of exhaust flicking from their cars' mufflers. The commuters looked angry as they searched for their spouses and children, as though somehow the swarmed sidewalks in midtown and the oversold train had been their families' fault, as though no matter how hard they worked to maintain homes in this town, they could never, in these first moments back, completely conceal their disappointment.

The cars disappeared in a line, like a motorcade, and soon the station was quiet and dark again, Larry's lights the only ones shining on the sandy lot.

"Miss *that?*" he said, his blue eyes tracing Anders's face up and down.

◆

There were all different kinds of inebriation, Larry insisted. There was the sort of buzz you got from a lunchtime sip or two, after which you squinted your way back into the world feeling joyful and empty, and there was the sort of sniveling drunk you descended into on the beach in winter when you were feeling sorry for yourself and downing all your friend's stolen minibar bottles. But if you could push past that, there was a happiness waiting to be reached that was worth all the trouble—a few healthy pulls of Cuervo with the car windows down as you careened past the twinkly mansions along the sound and you became invincible.

"Where are we even going?" said Anders. Larry hung a left at the entrance of Fairfield University.

"A little place I know."

There was a stone church, its two ancient steeples lit from beneath, and across a lawn there were dormitories with lit windows that revealed walls of posters and plastic shelving and, in one, an impossibly young boy reading in an empty lounge.

Larry pulled the car to a stop in the faculty lot. "What?" he said. "It's open to the public."

The bar had all the makings of an actual pub, with a long row of decorative beer handles and a polished oak bar. It even had neon signs in the windows and bowls of popcorn, but since it was attached to the student union, whose bulletin boards abutted its interior entrance, it had a cleanliness that made it feel more like an Applebee's in an airport. They ordered a pitcher and sat in a corner booth next to the stage, where a man with a walkie-talkie on his belt uncoiled a wire and tested the PA. The place was empty except for a table of teenagers who looked as though they might have been tasting their first sips of beer.

"Welcome," said Larry.

Though Anders understood it was how most of the population had fun, situations that were built around cutting loose and losing yourself for the night only made him feel worse about himself. Once in St. Lucia, after a bottle of wine with a beachside dinner, Helene had talked him into going to the local nightclub, a bumping shack with a pool and a hot tub and a clothing-optional area. After bobbing uncomfortably for two endless reggaeton numbers, he took a seat with his warm seltzer and had to watch as Helene danced for the rest of the night with a local kid in a linen shirt he left unbuttoned to his navel.

"Let's hear it for finals week!" said a young man at the microphone who was wearing a cowrie-shell necklace and a baseball cap pulled down so far that you couldn't see his eyes. There was a smattering of polite clapping; the microphone was turned up so loud that the smacking of the young man's gum seemed to vibrate their booth. "All *right*," he said. "Tonight we have some two-for-one Bud specials going on, and also we'll be treated to a visit from the Bud girls."

The teens at the far table clapped, and two young ladies in shiny red dresses stood up in the corner, waving blinky buttons. They made their way onstage and the taller girl uncoiled the microphone from the stand.

"All right, you guys," she said. "Just because there aren't too many of us here doesn't mean it can't be a party." She pointed at their booth in a way that reminded Anders of all the humiliating audience participation he'd been subjected to—Cirque du Soleil, Blue Man Group, that drag show in Key West. "So stick around, 'cause we have some awesome stuff to give away."

"Look," he said when the girls left the stage and turned up the music. He stood up. "I'm sorry, but I think I've seen enough."

"Sit down," said Larry. "Finish your beer."

Anders picked up his pint and downed the last of it. "I'll take a cab."

Larry let loose a powerful whistle that cut through the music and brought one of the Bud girls to their corner.

"I know *you*," she said.

"It's a pleasure to see you," said Larry. "Listen, my friend here thinks he's leaving."

"Why would he do something like that?"

"I haven't a clue."

"Well, hmm," she said and walked over to Anders. "How about another drink?" She smelled of vanilla, with a hint of something earthy, like maybe basil. "It's on me."

It was easier for Anders to take a seat.

"You know her?"

Larry smiled. "Heather."

Anders knew this was an act. The one time he'd stopped by Larry's house unannounced, he'd found him out back tending to his tomatoes, rows of leafy pillars that covered his entire yard. He wore soiled chinos and rubber clogs and a white bucket hat, and after he'd described everything that was planted, down to the blends of the compost, flicking gently at the bugs that landed on him and retwisting the occasional wire, he'd taken Anders inside to show him his plans for a greenhouse. Also, Anders had noticed, Larry still had a cloudy snapshot of his ex-wife hanging from his keychain.

"To your mother, your sister, and your bicycle," said Larry, as the three of them touched the wobbly glasses of complimentary shots. "Next one's on me."

And so it went, round after round, with Heather taking the microphone every half hour to direct a trivia question to the two tables, and even if they all answered it wrong, they got Budweiser koozies and more free beer. After a few hours, the kids at the other table left and she stopped using the microphone altogether, and since Larry was buying imports and top-shelf stuff, the girls stuck around, relieved, it seemed, to no longer have to talk about Budweiser and to drink for free while still, Anders supposed, clocking the hours.

And it was nice, the attention. The smaller girl, who said her name was Mona, "like the Lisa," pinned a blinky button on each of them, set Styrofoam cowboy hats on their heads, and finally reached into her plastic goodie bag, brought out fake mustaches, blond and curly, and diligently stuck one on each man's face. She did it all with a silent seriousness, never once cracking a smile. It was the way a little girl would play dress-up, placing the granny wig on her father's head and talking to him between sips from an empty plastic teacup. It reminded Anders of Emma, his granddaughter, who he knew had never felt comfortable enough around him to play, which he also knew was his failing, and not hers, and five or six drinks in, he made a private resolution to set that right.

"There," Mona said, standing back and looking at them, the two new cowboys who'd sauntered in. "Wait." She leaned forward and straightened the mustache on Anders's lip, touching it with four fingers. "Now that's right."

Heather clapped, and the men smiled bashfully, as though they were enduring something, though neither of them took any of it.

Heading to the men's room, Anders looked at his watch. He hadn't realized how late it was—nearly two—or how much he'd had to drink. The student union was dark, lit only by the exit lights; the music coming from the bar seemed boomy and far away. It was like being in an empty train terminal—it didn't feel right. There was something about it that he liked, though, the palpable excitement of college that lingered in the smells and the very walls of the building. He felt it in all of these student buildings, these little incubators of generations. He could feel it in the empty pizza boxes and the half-finished coffees that littered the big, dark room. Anders sat down on one of the sofas and leaned his head back. He thought of the info desk, Helene's name tag, the night he'd watched her from a distant table, pretending to listen to the Red Sox on his pocket radio. She'd had on a down vest and her hair was in a braid that was on the verge of coming undone. It was an image that made him enormously happy. The beginning. He thought of her in her nightgown at the Longfellow Inn, the smell of those dusty rugs, that big crackling fireplace and his head swimming in youth. That was a good place. That was a pure place. He could go back up there, stay at the inn, try a life as a professor. That would be a new beginning, a bold beginning, and it's what he would do.

He reached into his breast pocket and felt the stiff rectangle of Sophie's card. He took it out and tried to read it, but it no longer made much sense. It was the alcohol and the handwriting and the faded ink. It was the stupid amount of money he'd just asked for and the fact that he couldn't pay it back and the fact that, in so many ways, Sophie had been right. He crumpled the card in his fist, or tried to, but it was too stiff to be satisfying, so instead he tore it into fresh pieces and let them litter the floor.

He was spinning. He sat up, a little nauseated. He had forgotten how badly he needed to pee. He walked around a corner, a little off balance, past the dark wall of mailboxes and the red glow of a Coke machine to the blinding light of the men's room. The bank of urinals was new and gleaming, recently scrubbed with bleach, which lingered in the air, and as he swayed there, he glanced at himself in the mirror. He'd forgotten about the cowboy hat and the mustache, which was again crooked on his lip. He pulled it off.

Maybe he should grow a mustache. He stepped away and the urinal flushed quietly. He put the mustache back on, pressed the adhesive as hard as he could to his lip, chuckled at its sad lopsidedness, lost his balance, and grabbed onto the door. "Jesus, fuck," he mumbled, and was answered by the unmistakable sound of a child retching.

"You all right in there?" he said.

There was no answer. The stall door was unlatched and when he pushed it open, Mona was kneeling over the toilet, her rayon dress bunched awkwardly at the tops of her legs.

"You okay?"

She retched again, throwing her whole body into it like a long jumper. "Oh, that's okay," he said and handed her some toilet paper to wipe her chin. "You're gonna be fine." He reached forward to rub her back.

"Please don't touch me," she said finally and she spit into the toilet, then wiped her mouth with the back of her hand. "I know what I'm doing."

When she turned around, he saw her lipstick had rubbed off. She looked at his shoes, his crotch, and when her eyes made it up to his face, she said, "Can you go get Heather?"

He headed back through the dark union and to the pub, whose

doors were closed and, as Anders discovered, yanking on them again and again, very locked. The lights were off and the music had stopped and there was no one in there, not even a bartender wiping the tables — or, it turned out, his good friend Larry.

Mona was rinsing her mouth at the sink when he came back. "I called us a cab," she said, typing into her phone with her thumb and then snapping it shut and adding, "Heather's such a ho." She straightened her dress in the mirror, then reached up and pulled the mustache off Anders's lip and dropped it to the floor. "Sorry," she said. "That thing was making me really sad."

Anders half expected to pass Larry stumbling home through the frozen leaves on the side of the road, so he kept his eyes open, watching through the blurry cab window the entire way back to his house. And it wasn't until the cab pulled over and he looked across the back of the sleeping girl that he realized he'd given the wrong address.

Helene had decorated the place tastefully: garland around the front door, lit with a spot and twinkling with a simple strand of white lights. There was a candle in each window, and behind the glass the house was dark, peaceful, the sky above it huge and black. She had been their art director, instructing him from the ground on how to drape the garland and where to place the wreaths. She had an instinct for these things and she was always right.

The cabbie looked at him in the rearview mirror, waiting for payment. It was three o'clock in the morning, no time for serious decisions, and yet before he could correct the address, he was out of the car and on his way to the front door, ready to tell her, finally, what a terrible mistake he had made.

PART TWO

1

The numbers weren't adding up. She knew the computer didn't lie and that the cells of this particular program had been calibrated by her development director, who had a degree in statistics and who also didn't lie, but unless Helene had accidentally added a zero somewhere, there was no way the budget for this fiscal year would balance. Which was really just perfect, considering the timing—three weeks before the board arrived expecting bagels and a budget surplus—and she would have to spend her morning sifting through sheets of numbers to identify places to cut or somehow come up with a painless solution (*Money from trees!* That was essentially what the board wanted, *a forest of money trees!*) before the fiscal year ended in June.

With responsibility came numbers, and her new job was held hostage by them. Budgets, stats, literacy rates, statehouse funding. And also by time: calendars that were synced to all her handheld devices and governed her days with their buzzes and chirps. This month alone she had the board meeting and an audit and a best friend who was camped in the hospital with her son, and somehow in the midst of it all, the holidays were supposed to happen, the Christmas Eve dinner she had insisted on hosting for reasons of tradition she now regretted. She had thought it was familiar, and after the year that she'd had, she found herself clinging to anything familiar. In months like this, it was less and less clear why she had courted this job to begin with.

Through the slats of her blinds, the gray industrial compost of Bridgeport Harbor that she could see was always there to remind her: this was a bankrupt city on every level, littered with dormant factory chutes and docks that had rotted to their stanchions; the red-and-white smokestack of an outdated coal plant standing like the shaft of a giant, filthy candy cane. Even the new single-A ball field and college hockey arena—built for the Volvo drivers and the Volvo drivers' money—did nothing more than ensure that the only jobs available in the port of this city's name were behind a concession stand. On bright days like this one, at the brightest hour of the morning, all that postindustrial blight seemed to absorb the light. Helene had worked here, on and off, for twenty-three years, and while the whole country got rich, this city had stayed poor. Or at least the people who lived here had. The ones who ran the city and the ball field and the harbor-front lofts, the ones who cornered her at council meetings and spoke of a utopian future in which the creative classes were lured out on the Metro North, seemed to blame the city's misfortune on its own citizens and believed the best route to revitalization was simply to replace them. Which, of course, was why they needed all that state aid—to run out the riffraff. And to help pay the high property taxes on the developers' homes in the surrounding towns.

She smiled. This was what the numbers did—they provoked her vitriol; they made her political. You couldn't last in this job without staying in touch with the human element. Without it, there were just problems, big immovable problems, but walk through the center and peer into the classrooms, and there they were: people, brave people, sounding out the words to *Curious George* and transforming their lives in the process. Helping even one person in a year learn how to read—that was progress. That was a miracle.

She closed her blinds and called in her development director to go through the numbers; she didn't have the time to do it herself. Her boyfriend—well, you could call him something more than that, though she had never understood the politics of the word *partner*, and given that he now lived with her (which was a whole other story), not to mention the fact that they were both over sixty, *boyfriend* just seemed absurd—anyway, her *guy* had instructed her to meet him in the city tonight at some Italian place in the West Sixties. He'd been so earnestly excited—something that had been in short supply for the men in her life as of late—that she'd agreed, even though it meant she had to leave work early, and if she managed to do that, on this day of all days, it would be another kind of miracle.

But first, her nine o'clock, a meeting with a client who had levied some serious accusations against his tutor, a situation that would not normally have been her responsibility except that the tutor happened to be her son. Preston had been living at home for three weeks because he'd been unable to support himself in Chicago. She'd convinced the board, perhaps regrettably, to ignore the conflict of interest and give her son an hourly wage for doing the same work that the volunteers did for free. So she and her man-friend and her thirty-three-year-old son had all been living under one roof, in bedrooms that were across the hall, and Preston, who was so furious with his father, so absolutely unforgiving in his judgment, had refused to tell him that he was even in town or that he was living at home. All of which was beside the point, but still, she hated lying—it filled her with a dread that was always more excruciating than coming clean—and she also hated accusing others of lying, as she was going to have to do in her nine o'clock.

The client was one of her favorites, a Haitian man named Guerlens Baptiste who worked as a mover and was learning to read, he said, so he could help his daughters with their homework. He had been a board-meeting talking point, possibly the spotlight story for their annual appeal, but then he accused Preston of stealing money from him. Despite the fact that she knew this to be ridiculous—Preston might have had some wayward years but he was no *thief*—it put her in a highly unfortunate position: she had to either ask the board to take her word for it or fire her son. In any case, her morning would be spent documenting Mr. Baptiste's story with a finicky old tape recorder and writing a report, and she had to come to a decision that didn't reek of nepotism before tomorrow's meeting.

She had all her calls routed to voice mail and turned off her cell phone. The last thing she needed were the interruptions, the relentless calls of apology—highly subtle, densely coded, interpretable-only-after-thirty-years-of-marriage apologies—that her ex-husband had been making pretty much on the hour. *Bloomberg* had a piece on fund-raising in the Internet age, he'd send her a link; the forecast mentioned snow and he wanted to remind her to tell the guys not to plow the graveled part of the driveway; Stop & Shop had a special on the kind of gruyère she liked; there were geese in Hillspoint Pond, *geese,* if you could believe it, so if there was any other proof those people needed of the existence of global warming, as if the melting of half of Greenland hadn't been enough, he was staring at it right now in Hillspoint Pond; on and on, when all he really wanted to know was if she'd forgiven him for being a total lunatic and waking up the house at three in the morning. He should have just considered himself lucky that Donny had recognized him before the nine-iron had taken off his head and that the police had been so understanding, but instead, the messages were piling up, turning her phone into an electronic guilt machine that made her angry and ashamed at feeling guilty in the first place, a guilt she would never tell anyone about because it implied that she still cared for him, even after this, the last piece of bullshit in the massive pile of bullshit he'd put her through.

In the dim, cramped confines of her office, Mr. Baptiste was immoderately tall. Part of it was the room, which had been closing in on her with piles of unread *Times* and the near-daily reports on the rising illiteracy and shrinking incomes of the largely immigrant populations they worked with, but part of it was also his proportions. He was skinny, unbelievably so at the waist, with the broad shoulders of an Olympic swimmer and the sort of charming short dreads that (she hated herself for even thinking it) would photograph quite nicely for the organization's appeal. His flannel shirt was open to a tank top, and over his shoulder was a leather weightlifting belt that he'd punched with an extra hole nearly an inch past the tightest one. He must have been a mover who used his frame—the mere physics of his skeleton—to lift objects twice his size, a thought that brought to mind the absurd image of this man carrying leather sofas around the great rooms that had been tacked onto the sides of all the saltboxes in her town. She opened the blinds to let in some light and cleared off a chair for Mr. Baptiste.

"How's that?" she said. She placed the tape recorder, an ancient tool they still used for assessments, on the coffee table between them and explained that it was part of the organization's protocol for dealing with these kinds of situations, and he should just talk naturally and try to forget it was there.

Mr. Baptiste smiled at this and she wondered if maybe she needed an interpreter who spoke Haitian Creole.

"So," she said. "I understand there's been a dispute with your tutor?"

"It's not a dispute," Mr. Baptiste said, still with that smile. There was nothing in the least bit sarcastic or menacing about it. It was earnest, which made her wonder if maybe the man was cognitively impaired, even if the language was fine. "He stole from me."

Helene nodded. "Okay," she said. "If you don't mind, Mr. Baptiste, would you explain everything, including as many specifics as you can—dates, exact things people said, anything like that."

"He stole from me."

Again Helene nodded. "Okay. Mr. Baptiste, if you don't mind, I'm going to ask you some questions that will hopefully help you fill out your..." She couldn't think of the right word. *Statement? Testimony?* Both implied that this was some sort of hearing, which, considering the situation, would be terribly unethical. "Perception of the events."

"On November the twentieth," said Mr. Baptiste, "my tutor"—he paused and glanced at Helene—"your son, told me about an opportunity to make money."

"Okay," said Helene. He could obviously understand quite a bit. "What kind of opportunity?"

"It was a game."

"The opportunity was a game?"

Mr. Baptiste shook his head. He pretended to hold an object about the size of a racquetball and made a long curved motion with his hand, as though something were protruding from his knuckles. "Like this," he said.

"Lacrosse?"

Mr. Baptiste shook his head sadly. There was real disappointment on his face. "They throw the ball," he said and before she could say anything else, it hit her with an awful recognition what he was talking about.

"Jai alai."

Mr. Baptiste smiled.

"He told you that you could make money on *jai alai?*"

"My truck is broken. I tell him this and he tells me he can help."

Helene exhaled. This was more like it—Preston offering to help. Of course he would offer to help.

"I didn't have enough but he told me to bring him the money and in one week he would bring back more."

"I see," she said. "And did he tell you how he planned to bring you more?"

"He said he knew who would win."

Years ago, there had been a jai alai facility visible from I-95 somewhere around Milford, one of the stranger aberrations in this part of the world, and as a child, Preston had been fascinated with it. Because of the nature of the sport and its huge dependence on gambling, she'd refused to let him attend the games (you didn't bring a kid to the dog track, did you?), though he did two reports on it for his Spanish class, hot-gluing photos he'd Xeroxed from the encyclopedia to a poster board. His reports, what she could understand of them, always emphasized the danger of the game—the injuries that could occur when a ball was moving at high speeds—and so she'd assumed his fixation with the place was just an early-adolescent curiosity with the forbidden. Though she could've sworn that the facility had been closed since the first Clinton term, something about Mr. Baptiste's story was making her uneasy.

"Did he say *how* he knew who would win?"

"Your son," said Mr. Baptiste, "is very persuasive."

"But what did he tell you?"

"He told me he knew a man who knew who would win—it was unexpected, nobody would guess. He said he was putting in all of his money—"

"I'm sorry, what?"

"He said he was putting in all of his money."

Helene composed herself, nodding.

"And that if I wanted a new truck, I should give him what I had. Like I said, your son is very persuasive," he said. "So I brought him my two thousand—"

Helene held up her hand. Two thousand was too much. It took this out of the realm of a good-hearted but boneheaded suggestion and into plain-old con.

"I'm sorry, Mr. Baptiste. How much did you say it was that you gave him?"

"Two thousand dollars," he said.

Helene leaned forward and clicked off the recorder.

◆

She taped a note to her office door and slipped down to her car. She tried Preston from the highway and was greeted over the stereo by the solicitous chirp of his voice mail. She hung up and merged into the fast lane on I-95, which, during the hours it wasn't clogged with traffic, was something like the Autobahn. Instinctively, she'd gotten on the highway heading south, toward home, but it was already after noon, and something in her gut told her to turn around. She exited at Black Rock, took the roundabout without braking, and floored it up the ramp. She'd had a better idea.

According to the Internet, there was a new jai alai fronton not far from the old one, which, she could see from the exit, had been turned into a sports bar with a vast, empty parking lot. The new arena had been built beside a batting cage at the end of an anonymous office park, and it was clear that no one was there. She supposed that after noon on a weekday wasn't a big time for underground gambling, but she did notice a few cars parked along the side of the building, so she rapped on the locked door until somebody came to answer it, a small man who appeared to be cleaning the floors. Behind him, pinned to the bulletin boards, were flyers for youth leagues, camps, in-house tournaments, all brightly colored and welcoming, in both Spanish and English. The place smelled less like an OTB parlor than a rec center, and as the man looked at her, she felt suddenly foolish.

"Hi," she said. "This is the—fronton?" She wasn't sure how to pronounce it, and every way she said it made it sound like she was ordering Chinese. "Jai alai?"

The man stared at her. He was sweating, and it occurred to her that what she'd assumed was a janitor's jumper may have been what people wore to play the game. In fact, that was certainly what it was. She was interrupting a game. "You know what?" she said. "I apologize." She cringed a moment. "But is there—is there gambling here?"

The man said nothing.

"Listen." She tried again, this time a lot less polite. "I'm looking for my son." She'd brought along a snapshot of Preston that had been taken at his graduation, capped and gowned between her and Anders, literally just hours before everything fell apart. The man's eyes lit up when he saw it. "Do you know him?"

As he smiled, she allowed herself a tiny pleasant fantasy—perhaps Preston was actually volunteering out here, helping to organize these programs, putting his degree to use, helping people. Perhaps everything with Mr. Baptiste was a mix-up.

"He comes at night," the man said.

"To play?"

He smiled again and shook his head. "To make money."

Helene wished she understood something about men: why they'd rather fuck up and be forgiven than not fuck up in the first place. Or maybe it was just the men around her who were like that; they stayed boyish and stupid because they knew she'd always forgive them. Maybe the problem was her. Sophie called it patience but mostly it felt like being a sucker. She thought about phoning her from the car, unloading some of this, but she couldn't burden Sophie with it, not now. And if she was honest with herself, she also couldn't call because she knew Sophie would tell her she had to fire her son and kick him out of the house—consequences! real, tough consequences!—which would force her to defend Preston and swallow her rage or vent it in some other way and end up ambushed with guilt, and these days she really, really didn't need any more of that.

All of this was roiling inside of her—mostly, she knew, because yet again she'd been made to feel stupid—but before she could get on the highway and break the speed limit getting back to the office and then bury herself pleasantly in work, she noticed a highly familiar Toyota 4Runner sitting alone in the gray expanse of that sports-bar parking lot.

Preston was sitting at the bar. The tables in there were lit with dramatic spotlights, and the rest of the light came from the televisions that blinked at you epileptically from all angles. Seen from across the room, he looked skinnier than usual, and paler; his hair was stringy as it hung behind his ears, though in fairness nobody looked healthy in the glow from a TV. He had a plate of food in front of him, which was encouraging, and what appeared to be a Coke in a pint glass. He was fixated on a screen. Helene had to rest her hand on his shoulder, a sharp angle under his flannel shirt, before he turned.

"Hello." His eyes flicked back to the screen, which was showing a soccer game. Helene sat on the stool beside him and put down her bag.

"I've been looking everywhere for you."

"This is pretty impressive," he said. "Did you have me followed?" He smiled in that vague way she'd never been able to understand, as though he were saving the joke to tell someone later, and it was this, combined with the fact that after his initial glance at her he hadn't looked away from the screen, that reminded her of exactly how pissed off she was.

"I had a very interesting meeting today," she said.

"I didn't steal the guy's money."

He said it matter-of-factly, as though he had already heard the entire tape.

"Two *thousand* dollars?" she said. "Two thousand dollars from an *illiterate* man?"

"I thought you didn't like to use that word."

"Goddamn it, Preston. *Look* at me."

He turned and fixed his big green eyes on her. "He gave it to me," he said very calmly.

"For you to gamble? On *jai alai?*"

"Do I get a chance to tell my side of the story?"

She glanced at her watch. "You've got two minutes."

"He was desperate," he said. "He was thinking of asking some guy in his neighborhood for a loan, not the sort of guy you want to owe anything to. I explained to him how these things work, how he could end up very hurt if he didn't pay it back right away, and how he'd end up paying a lot more than he needed to. He said the other thing he might do is go to one of those car lots and take one of their jacked-up financing options—and, Mom, I know. It's what he should have done. But he asked me if I knew of anything else."

"And you thought, *Oh yeah, there's that underground gambling I'm involved with.*"

Preston shook his head and turned back to the screen. "Let's just get this over with," he said.

"Get *what* over with?"

"The firing. The sacking. I get it."

Helene tried to catch her son's eye. His profile was so delicate; she was once again amazed at the sorts of places she had gone to collect him in his short life—a disgusting squat in Burlington, Vermont; a dingy detox in LA; that apartment in Evanston with six dissertation-prolonging roommates and apparently not a single sponge; and this, an amateur jai alai center, where her delicate boy, she could now see, was certainly being hustled.

"Listen," she said. "I'm in a tough spot."

"I understand."

"Even if you meant well, Preston, it looks like nepotism if I don't fire you."

"You don't have to explain it."

"Preston, how much money have you lost?"

He looked at her.

"What makes you say *lost?*"

"Come on."

"None," he said and went back to the game.

"How much money do you have on this game?"

He shrugged. "I like Champions League."

This was a classic Preston nonanswer. Her son wasn't so much a liar as a withholder, a half-truther who strategically released information when he knew it would get him off the hook. When he called to say he wanted to go back to school and get a degree in social policy, of all things, she'd found herself telling the most unlikely people—the fellow in the parking booth at work, the lady behind the loud chrome machine preparing her macchiato—explaining all the details of his matriculation, how his grab bag of credits would transfer, how many courses Northwestern required, how many times she found herself saying the name Northwestern, the unexpected pleasure it gave her, its proof that all her leniency—all those claims that Preston was "finding his way"—had been right and her son wasn't a loser and she wasn't an enabler either.

It was true he had finished the degree, a surprise to both her and Anders, but there was a part of her, the most cynical part, that knew he'd needed money, money that his father had long ago sworn off sending him, and Preston had understood that the only way to get a regular check in the mail was to tell his parents he was doing what they'd always wished he would. It was often shocking to her, after all her years as a parent, how little she actually knew of her children.

"All right," she said, and she stood up. "You're fired. And you have a week to find another place to live."

She wanted to walk away but lingered to see if he even turned his head, and in that hesitation, her guilt returned. She could never stay angry long enough for the anger to protect her.

"Well, you should probably find a place too," he said.

"Excuse me?" She had on her best teacher face, the one she'd perfected when she was working in the Bronx in the seventies, but he didn't notice because his eyes were still on that boring goddamn game. The score was zero to zero. He might as well stare at a green wall.

"Dad's not paying the mortgage," he said.

"What?"

"Hasn't in almost a year. Tommy told me. So you should probably find another place before those guys in nylon jackets come and padlock the doors or whatever it is they do."

Helene sat back down.

"Tommy told you this?"

Preston slurped the bottom of his Coke with his straw. "Yep."

"A *year*? He said it'd been a *year*?"

He nodded, and for the first time since she had arrived, he seemed to actually see her. "Sorry," he said. "I guess that's bad timing."

She picked up her bag.

"You're still fired," she said.

2

By four o'clock she was on the express to Grand Central with two tote bags of work and a new budget to review. Outside the sky was bruised, the marsh grasses and estuaries of the sound slipping past. She never understood the disdain all those commuters had for this trip. It was quiet and relatively scenic and she had a fondness for the roll call of bedroom communities the conductor rattled off at every stop ("East Norwalk! South Norwalk! Noroton Heights! Darien!"): the ritual, on this end, of entering the Great Metropolis and, on the other, of escaping its chaos for the warm envelope of home.

It was her first lull in an anaerobic day, and, against her better judgment, she decided to check her messages. There were six—five from her ex-husband and one from Donny—each with a ripe blue dot beside it. In the first, Anders rambled for two and a half minutes about quinoa, which he'd just now discovered thanks to the good people at the *Wall Street Journal*, and even though there was a big red Delete button on the screen, the funny thing was she found herself leaning against the window and listening through to the end of that message and all his others. It was habit, mostly—forty years with a man who treated communication as a reward would do that to you.

Though, really, the habit was formed in those last few years, when he would show up at home an hour after his train had gotten in, saying he'd left his car at the station and decided to walk, in the middle of winter, in his Italian leather bucks, the tip of his nose red and runny, and even still he'd barely touch his dinner, which admittedly tasted weird, because it had been warming on low for over an hour. Of course she'd had her theories, thousands of them, about the job souring and the slog of the commute, about how their lifestyles had ballooned and stuck him with the bill, but they were just theories. She searched for clues in whatever communication he would give her, but in the end, all she really knew was his exclusion of her, and so, after he would retreat to bed early, reading article after article with his head propped on pillows, she would dump half a bottle of chardonnay in her glass and stay up long past midnight, playing computer solitaire in her robe.

It wasn't her proudest time, and she had come to associate its sedentariness and spiraling introspection—and mostly its powerlessness—with the end of one stage (middle age, maybe, or motherhood, or the clarity and comfort of the nuclear family) and the beginning of another. Whatever that new stage would be (a sort of pre–nursing home, postchildren second adolescence?) had yet to be fully defined, except that was also when all the trouble started, when her world went gravityless and she could feel everything down to the floorboards coming apart around her.

Looking back, she could see that its beginning was so common as to be boring, but at the time, it was something of a wonder to receive an e-mail in the middle of the night announcing that Donald Fitzsimmons wanted to be her friend. The board had recently decided, along with the rest of the world, that the key to fund-raising was in social media, so on her lunch break one day she had clicked through a series of blue boxes, entered her life statistics, uploaded a headshot from the staff page, and thought nothing more of it. Within an hour she was inundated with requests from Tommy's childhood friends, names she hadn't heard in years, many of whom had ultrasounds as their profile pics, it seemed, to advertise their induction into the phase of life she was just leaving. It was pleasant, she supposed, to click through all those photos and glimpse all those lives, but otherwise the whole thing felt to her like a grand party that had started long before she had arrived, one with its own language and demands, and there was nothing worse than arriving late to a party whose jokes you didn't understand. But at the lowest hour of her night, after five full rounds of solitaire and about as many goblets of wine, the intrusion of a *real* old friend, one that announced in the subject line of the e-mail that he *wanted to be her friend,* made all the noise of that grand party suddenly feel as intimate as a whisper.

And so whisper they did. What started as a friendly note—*So how's the smartest girl I know?*—became a kind of furious banter. Her solitaire time was now spent firing off notes and refreshing her browser, and soon the conversation leaked over into IM chats at work, endless meandering typing, so that as long as she was near a screen she never felt alone because there he was, in that bottom right corner, waiting to respond. When the confessional stuff started, all those long, long e-mails about their desires and the boredom of their real lives, about the winter light in Londonderry and the way that the row of rusted container cranes out her window at work looked to her like a family of sleeping swans, she knew it was only a matter of time before they decided to meet.

They chose a hotel in Portsmouth. It was fall, and though they had never discussed it, she assumed they had picked a spot on the New England coast because it was where they remembered each other. Though how she had remembered him was *smaller*. It was true that in his photos he had looked hulking and bearded (so much so that Sophie had dubbed him the real-world incarnation of Fred Flintstone), but those photos had been taken with the peewee hockey squad he coached, its players all smaller than whatever trophy it was they were hoisting over their heads, so she figured it was a trick of proportion until the moment he stepped out of his car in Portsmouth.

According to a frayed patchwork of sources—old friends, alumni newsletters, and a recent scouring of the Internet—Donny Fitzsimmons had lived two distinct lives in the many years since she had seen him. The first was as the manager and eventual co-owner of his cousin's heating-oil business in Nashua, a mom-and-pop outfit that, according to a local article, Donny had built into a regional powerhouse with a fleet of trucks roaring across southern New Hampshire and a series of AM radio ads that sang his name between the innings of Red Sox games.

Donny's second life, though, was a little less clear. It began after a spectacular lawsuit filed by his cousin, the business co-owner, for carrying on with his cousin's wife what, according to some salacious rumors at their college reunion, amounted to an extended covert fuckfest. Whether it was true or not, he surrendered his half of the business, moved up the road to Londonderry, got sober, and became a peewee hockey coach. That new life, as far as Helene could tell, had held stable for a solid decade and despite her obvious concerns about his moral character, she was the most puzzled about why, even after his rebirth, after he had become wildly successful as a consultant for the natural-gas industry, he still had never married. It was a question that, at her most cynical, left her with a much sadder impression of his life, one of take-out cartons and porn subscriptions and an eHarmony profile he kept at the urging of his sister.

When she first saw him, he had his hands in the pockets of his slacks, a tall wall of a guy, bellied, wearing an orangey cable-knit that could pass for either a yacht owner's or a chowder spokesman's (a color that didn't do much to silence Sophie's voice in her head bellowing, *Wiiillllma!*). He was as handsome as she'd remembered, handsomer even, with the infuriating pixie dust of male wrinkles and a natural easiness he seemed to have grown into. He didn't have to try so hard to make people like him; in fact, in the way of all gentle giants, he didn't have to try at all. He hugged her and he smelled just-out-of-the-shower clean, and all the stiffness she'd projected onto their transition from the online world to the real one fell away.

They walked politely from shop to shop and chatted politely and had a polite dinner in a restaurant overlooking the harbor. It occurred to her, as he was pulling out her chair, that she had skated through life without ever going on a formal date, and what was thrilling about finding herself on one wasn't all the coded communication or the evaluative dance but rather the sense that there was another person inside of her that suddenly seemed available. Most of being young, she had always thought, was playing a game of elimination with an army of different selves until you settled on one, usually by circumstance. But what made her grin, sitting across a starched white tablecloth from a man who seemed to actually listen to her, was the feeling that all those other selves weren't dead. They were still alive—multitudes of them, waiting inside her.

On the drive up to Portsmouth, once she had admitted to herself what she was doing, there were only two ways she could think of it. One was as a simple transgression: she could embrace the act as a pure expression of the heart. To this, she thought of the Stevie Nicks song, one of her favorites, imagined a willowy woman in scarves at a microphone, sur-rounded by men, her fist in her hair, telling the world not to blame her but to blame her wild heart. Sure, the song was a little corny, but it was tempting to frame infidelity as *more* honest, not less, even if, deep down, it seemed to her like a pretty sure recipe for dying alone. The other way to think of it was to use microlevels of justification, to tell herself at each stage—every time she refreshed her in-box, every private feel-ing divulged—that she was still completely aboveboard and if, say, her husband were to find out, he would probably be fine with it. And even though she sang along to Stevie Nicks at the top of her lungs all the way to Portsmouth, Helene was defi-nitely in the second category, which was why she had refused to remove her wedding ring even when they were in bed and why she had closed the blackout curtains and had wanted to pull the blankets up over their heads and stay in that quilted cocoon until Sunday morning.

Also, she refused to have sex. This, you might imagine, would be the hallmark of a terrible mistress, and you would be right. The whole time she could think only of Anders, not so much the recent man but the one she had married, and less about how much it would hurt him than about how simply *con-fused* he would be, how little any of it would square with what he thought he knew of his wife. She spent most of the weekend apologizing and crying while she felt Donny's big arms around her and she listened to him repeat, in his consummately considerate way, that it was all right, he understood, it was all pretty complicated.

On the way back she figured that would settle it, that would drive away Donny and solve her problem. But when she made it home, invigorated and ready to cook them a big dinner, it seemed Anders had not moved from the sofa and, although he'd left a queue of dishes for her on the counter, hadn't seemed to notice she was gone. So she dropped her sack of groceries on the counter, the baguette vertical, popped two Lean Cuisines in the microwave, and, without bothering to ask him about his weekend, headed back upstairs to her computer.

Which was when things got serious. All the flirting and teasing and poetic earnestness gave way to explicit plans. Whereas before she had avoided mentioning Anders to Donny at all, now he was named and all of the inner workings of her marriage were dumped into Facebook messages, which Donny seemed to patiently tolerate as she concocted the grand scheme for her escape. No matter how complex her variations, it was a plan that amounted to packing a bag and getting in the car and driving north to what was, she assumed, Donny's very nice fairway-side condominium. It was a plan that involved leaving Anders, finally, to his goddamn paper and his goddamn dishes and seeing how long it took him to even notice.

But he didn't notice, because of course she continued to do the dishes, as always, and left him alone to read, as always, and the only place all her newfound rage took her was a Hampton Inn on 495, somewhere in the vicinity of Worcester. There, all of the gestures toward romance of Helene and Donny's first failed rendezvous were replaced by a kind of determined disrobing, followed by a somewhat automatic process that was instigated by her and therefore tinged with a vengeance that made the whole thing feel about as sexy as a pelvic exam. Afterward, they ordered Domino's pizza and ate it in bed with the warm box on their laps. She turned to him then and confessed, with a mouth full of pepperoni, that this finally seemed to have enough self-loathing and lovelessness to qualify as an affair—a joke! An admittedly unfunny-and-also-kind-of-true joke. Donny's face went white, and though he played it off well, he still climbed out of bed and put on his T-shirt.

This time she drove home relieved and stopped at the gourmet market for Kobe steaks and wild-caught salmon, determined to finally cook that big meal even if it meant eating it across from a husband who was about as appreciative as a totem pole. They ate the meal, which Anders even mentioned was delicious, and for the first time in perhaps a year, she went to bed at the same time he did, feeling wifely and good as she read beside him on a matching hummock of pillows. So what was it that made her get up in the middle of the night and turn on her computer? What was it that kept her there, reading the three long messages that were waiting for her about how for Donny it wasn't just an affair, that he understood she was in a difficult spot, but for him it was never any question what he wanted—he wanted her, he had always wanted her, a woman he had loved since he was nineteen and who it was clear deserved to be treated much, much better.

What was it then that made her write him back, even though she knew it would all start again, her dual life, what made her say to herself that she would be happy if she could somehow have both, one in person and the other on a little phone in her pocket that vibrated when it was time for some attention? And most important, what made her go on to *have* both, months and months of a split life, more Hampton Inns and invented conferences, more Domino's pizza and quilt cocoons and much, much better sex, all of it coming easier, with fewer tears and a lot more Stevie Nicks? And then what was it, seemingly out of nowhere, that made her end it, just as easily as it had begun, with a Facebook message in the middle of the night saying she could no longer see him?

Sophie told her it was because of her conscience, because she was a genuinely good person, but Helene knew the real reason, one she wouldn't admit even to Sophie, and it had nothing to do with guilt. The real reason was that when she made it home at the end of the night and logged on, she found herself more interested in playing computer solitaire than responding to another one of Donny's impossibly thoughtful letters. Of course, she couldn't have known the absurdity of her timing, that she had cut it off only weeks before Anders declared his decision to divorce and that a tumor the size of a marble was growing strong in her left breast.

Illness in its own way is embarrassing and private. At times, it felt like the most private thing she had ever experienced, so Anders's aloofness was just what she needed. If he had been an eager puppy who read the cancer books along with her and insisted on telling her she was beautiful as she lay in the recovery room, she would certainly have pushed him away. And though this was an aspect of him that her friends had never understood ("There's a difference," Sophie had said, "between someone who's depressed and someone who treats you like shit"), she knew enough about herself to understand that his distance was also the thing that made him attractive, the thing that, even when they were nineteen—and she had been, unbelievably, choosing between these same two men—had always captured her interest: his unavailability. The fact that he needed her completely and yet was so far from admitting it that he couldn't admit it to himself. Which of course for her was a blueprint for its own kind of unfulfillment. Yet she knew enough about herself to understand the sway he still held over her.

So when, after the rabbit hole of amputation and intravenous drugs that was her treatment, Anders had opted to stick with his original plan—which she *knew* he would, she wasn't stupid—she had poured herself a glass of wine and, knowing exactly what would happen, logged back on to her Facebook account. Within six months, Donny had moved south; within eight, they shared an address.

And Donny was *great,* he really was, even though he was a Republican, which wasn't a reason not to be in love with someone. She just couldn't figure out why she kept ending up with these individualist cowboy types. Anders's politics, like everything else in the last year, had changed to something indiscernible—anarchy?—though he had become fixated on global warming, which was yet another system in the giant system of systems that was being unjustly exploited. And you would think Donny, with his lifelong involvement in athletics, who had preached to his players about the importance of team and who seemed to value the fraternal bonds of that group over just about anything else, might extend that thinking beyond the locker room. But when it came to making a living, it was all myth-of-the-individual stuff, just like Anders (who, inexplicably, had voted for Perot *twice*). Donny seemed to read only fat biographies of people like Churchill and Carnegie, seemed to hold unwavering admiration for nearly all titans of industry, who, at least in the narratives of their ghostwriters, had overcome tremendous adversity with little more than hard work to stand on the very top of the human pile. Besides their lack of cooking skills, it was the most boyish thing about these men, all of it some prolonged cowboy stage, and when she pictured them together, she couldn't help seeing them in John Wayne hats, snapping cap guns at each other.

But otherwise Donny was *great*. He had gladly moved his hideous leather sectional and sixty-inch sports screen down to the basement, along with his hockey bag and bucket of pucks, and when she returned from work one day that first week, he had filled the whole house with plants—jade and gardenia and even a miniature Meyer lemon tree—because she had been in a terrible mood when she saw all his stuff intermingled with hers and had told him, oddly, that all that leather and plastic just reminded her of *death*, and more and more these days what she needed was to be around living things, happy living things. Hence the plants, which he watered and she did enjoy, and hence the house, which still looked nearly identical to the way it had for the last thirty years. It was all a transition, a big monstrous transition that she knew she couldn't have managed without him, but now that the pleasant weight of him beside her in bed had become normal, and the little green stoppers he brought her from Starbucks so she wouldn't spill her coffee on the way to work had accumulated into a sticky pile in her glove compartment, and now that she was no longer even uncomfortable standing naked in front of him with her new breasts (which were a half a size bigger and looked terrific in a bra but were frankly gruesome when bare), she was starting to wonder if maybe, just maybe, she had rushed things.

Now, the train hissed to a stop in Grand Central, and she filed with the others onto the hot platform and up into the giant marble chamber, whose barrel-vaulted ceiling often left her standing, even in the swarm of rush hour, with her head back and her mouth open. It was painted the deep Atlantic green of the sky just before dawn, a peaceful, private time of day suspended above the frenzy. This giant space, this magnificent, manic hive, had always been connected somehow to her own living room—it was the nexus between work and home that made that life possible, a thought that suddenly caused her stomach to drop. If Preston was to be believed, which she had a sinking feeling that in this case, he was, then they had finally found the end of their thirty-some-year experiment in the suburbs. Funny how it wasn't the divorce so much as losing the house that defined that ending for her, and funny how she wasn't angry so much as wistful, the way you were when you could finally see the whole of something. This was how it all ended. This was where it all ended up.

Her cab flew up Sixth Avenue, skirting the acid trip of Times Square and turning onto Central Park South, where horses pulling tourists clopped along beside the cars and all the hotel windows were wreathed with giant green boughs. They inched through the swirl of Columbus Circle and finally onto Broadway, where she stopped the cab two blocks from the restaurant and, even though she was already late, ducked through the plastic flaps of a Korean produce stand.

Over the past few months, she'd made a habit of slipping out of work and driving to the closest grocery store, a worn-down Pathmark whose shopping carts had mostly been stolen. There, she would search the cardboard bin in the produce section for the roundest grapefruit she could find, which was often more like a yellow cube, and bring it back to her car. She would feel its satisfying weight in her palm, hold it up to her nose and run its surface along one cheek, then the other, before plunging her thumb through the skin and taking her time peeling it, top to bottom, in one continuous spiral. She never ate the fruit—usually it went back into the bag and the bag went into the nearest garbage can—but the citrusy smell would be pleasantly under her fingernails for the rest of the day. It was admittedly peculiar behavior, and something she could explain about as well as she could her dreams, but in the past month she had probably gone through a crate of cheap ruby reds, which made the one she was holding now feel round and firm and essential. She paid for it and slipped it into her purse.

She was twenty minutes late by the time she found the address. She had expected to find Donny waiting patiently at the bar with his Diet Coke, she had expected to apologize and kiss his cheek and chalk her lateness up to her crazy day, but she hadn't expected that the Italian restaurant she had traveled all the way into the city for would actually be a pizza joint. Donny was sitting in the fluorescent lights at a table in the back, an orange tray in front of him with four cooling slices on two paper plates.

"Surprise," he said and slurped from his soda.

As he stood and enveloped her in a hug, she felt something inside her release so that her knees nearly gave out, leaving her dangling from his neck.

"You okay?" he said and she stood up, straightened herself.

She took a deep breath and smiled.

"Now I'm wonderful," she said.

She had skipped lunch, so she was halfway through a slice before Donny had a chance to ask her about her day.

"Long," she said.

"How'd it go with the accuser?"

"Oh." She pictured Preston hunched over that huge bar, watching soccer. "Fine."

"Fine?" he said. "Problem solved?"

"Yeah."

Why she was withholding it from him she wasn't totally sure. She was already feeling terrible about tossing her son onto the street, but she knew it wasn't as much about Preston as it was about the house and therefore about Anders, whose failures no longer surprised her as much as her instinct to protect him did.

"Disappointed in the meal?" he said.

She held up her paper plate, dropping crumbs across the table. "I am."

"We better get moving." He took the tray to the garbage bin. "The show starts in twenty."

On the table in front of her, as if by magic, were two tickets to *The Nutcracker*.

Donny winked from the door. "After you."

He took her bags and she took his arm and they walked across Broadway and up the steps to Lincoln Center, its great fountain dormant for winter. They made their way into the velvety red lobby and to the tenth row of the orchestra. Numerous balconies towered above them, the proscenium itself tall and wide enough to house a downtown apartment building. The whole complex felt out of fashion, a holdover from the sixties, yet inexplicably elegant. Donny had crammed himself into the little theater seat with his hands gripping his knees as if he were holding his whole body together. None of this—the ballet, the ladies in furs, Lincoln Center—was his thing, and she would have been just as happy to go to a Rangers game, but seeing him folded in that seat, his face already flushed, smiling mildly as the woodwinds in the pit tested their reeds like a flock of sad birds, made her reach over and run her hand along the fine hairs on the back of his neck.

The lights went down and the music started and soon the curtain rose high into the rafters, exposing yet again that happy family on Christmas Eve surrounded by presents and celebrating before the family went to bed, and the mice appeared, and a girl watched the tree grow three times its size before her very eyes. It was classic Balanchine, unchanged in its schmaltz since its New York premiere in the fifties—same cartoony Russian costumes, same tights and tutus, and of course the same nineteenth-century grandeur in the music, music that had been appropriated for Macy's commercials and *Home Alone* montages—and yet somehow she found herself, in the ambient glow of the stage lights, utterly ambushed by it. It seemed as though she felt every trill under her fingernails and heard every theme as if for the first time, so that when the snow started falling on the stage, floating in the footlights, a magical thing, and the harp came in with a children's choir not far behind, the crash of cymbals and the swelling of strings and horns—Jesus, *horns*—all of it combining at once, relentless and familiar and a relic of her not-too-distant past, she found herself in tears on the floor of the New York State Theater.

When the lights came up at the end of act 1, she was sure her face was a puffy mess, so she excused herself out of their row and into the line for the ladies' room. She found a balled tissue in her purse and tried her best to do some damage control, and when she brought the tissue back from her face she noticed she was shaking. She was fine; it was silly, this reaction, crying at *The Nutcracker*. It was a children's show! She was fine. When she made it into a stall, she closed the toilet lid and reached into her purse.

The grapefruit was smaller than she remembered, a cool orb in her palm that she brought up to her nose and then to each cheek. Maybe it was a good thing that she had to move. Maybe she could truly start again, devote herself to her work and her garden and maybe do what the rest of her family did—worry only about themselves. Maybe then she could sit through the first act of *The Nutcracker* like a normal person and sleep through the night without anesthetizing herself with Benadryl and maybe, just maybe, stop feeling guilty about the fact that more and more when she thought about her family, all she felt was betrayal.

She had been telling herself that she wasn't angry for so long that she didn't know what she felt anymore. She had wells of fury inside her that had no place to come out, anger they would never know, anger that she didn't even understand. It was like poison in the groundwater; it leached out whether she wanted it there or not. And in the past year, when she was cooped up in recovery, covered in blankets and on a morphine drip, and her three men—Tommy and Preston and Anders—just stood around her, wordless, with their arms at their sides like a pack of baboons, she'd become something more like a Superfund site. In retrospect, she understood the inherent clumsiness that husbands and sons have around ill women, but it didn't stop her from being furious that she'd reached a point in her life when none of them cared enough to need her anymore.

The peel came off easily—a good clean spiral, no breaks— and she was steadied. There were new town houses in Black Rock down by the water. She could afford one without money from anyone, be closer to work, trade in her Audi for something sensible. Simplify. This felt right—it felt, in a term she had always loathed, *age appropriate*. There was no reason to hold on to the house or any of the fantasies that had come with it. Let them all go, be free of them, be free of all of them, and with them all her needless worries.

Donny was waiting for her outside the ladies' room with a cup of champagne.

"Everything okay?" he said.

"Of course." She kissed him.

"What's in your hand?"

She looked down. She had forgotten she was still holding the fruit and the peel.

"A grapefruit," she said.

"I see that."

"You want some?"

Donny took the grapefruit and replaced it with the champagne.

"Cheers," he said and held up the skinned fruit. She tapped the plastic cup to it and when she brought it down something in Donny's eyes had turned deeply serious.

"Are you having a good time?" he said.

"Donny," she said. "It's perfect. I'm having a *perfect* time."

His face seemed to soften with relief. "That's good to hear."

"*Relax*," she said. "You did good."

There was a moment when she thought that perhaps this affirmation had been enough to take his legs out from under him or that maybe he was having a major medical event—how very Donny it would be to be so concerned about her comfort that he didn't even notice the tingling in his shoulder—either of which would have been much less surprising than what was actually happening, which was that Donny had dropped to his knee, right there on the plush red carpet during the intermission of *The Nutcracker*, and was holding up a box with the single biggest diamond she had ever seen.

3

Anders figured he knew how it would all go down. Larry would know a guy, probably a kid Tommy's age, a hedgie who worked from a laptop in a shed in his Darien backyard—the future, Larry would say, the sort of kid who had made a billion dollars last year in his Adidas sandals. Larry would tell Anders not to worry about it, it was just money, they could make it back in an hour; all Anders had to do was give him a number and Larry would place the order. He'd slap him on the shoulder and tell him to relax, it's what friends were for, and toast him with his third drink of the morning.

Larry lived in the original farmhouse on Beachside, a property that had been divvied up into an entire avenue of waterfront estates, walled-off monuments with service entrances and wrought-iron gates and hunks of modern sculpture strewn about the front lawns. His greenhouse came off the side of his home, a tall glass structure that looked like it might hold the food court of a major museum. Inside, it was something of a gymnasium of flora—all leaves and humidity, dirt and cement. He led Anders down a long row of what appeared to be pots of earth. He was barefoot, the cuffs of his Dockers rolled, and as he walked, he'd occasionally touch the beds of soil with his thumb and then smell it. "Tells me if they're healthy," he said. "You develop a knack for it." He went over to the corner and ran a pitchfork through a steaming heap of compost. It was black and as he turned it, some vapor escaped. "Put your hands in there," he said. "Go ahead. It won't hurt you." It was surprisingly smooth, soft, really, and gave off a rich scent of organic matter. "Cleanest thing on the planet," Larry said. "From garbage to the espresso of soil in a couple of months."

When he had a lot of work to do, Larry said, he turned off the ringer. Anders had assumed that by "a lot of work to do," he meant something like managing his portfolio, but Larry meant planting a kind of heirloom called Mr. Stripey. Raising tomatoes, he said, snapping a brown leaf from the bottom of a nearby plant, wasn't just about bearing witness to the cycles of life—all that living and dying and producing of fruit—but about putting your hands in the ground. "Touch the place where we intersect with the earth, where our food comes from and where we're eventually headed, get that stuff under your fingernails," he said, "and you're changed forever." He'd been inviting classes from Bridgeport out there, elementary-school kids who had no idea their hamburger was cow and thought food came from bodegas. "Mostly I want them digging in the dirt," he said. "That's enough. I discovered the hard way they're all plant murderers."

In the week since Anders's humiliating scrape with the law—a ridiculous incident, when he thought about it, the behavior of a crazy person—he'd been doing some evaluating. From what he remembered of that night, which unfortunately was almost everything, he recalled elucidating for the police officer that it wasn't breaking and entering if he had a key to the front door, not to mention if the house was in his name, and especially if his wife—ex-wife, whatever—was standing right there. He remembered pointing, a lot of pointing, and though all the cop had done was scribble silently in his pad, the lights on his car still whirling, and all Helene and Donny had done was stand there staring at him in their pj's and terry-cloth robes, that was enough. He'd ridden home in the back of the squad car with his forehead against the window and a Budweiser button still blinking on his lapel.

What followed, though, was a morning of such raw clarity, such sober awareness, that he found himself waking at dawn, flinging open the curtains on the low cotton sky and cleaning his condo to the grout. He filled his cabinets with groceries, bought end tables from a design store, and rearranged the furniture until it felt like a room that a person might want to be in. He took a brisk morning walk and spent the evening with books, adventure stories mostly, though over the week that followed he also ventured into the shelf of self-help tomes that Helene had pushed on him, books that turned out to be smarter than he had thought, that pinpointed some of his feelings with embarrassing precision and almost always ended by recommending meditation. Which he tried—he tried everything. He apologized to Helene on her voice mail and he ate less meat and he cut out most of the caffeine and all of the booze and with them the twin drugs of rage and self-pity, waking in the morning refreshed and calm and with a rare sense of clarity about the life he was no longer ashamed to say he was wrong to have left.

Larry and Anders wheeled the top dressing over to a row of pots and packed it with their bare hands. "Not too tight," Larry said. "Like you're tucking them in." They worked in silence. Occasionally a fine mist would spray over the rows like in the produce aisle at a supermarket but otherwise it was still and quiet.

"So," Larry said when they had them all packed. "Should we talk numbers?"

"Why don't we go inside."

Larry's kitchen was an open palace of granite and brushed steel that made even Anders's renovation seem modest. The range had eight different burners, none of which seemed to have been used, and the refrigerator was one of those restaurant-grade bunkers, the kind with a door that you had to use your whole body weight to open. They scrubbed their hands at the sink with a rough powdery substance that Larry said could also take the stain out of the tub, and he punched a button on the coffee machine. The afternoon sun burned through the clouds and for a moment the countertops were ablaze, the whole room awash in white. There was no way Larry had designed this kitchen himself.

"Nope," he said when Anders asked. "Course not. This was her last project—took two full years! Turns out nothing says 'It's over' quite like a warming drawer."

The coffee machine gurgled. Larry poured them two mugs and held his to his lips, smiling. "So," he said, the steam fogging the bottoms of his glasses.

Anders told him what he owed.

Larry took a small sip, seemed to let it linger on his tongue, and swallowed. "And here I thought you might have come by for a visit."

"Look," Anders said. "I don't want you to loan me *all* of it."

Larry crossed the kitchen to a drawer that held a leather binder of checks.

"Seriously, I was thinking maybe about an investment," Anders continued. "Didn't you say you knew a kid who was into some new high-yield—"

Larry wrote the check, tore it out, and held it for him.

"Look," said Anders. "You know I can't take that."

"You still love her?" said Larry.

"I'm sorry?"

Larry held his gaze. "You heard me."

Anders took the check.

He helped Larry until the sun was low and even the greenhouse was dark. His hands and his pants were filthy and as he drove home he could feel a smudge of dirt on his brow and a calm sense of accomplishment. It had been ten days since the party and already he felt renewed. Ten more like this and he might end up with a decent Christmas after all.

Driving past the clean rows of his neighbors' condos, which were wreathed in garlands, he caught sight of the blinking halo of light that emanated from his place. Despite the complaints ("tacky," his neighbors called it; "embarrassing"), or likely because of them, he had been leaving his display blazing through the night while he sank into the pleasant indent of his memory-foam mattress.

There was nobody around to complain—the streets, as usual, were empty and silent—but when he made it to the spectacle of his property, there was an unfamiliar car waiting for him in his driveway. It was a dark Escalade of the sort that carried diplomats and drug dealers. It was still running, mumbling some kind of talk radio, and had a license plate, he noticed when he got out of his car, from New Hampshire.

"*There* he is."

Donny climbed out of the driver's seat, his big car dinging, and offered Anders the engulfment of his hand. "Quite a place you got here." He was grinning, as if acknowledging a joke. He had on a tie and a nice camel-hair overcoat with a pink ribbon on the lapel. It was all more private bodyguard than Wall Street. "Sorry to barge in on you like this."

Donny, he noticed then, was looking at him with worry more than anything else. It was a look that triggered in Anders a vague memory from the other night of pointing at Donny's terry-cloth monogram and shouting, "*He's the criminal! He's the criminal!,*" which was not only dumb but humiliatingly dumb. Beside them, a group of inflatable carolers were beeping noisily through the end of "Silent Night."

"Come on," said Anders. "Let's go inside."

During his final years at Bowdoin, Anders had expected to answer his door at 2:00 a.m. to a drunk Fitzy waiting to toss him around by his lapels, but it had never happened. After Helene moved in with Anders above the Penobscot, something in Donny had changed. The Fitzy who could drink a case of beer himself and had used their dorm-room chalkboard to illustrate for Anders the colorful definition of a dirty Sanchez was replaced by the quiet history nerd who had always been lurking inside him. He became sullen and studious, walking around with a large green library tome under his arm and the distant, vaguely cross look of someone who'd spent the day reading. The irony, of course, was that Anders found this side of Donny much more interesting and so, when he saw Donny ambling across the quad or barricaded alone at a table in the library, there was a part of him that wished there were a way to reconcile their rift, that wished, in short, that there was still room somewhere for the three of them.

So around graduation he stopped by Donny's house, the A-frame out on Merepoint he rented with some other guys from the team. There had been a party there the night before; the yard was littered with bottles, and Donny was the only one up, sitting on a log in his sweatpants and slippers, reading the paper with a plug of Skoal in his lip. It was mid-May and the summer folks would soon be back to claim their houses, hurling them all into the workforce for good, so there had been an end-of-days quality to the week, with lots of arms around shoulders and professions of love, and Anders had awoken that morning with the need to set things right. He brought a box of doughnuts and some coffee and a leather-bound copy of Marcus Aurelius, none of which seemed to surprise Donny, who was mostly interested in spitting his hangover into the bottom half of a beer can.

"*Meditations,*" Donny had said, holding up the spine of the book. "I like Aurelius."

"I know. You took my copy."

"Oh yeah," Donny said and handed it back to him. "I already have a copy."

"C'mon, it's a gift."

"Stuff's all packed."

"Okay, listen," said Anders, standing with the coffees balanced on the box of doughnuts. "I'm sorry."

Donny spit into his can. "For what."

"What do you think?"

He stared up at him. "Haven't the slightest."

Anders looked for a place to sit but there wasn't one.

"For Helene," he said finally.

Donny wiped his bottom lip with his thumb.

"What about her."

It didn't take long for Anders to spill the exact terms of his regret, down to his guilt about having bluffed his way into the scholarship dorm to begin with, though he also mentioned that while he knew it probably seemed that he had broken the cardinal roommate rule, from Anders's point of view, he had seen her first, and while that might seem like a lame excuse, it was the truth, and he knew that Donny knew that too.

Donny did little but smile and replace his wad of dip. "Feel better?" he said when Anders was done.

"Not really."

At commencement, they sat alphabetically, so there were only five students between the two of them, and though Anders had looked to Donny several times for a nod or a smile or a shrug of recognition, Donny hadn't once looked back.

"Here," Donny said now, walking into Anders's condo. He was holding out a bottle of something in a paper bag as an offering. "This is for you."

"This is for me?"

"It's a gift."

Anders opened the bag to find a twenty-five-year-old single malt that, as if to prove its authenticity, had a fine layer of dust on the cap. It must have been the most expensive thing in the store.

"Christ," said Anders.

"The man at the store said if you're a scotch lover then that's the one."

Anders examined the label.

"You're a scotch lover, right?"

"Bourbon."

"Bourbon!" Donny shook his head. "Shit, I never could tell the difference."

"It's fine," said Anders. "Believe me." He hesitated, looking down at the bottle.

"You don't have to drink it now," said Donny.

"You don't want any?"

"After sixteen years, you don't want me to have any."

He had confidence. It was something in the way he stood, in the easy way he waved off a drink, and, Anders had to admit, watching him from the kitchen as he relaxed into the sofa, in the comfort he seemed to have with his big body squeezed in a suit.

"It's nice in here," Donny said, looking around the room. Anders had replaced the gloomier Winslow Homers with a few prints that featured the New England coast without the grays and purples of gathering storms, and he had matched them to furniture that he found at an antiques store, bookcases and whatnots and an old lobster trap that served no practical purpose except that it reminded him of a happier time.

"Listen," said Donny. He had leaned back into the sofa, had his ankles crossed in front of him. "I'd like to apologize."

Anders came in with his scotch and handed Donny a glass of water. "Apologize?"

"For the way that everything has happened. I just feel terrible. I should have called you in the first place."

Donny's suit jacket was open and his tie had fallen to the side of his belly in a way that made Anders think of the lolling tongue of a dog.

"So I want to be completely up front with you now," Donny continued. "Full disclosure. The older I've gotten, the more I've realized it's all about communication."

"What's all about communication?"

Donny looked at him a second. "Relationships. People."

There was something disarmingly genuine about him, a trait of his Anders had forgotten. He didn't seem to feel shame the way most people did, and in his openness, he seemed to loosen the rest of the room too. It was with Donny that Anders had had his first negotiation about masturbation (*Just keep it in the bathroom and everybody's happy*) as well as his first honest discussion about blow jobs (*I just want to say to them it's okay to yank a little; no good blow job's a timid blow job!*), and now, amazingly, it seemed he was having his first conversation about another man dating his wife.

"Don't worry about it," said Anders, sitting down. "That's all in the past."

Donny watched him for a long moment. "I appreciate that," he said. "And if it makes you feel any better, I wanted to let you know I don't blame you for what happened last week."

"You mean my being an idiot?"

"Believe me, if I had a dollar for every regrettable thing I'd done after I'd had a few too many…" Donny shook his head. "Sorry about the golf club. You hear someone trying to get in at that hour and, well, everything in that house seems louder than it is."

Anders looked at him. "I guess it does, doesn't it."

"Old houses," said Donny.

Anders sipped his scotch.

"Well, anyway," Donny said.

"How is the house?"

"The house," said Donny, nodding. "Well, this is actually something I wanted to talk to you about."

"How long have you really been there?" said Anders.

"A couple of weeks."

"Weeks?"

"Maybe months."

Anders looked down, took a deep breath. His scotch was half gone. "And neither of you ever thought to say anything to me?"

"Anders."

"Considering I was the one who was paying for it?"

"Anders," Donny said again. "I know that's not true."

"Excuse me?"

"I know about the mortgage. And I don't blame you for any-thing. A lot of people were screwed over the past few years and there is no shame in it—I want to make that clear—not in this economy."

"Who told you that?"

"I think we both want the same thing."

"Was it Tommy? Did Tommy tell you?"

"Look," Donny said. "Nobody wants to lose the house."

Anders tried to rattle another sip out of his scotch. He had already finished it.

"I have it taken care of," he said.

"Look, I'm still working and things are going quite well for me right now. It doesn't make any sense for you to be burdened with it."

"It's not a burden."

Donny nodded and uncrossed his legs and put down his wa-ter. "Okay, look." He sighed. "I'll give you ten percent over market value."

"Excuse me?"

"I'm making you an offer."

"Do you know how much that is?"

"To be honest," said Donny, "I don't. But it doesn't really matter."

Donny had come a long way from tarring cracks on the state highways, and it seemed he was more than happy to make a show of it. In fact, Anders now remembered, he'd some-how gone from the quaint mom-and-pop world of heating-oil delivery to working for the natural-gas industry, a move that explained his suit and his corporate lapel ribbon and the gas guzzler in the drive, not to mention the bottle of exorbitantly expensive scotch he'd brought with him and didn't expect to drink. Donny had a lot of money, and it occurred to Anders that he had come over not to apologize, but to try and purchase what was left of his life.

"The house isn't for sale," he said.

"I can pay you today. Right now."

Anders shrugged and put his glass on the table. "I'm not interested."

Donny crossed his legs and settled into a pose that was vaguely feline. Outside, the wind had kicked up and they could hear the rattle of lights against the siding. "If I can be honest," Donny said. "For a guy who worked so long in finance, I'm a little surprised."

"That I'm not interested in money?"

"That you're not interested in reason."

"*Reason*," said Anders, more amused than anything else. "You're appealing to reason."

"Come on," said Donny. "You have to admit, this situation doesn't make sense for anyone."

"How old are you?" Anders said all of a sudden.

Donny exhaled and a short silence fell between them.

"Same as you," said Donny. "Why."

"Seems like an unusual time to suddenly want a family."

"Anders," said Donny. His tone had changed. "This crap has to stop."

"Let me explain something to you," said Anders, leaning forward and pushing his glass aside. "You may think, waking up in that old house and watching all those sprinklers come on at once, that you're doing the right and good thing in your

151

life by playing the breadwinner. You may think that; you may even believe it. But take it from me: you're kidding yourself. You want to come here and flaunt your money, that's fine. But don't come over here and tell me I'm not being *rational* when you're more than sixty years old and you suddenly want a family."

Donny's eyes had glazed over in the way Anders's sons' used to when they were enduring one of his lectures, and, in the pause that followed, Donny's gaze seemed to settle blankly on the coffee table.

"Look." Anders stood up and clapped his hands together. "I appreciate the effort," he said, heading over to the door to show him out. "It's admirable, the honesty. But to tell you the truth, you don't know what the hell you're doing."

"Anders," said Donny. "Helene and I are getting married."

Anders felt the plush carpet under his feet. There was a faint shadow of soil, he now noticed, running down the front of his pants.

"You're what?"

"In February. In Hawaii. The big island."

"Huh."

"I'm sorry," said Donny. "We didn't want you to find out this way."

"How else would I find out?"

Donny stood up. "I should probably go."

"No, hang on, hang on," said Anders, heading back to the kitchen with Donny's glass and his own. "Let's have another drink."

He refilled Donny's glass from the faucet and poured himself another scotch, a little more than he'd intended, so he took a few gulps from the top in an attempt to be discreet, which made him cough and made his head feel unsteady. When he caught his breath, Donny had his coat on.

"Here," said Anders, handing Donny his glass. The booze had left his throat feeling scraped. He touched his tumbler to Donny's water. "To your happiness," he said.

If he went ahead and pictured the luau of his wife's second wedding, with its grand roast pig and oldies playing on an outdoor terrace, with its guests' flower-print skirts and linen suits, what he imagined her friends talking about when his name came up was that they didn't understand his decisions but that, as Helene had said so many times it had become a kind of mantra, they hoped he'd figure it out. And if he pictured the invitations and the toasts and Sophie Ashby reading from First fucking Corinthians, what made him tremble all of a sudden with the booze rising to his head was the thought of all that midlife reinterpretation, all those platitudes—about how love was long-suffering and love was not resentful and true love never ends, even if it took a couple of tries to get right.

He finished the scotch and put the glass down.

"So what's with the ribbon?" he said, wiping his mouth.

"I'm sorry?"

He pointed at Donny's lapel. "That."

"We're doing a thing."

"A thing?"

"Instead of wedding gifts, we're asking people to donate. Cancer research. Helene has a vision of the whole wedding wearing these."

"That's really nice," said Anders and he pulled out his wallet.

"Anders. Don't do that."

He took out some twenties, easily a hundred dollars.

"Please," said Donny.

153

"It's a *gift*," said Anders. "Here." He fanned the bills in his hand. "I'm not going to beg you." Donny didn't move. "Going once…going twice…" Anders opened his hand, and the money fluttered to the floor. They stood for a moment, looking down at it. Eventually Donny bent over and picked it up.

When he was gone, Anders found himself alone in his kitchen, staring at the ribbon in his palm as if it were an insect. The wind was howling now, pattering the lights against the siding like hail, and it occurred to him just how gaudy his decorations actually were. They were awful, those lights. They were pathetic. He opened his door and stood on the spotlit slab of his landing, his breath coming in dramatic white puffs. It was nearing the winter solstice, the black total beyond the glare of his lawn. He walked out to the spotlight in his socks and yanked it from its cord. The relief was immediate. He did the same for the inflatables and the deer, then tossed them together in a pile. A moon appeared, bright and tiny, and across the street a night owl sounded. He popped the valve on the inflatable carolers and stomped on them in his socks, trying to get the air out, and when that wasn't enough, he rolled on them with his whole body until they were flat. He did the same for the inflatable snowman in his globe and the hamster in a Santa suit, using his fists and his arms and his knees until he was lying in the yard, spent, exhausted, and staring up at a silver raft of stars.

4

There were guys who bought Porsches, even Ferraris, and drove them to the station during the summer months, stepping out on Monday morning in shades as if to imply they had just rolled in from a weekend of entertaining girls and fighting crime. The Thing, though, was the opposite of that. It was a faded orange contraption from the 1970s, made by Volkswagen, with the angular body of a military vehicle and a leaky canvas roof that could, with a team effort, fold back to make the car a convertible—a process akin to dismantling a circus tent. Anders had first seen it parked on a front lawn across town on a warm spring day after Helene had informed him she was again pregnant; he had set out to buy her flowers, a gesture that felt right because it was good, another child, damn, a blessing, but before he made it to a florist, he came across the Thing and stopped, needing desperately to own it.

It turned out to be a steal. The guy took cash for it, an even grand, and let Anders pick it up that evening with Helene, who took one look at its Beetle-like headlights and orange body and shook her head and kissed him on the cheek in a way that he knew meant she hated it.

"C'mon, let's take it for a spin," he said.

"How 'bout I follow you home?"

And so he drove it, this oddball car, at daybreak and long past dusk, puttering up the road to the station, audible for several blocks, grinding the occasional gear, and making, for at least the first few years, a bit of a scene. He loved to drive up to the platform in the Thing in the same way he loved to inform people that his particular town, right here on the gold coast of Connecticut, had in fact been settled by artists, was where Fitzgerald had supposedly written the opening of *Gatsby*, where Salinger had once lived, where drugged-up Robert Stone had banged away for a National Book Award. It was quiet and affordable and *funky*, he would say, as if to imply the last word was somehow the most implausible. Funky. A place with its own sense of self. A place that valued differences. The sort of place where a guy could drive a loud, orange Euro-jeep that announced its arrival each morning to a platform of men reading newspapers meticulously folded into single-column strips.

It became his signature, so that his favorite part of the day was when he was back in the Thing with the windows down, listening to its rumble like a melody and smelling its exhaust as he followed the long, serpentine train of taillights that wound their way toward his home. In the warmer months, Helene gathered the playgroup for barbecues, a weekly reunion of commuters and stay-at-homers in the long summer dusk. They were lovely get-togethers, with charcoal and cold beer and cut-up hot dogs on Styrofoam plates, but around the fourth drink, conversations tended to split along gender lines and turn argumentative. By dark everyone would have dispersed except Mitchell and Sophie, who liked to steer the discussion to Major World Problems and force Helene and Anders to take

sides, with Helene supporting Sophie no matter her position —
a move that somehow forced Anders into an uneasy alliance
with Mitchell, who often said *irregardless* and when he drank
could be terribly mean.

"I don't see why you guys have to get all know-it-all-y," Helene would say in the tense moments after they had finally left.
"You talk at us like we've never read a newspaper."

"*I* don't do that."

"Oh, really? You want to remind me one more time where
New Guinea is?"

"Well, it isn't in *Africa*."

"There." She pointed at him. "That's the tone."

"Helene, please, it's been a long week."

"That doesn't sound anything like an apology to me."

"I'm sorry, okay?"

She nodded and put her head on his chest, playing absently
with the hair there. "If it's not in Africa," she said, "where the
hell is it?"

It was on one of those nights, about the time the others had
begun to leave and they had run out of ice, that he received
the call about his father. It was the pancreas, his brother had
said as Anders stared into the empty ice bowl he was holding.
When he hung up and looked out at the porch, Helene had
someone's baby in her arms and Mitchell was trying to shake a
sip from a cup full of crumpled lime wedges.

The reserves were in the basement freezer, which was filled
with ancient Popsicles and ice trays that required cracking one
cube at a time. He went down there and took a moment, easing himself into a leaky beanbag chair and letting his head
loll back. It was already dark, which meant it was much later
than it seemed, and the talk on the patio had turned from the

schools problem to the homeless problem, a subject that had already made the whole table hoarse. He often took a moment down here with the lights off and the faint mildew smell of the carpet—a habit that was becoming more and more frequent during these barbecues; sometimes he brought his drink with him and finished it in the dark—but he had never before been overcome by the feeling that he would have to stay here the rest of the night.

His father, in all those years, had never come to visit, and though Anders knew it was a matter of principle—a grudge he would never relinquish—what he couldn't reconcile himself to all of a sudden was that it had never been discussed. Instead, on his terrible visits home, he would find himself sitting across from his father in his wingback chair, the screen door open and the crickets singing and their drinks gone to water, and feel the need to mortar their silence with the many pleasant details of his life. His father would listen as Anders prattled on about executive training or the apartment they might buy or the flower guy on Seventy-Third who knew Helene by name, and, though his every expression seemed shaded in judgment, his father wouldn't say a word. It was absurd, this battle of pride, and as Anders slumped in the basement in the dark, simmering with judgment of his own, the idea for the video had come to him.

It would be, as he described the project to Helene in bed that night, a modern greeting card, a postcard come to life for his suddenly ill father. Though if he was completely honest with himself, having just settled in their house in the burbs, a colonial so finely restored the clapboards looked synthetic, he knew the video was actually an attempt to answer, through the wonders of technology, the unspoken questions he had felt in the tinkling of his father's bourbon.

What followed was a perfect July Saturday, a lush, bright morning where the leaves shone silver in the light and even the yellow stripes on the pavement looked new. After heaving the outdated mower up and down the yard and squaring the corners of their hedge, he sat on the bed while Helene tried on six summer dresses until he found the one that most closely matched the dress in the video in his mind. Downstairs, he snapped off the cartoons, pulled his boys into clean shorts, and took them outside, where he unwrapped a Wiffle Ball set and, using gardening clogs as bases, explained to them the fundamentals of the game. They were too young for it, easily distracted, and when the videographer arrived with an entire suitcase of equipment, Preston was toddling around the front yard, taking swings at the ball in the grass as if the bat were a golf club.

The shoot took all day; even the opening frame—fade up to find Anders and Helene standing in the front yard, arm in arm behind their boys, all of them smiling before the high square facade of their home—took over ten takes because the boys weren't looking at the camera, or the sun slid behind a cloud, or a car with a muffler problem roared past, and by the time they had been to the beach and the neighbor's pool and had taken the Thing for a tour of town, even the videographer, whom Anders was paying handsomely by the hour, had lost patience.

"All right, Preston," said Anders during their picnic in the park downtown. "Before you take a bite of that sandwich I need you to come over here and sit on my lap."

The boys hadn't eaten since breakfast, and the picnic, which was supposed to have happened four hours earlier, had the labored pageantry of a chore. He pulled his younger son into his lap, and before they could get the shot set up, Preston threw his PB and J in the dirt. When Helene picked it up, she gave Anders the look that meant he had ten minutes, tops, so he took the sandwich from her, tore off the sandy part, put it back in his boy's little hands, and commanded him to eat. Preston threw it again, launching it this time to the edge of the river, where a pair of gulls took turns mauling it. Anders knew he couldn't let loose on a four-year-old, not the way he wanted to, so when Helene lifted Preston from his lap and announced she was taking the boys home for dinner, he let her go ahead to the car even though there were four locations left on his itinerary. He started to clean up, stacking plates and cups around the picnic table, and when he could see they had closed the car doors, he slammed his fist onto the table again and again, until his pinkie was fractured in three different places.

He couldn't open his hand, and before he could call to Helene, he noticed the videographer was still standing there with the red Record light on. "Turn that off," he said, but the black eye of the lens just stared, and, in the camera's silence, he felt his own father's gaze beaming all the way up from North Carolina. So he turned to it, held his fractured finger against his stomach, and said, "As you can see, Dad, I've got just about everything under control."

The final cut arrived two weeks later, in a black plastic case like a Hollywood movie, and he gathered everybody in the living room to watch it, the curated film of their lives. He was pleased at how vibrant it was, how colorful everything looked, how even the brown swirl of his own hair seemed to glow in the light. The children were thrilled to see themselves on TV, and even Helene, who had suffered graciously through the whole ordeal, seemed taken with it, squeezing Anders's good hand so tightly it made him flush with pride. *Look at us*, she seemed to say. *Look at what we've made.*

But somewhere during the long splashing shots at the pool, when the loud buzzing of a plane overhead obscured the audio completely and Anders's swimming lesson with Tommy—a shot he had insisted on, instructing the cameraman to keep it rolling until the boy could doggy-paddle on his own—felt interminable, Preston dozed off and Tommy began drawing a design in the carpet. So Anders paused it and put the boys to bed and let Helene disappear into her paperback mystery, then came back down, alone, to watch the remainder. What he couldn't help noticing, besides the color and the sunshine and the way the breeze kept blowing out the microphone, was that at the side of almost every shot, he saw himself standing with his clipboard tucked under his arm, glancing nervously at the camera. It was the same expression, he was sure, his father had been watching for years from between the leather wings of his Chesterfield. And whenever the camera focused on him, he would turn to it and address it directly—"The water around here, Dad, is quite chilly"; "The convertible takes a while, so bear with us, but we're experts at getting this roof down"; "This downtown, Dad, is probably about the size of Fayetteville, and look, Tommy's school is just across the river." And he kept repeating, as if it were scripted, as if he had forgotten that the whole production was just a way of saying *We miss you* and *Get well soon*: "Dad, I think you would really like it here."

And he wasn't faking. He *was* proud of his life, proud of the whole domestic spectacle, the little bubble of safety and opportunity he had created, already, for his boys. That was adulthood, wasn't it, the creation of a world just a little better than the one you were born into? And why not show it off, why not, in an hour-and-a-half-long pageant, show your father the life that, like it or not, he had helped to build? This was why Anders had sent the tape to him, even though he had had to force himself to watch it all the way to the end, to the moment Preston had thrown the sandwich and his family had retreated and Anders had banged the table, and all of it was still in there, including his strained look of disappointment as he clutched his hand to his belly and his sad little laugh and his admission to his father that, despite the hour-and-a-half inventory he had just watched of Anders's very good life, he had no control at all.

His mother died not long after his dad, and when Anders returned home with his older brothers to clean the place out, he found the video in a boxful of letters dating back to World War II. It was still in its black plastic case, and Anders saw, when he popped it open, that it had been stopped halfway through. Someone had watched at least part of it. And though he could picture his father propped up in his hospital bed and grinning at Preston's misuse of a Wiffle Ball bat, he knew that there was no way his sick father had made it all the way through and then started it again from the beginning, and so the only unscripted moment, the only moment that felt to Anders like an honest reflection of his life, his father had never seen.

He finished watching the video at about the same time he finished his fourth scotch, his screen becoming a bright wash of blue. He was rewinding it to start the thing again when someone knocked on his window. He assumed it was his neighbor and was surprised it had taken her this long. He'd left just about every light from his display strewn across his lawn so that the yard had the inert quality of a massacre. He slumped down on the couch and took a pull from his glass. She tapped again, this time more insistently, as though Anders's mess were somehow a problem that had to be solved now, in the middle of the goddamn night.

"Dude!" someone shouted. "I can *see* you."

When Anders sat up, Charlie Ashby was at the window, his face haloed by the shaggy mushroom of his hair.

"Evening," Charlie said through the glass. He had a camping headlamp strapped to his forehead.

Anders opened the door. Charlie was knee-deep in barberry hedges, wearing only a thin hooded sweatshirt and a strappy mountaineering backpack that sagged off his shoulders. He broke into a grin. "I had a feeling you'd be up."

"What're you doing here?"

"I was in the neighborhood," he said. It was two o'clock in the morning. Behind him, a lone tangle of lights blinked anemically beside a felled plastic deer. "This place," he said, turning his headlamp off, "is insane."

Anders wasn't sure what to say, and as he stood there, Charlie waltzed past him into the condo.

After he'd been expelled from school, Preston had made a habit of disappearing in the middle of the night to God knows where, then strolling in a day or two later with his clothes rumpled and the fervent belief that he owed no one an explanation. Helene had seen the whole thing as a stage he would grow out of and shrugged it off the same way she shrugged off all the vagaries of that age, all the Saturdays he spent sleeping until two and the laundry glued with semen and the cubic feet of food he consumed. "He's pushing us," she said. "Don't give him the pleasure of your outrage." But after his third reappearance, as

Anders watched his son root around in the fridge without having said hello—an openly hostile act—sniffing the milk and showing theatrical disappointment in the leftovers, he couldn't help but take the bait.

The scream-a-thon that followed—about the cost of food and housing and tuition for an unrefunded semester at St. Paul's; about the beautiful things this family had given Preston and the minuscule bit of respect it asked in return; about the basic tenets of responsibility and fairness and decency that, when ignored so flagrantly, gave the boy the ugly stench of entitlement—was all straight from the moral-high-ground handbook, and therefore it was easy for his son to smile, thank him, and sit down at the table with his five containers of leftovers.

Fairness, it seemed, was a ridiculous thing to plead for with children, considering they had no say about coming into the world or about the rules they had to follow—and, in the case of Preston, no choice about virtually any of the institutions his parents continually reminded him he should be grateful for attending. Therefore, in the calculus of parent-offspring responsibility, he owed them nothing, while they, like it or not, owed him everything. This was a logic Anders himself had used on his own father, and so, after watching his son devour the very same tray of wild-rice casserole he had proclaimed to his mother's face the week before was "inedible," he decided to get personal. He told his son that he was making an ass of himself with his long greasy hair and all his naked desperation to seem cool and transgressive, because someone who truly had the character to run away, who had even half the courage needed to spurn everything and disappear, would never come home for leftovers.

Preston had planted his fork vertically in the square of casserole and walked out the front door.

"Here," said Charlie now, holding up the Klee book with its faded cover. "It's overdue. I figure this shit's getting expensive."

"Are you running away?" Anders asked. Charlie sprawled on the sofa. On his wrist, he was still wearing the sad pink bangle of a hospital bracelet.

"I'm taking some time."

"Do your parents know?"

Charlie looked at him.

"Dude, if you're going to call them, I can just get out of here."

"I'd really like to avoid doing that," said Anders. "Believe me. That's pretty much the last thing in the world I want to do right now." He was feeling the scotch; he had finished half of the bottle.

"I need a favor," said Charlie.

"I can't let you stay here," said Anders, plopping down on a chair. "I'd love to, since your parents annoy the shit out of me. But they'd probably have me arrested."

"It's not me that needs to stay," he said and he unzipped his pack.

Charlie's turtle had been wrapped in a pillowcase and carted over in the top compartment of his backpack. He pulled it out—a high, domed shell, the turtle shut in tight—and held it in his palm like a stone.

"You brought over a turtle?"

"You remember Relic."

"Why did you bring over a turtle?"

"Because he's basically my best friend in the world. And I need someone to watch him for me."

165

Anders shook his head. "Are you serious?"

"He's a kind old man," said Charlie. "Here, hold him."

Charlie put the creature in his hand, and Anders held it by its smooth undershell. It was still and surprisingly light. "You sure he's in there?"

"Give him a second."

Sure enough, soon the bottom of his shell hinged open and a small, bald head peeked out. He had the half-squint and glassy eyes of a stoner, but when he emerged completely and looked up at Anders, he held his gaze.

"Look at that," said Charlie. "He likes you."

"Look, your parents will take care of your turtle."

"My *parents*," said Charlie, suddenly angry, "won't even feed him. They think he smells, but that's only because they don't clean his tank. Yelena's supposed to do it but she's scared of him, calls him *el reptil*, so now they think he's too much work. They won't say it to me, but I know they're going to give him away. My *parents*," said Charlie again, "are assholes."

Anders looked at him a moment and the situation was suddenly clear.

"You're not planning on coming back, are you?"

Charlie glanced over his shoulder, as if someone might be watching.

"Probably not."

"Where are you going?"

"I have a plan, okay?"

"To Seattle? To your sister?"

Charlie didn't answer.

"Sorry," said Anders. "Lucky guess."

When Preston had stormed out, Anders followed his son out the door and across town to an unmaintained ranch house marked by a wet pile of newspapers and a wall of evergreen bushes that had gotten out of hand. The house, it turned out, belonged to Davis Lestrade, a cast member from an iconic mid-eighties sitcom who now taught middle-school drama in town. Never mind how he ended up teaching a generation of students who took winky pleasure in the badness of his show or that his only friends seemed to be adolescents who were the same age he was at the height of his career, because according to Preston, he and Davis Lestrade were "good friends." Lestrade wore a high-necked heavy sweater that obscured his belly and a ring on each pinkie. He wasn't particularly surprised to see Anders, though he never seemed to be particularly surprised about anything ever; his default mode was the droll sophistication of a Tennessee Williams heroine.

"Oh, Preston," Lestrade called into the house, as if in lament, "the authorities have found you." Lestrade held a spherical lowball glass that tinkled with a giant ice cube and had a black cigarette tucked behind his ear. He looked up. "I can't remember," he said with a wince. "Are you The Dad?" Anders pushed by him and into the house.

Down the hall, three teenagers were lounging on a sofa in a haze of cigarette smoke, watching a black-and-white Italian movie with English subtitles. Inside, the house was pristine, with ornate chaises and love seats upholstered in burgundy and lots of beaded lampshades and large potted plants, all of which combined to create the feeling of a high-end bordello. The kids smoked casually and drank from their own lowballs casually and generally mimicked the air of sophisticated boredom their mentor had modeled for them. Preston was slumped in a beanbag chair, drinkless and smokeless but like everyone else absorbed in the gray flicker on the screen. Anders stood behind

167

him, waiting for his son to turn. Finally, he put a hand on his shoulder.

"Go away," said Preston.

"Shh," said someone behind him.

Anders crouched down so he could speak into his son's ear.

"I'm your father," he whispered. "You can't keep leaving like this. It's not fair to us."

"Can you guys go in the other *room?*"

"Once you're eighteen you can do what you want, but until then you live by my rules, do you understand me?" Anders said. When his son didn't respond, he stood up. "Do you understand me?"

"Okay," said Lestrade from the back of the room. "Either leave or sit down and enjoy the film like everyone else."

"Excuse me?" said Anders.

"It's Antonioni," said Lestrade, stepping toward him in his argyle socks. "And it's a masterpiece. I think you'd like it."

Anders looked at Lestrade's smile, saw his confidence and his protectiveness of his little disciples of culture. He looked down at his boy and his ridiculous hair and his ill-fitting cords with the wale worn clean off the front, saw his posture—he was so clearly in distress, so clearly confused and isolated and angry for reasons no one understood—and eased himself down to the floor, where he sat, cross-legged, for the rest of the movie.

And the film *was* good. He had seen it in college and it had held up. When it was over, he thanked Lestrade for his hospitality and let himself out. The next day he reported the whole thing to the superintendent of schools; Lestrade was dismissed before Christmas.

He never admitted it to Preston or even thought much about it, at least not until his son turned eighteen and disappeared completely. This one, it turned out, was not a drill. No one at Boston University, where Preston was at school, seemed to know anything. His roommate, who could barely look up from the macho soap opera of professional wrestling, could only shrug and claim that that hippie would never talk to him. So after a night in which his fits of shut-eye amounted to less than an hour of sleep, he got in the Thing and drove to Lestrade's. It was a Saturday, and he had heard the guy was still around, pulling espresso shots in a grimy green apron and offering children's acting lessons on Craigslist. The place was a wreck. The grass hadn't been cut all summer and had withered into mats of brown. A hole had been punched through the cheap front door and plugged with a hand towel. When Lestrade finally answered, in a kimono robe and with a thatch of light-socketed bedhead, he was shockingly frail, half his former size, his round face shrunken and bruised half-moons under his eyes. He leaned on a cane, waiting for Anders to speak. "I need your help," Anders said eventually.

Lestrade swore that he knew nothing, and something in the way Lestrade had paused to consider the situation displayed concern for the boy, who he had heard was gone and who he knew had a penchant for idiotic decisions. "Well, who *would* know?" Anders said, and Lestrade, who had every reason to hate him, who had every reason to wish this terror and so much more on him, yawned in his feline way and told him he'd look into it.

Why exactly the man had helped him after everything was a matter he couldn't explain except to think he was genuinely concerned, except to admit that maybe Lestrade actually was one of his son's good friends. Lestrade called him that afternoon and told him his son was driving around the country following a band. "It's a thing for some kids," he said. "A sub-culture. The music is *dreadful,* but if you find the band, you'll find your son." Anders tried to figure out how to thank him but everything he came up with seemed slight or silly, especially in light of the man's health, and by the time Lestrade showed up in a *Times* obituary, Preston had resurfaced and the whole episode had the distant, ludicrous quality of a dream.

The photo the *Times* had printed was a headshot of Lestrade from his healthier days. Anders had seen it on the train, the picture staring at him from the back of a newspaper the man across from him was reading, and he asked to borrow the paper. The writer called him a "cult-sitcom favorite" and cited his ca-reer as an educator and a mentor (though nothing of how it had ended), filling the obituary with glowing quotes from for-mer students about his compassion and his faith in them, about his empowering belief in their abilities. Reading it, Anders fi-nally understood the reason his son had run across town to this peculiar man's home. Lestrade may have been frozen in the psychological landscape of adolescence, but he had made him-self available to the emotional lives of young people—a simple thing—and it suddenly broke Anders's heart that his son had needed to go and look for that elsewhere.

Anders handed the turtle back to Charlie.

"Where are you going?" said Charlie.

"To call your parents."

"For real?" he said. "That's how you're going to play this?"

"I don't really have a choice." He headed toward the phone in the kitchen.

"I should probably warn you that you're not exactly their fa-vorite person right now."

Anders laughed. "Tell me something I don't already know."

"Okay," said Charlie. "They're suing you."

Anders came back in the room. "What did you say?"

"They're suing you."

"For what?"

"What do you think?"

"I can think of a handful of things, actually."

Charlie's look begged him not be dense.

"They know?"

Charlie sighed and shook his head. "I swear to God, I didn't tell them."

"They *know*?" Anders looked down at the stickered spine of the Klee book. Howard was never getting his book back.

"You know what?" he said. "They can do whatever they want. Tell them that. Tell them they can have everything I own if it makes them feel better. I don't care anymore. I just don't *care!*"

When he looked up, Charlie was grinning at him.

"My parents are assholes," he said. "They're suing everyone, if it makes you feel any better."

"I was tricked into smoking that crap with you—you know that. You'll testify or what have you, right? You'll tell them the truth?"

Charlie raised his right hand. "So help me God."

Anders nodded. All he could think about all of a sudden was Davis Lestrade, shrunken in his kimono. "I didn't do anything wrong."

"That's right," said Charlie. "You didn't. My *dad* even smoked grass with us that night. We have a one-bowl policy."

"Aha!" said Anders. "See?"

"And I don't think you can technically 'abandon' your kids if they're, like, full-grown adults."

"What?" said Anders.

"Oh, it's just a thing my mother keeps saying, like her proof for the whole situation."

"What is?"

"Nothing. It's dumb. She gets all calm and weird when you come up and then she says this stupid thing."

"What."

Charlie shrugged. "Give me some of that scotch and I'll tell you."

Anders didn't move.

"*Anyone who abandons his family can never be trusted,*" he said in a pitch-perfect Sophie Ashby.

"Yeah." Anders pursed his lips and tried to concentrate on his breathing. But there it was, the unspoken indictment. In some ways it was a relief to finally hear it aloud. It was incredible to him that after this, after all of this, he could find himself labeled *irresponsible. An abandoner. A deadbeat.* It astounded him how quickly everything in a life could be undone.

"Wait," said Charlie. "Seriously? *That* gets to you? She's full of shit, dude. Both of them are—you were the one who told me that. You can't stand them, remember? You find my parents unbearable." Anders shrugged. "How can you let someone you don't even *like* have that much control over you?"

"I don't."

"That's right, you don't. You *don't.* And neither do I. I never will. You gotta think about it the way my sister does. She says, 'Until they accept me for who I am, until they stop seeing my decisions as mistakes and my life as a phase, I will happily live without them in it.'"

"Good for her."

"Yeah, she was kinda homeless for a year, but still—fuck 'em.

Fuck. Them. You have the balls to live your life, man, you have the balls to do what you want, and *that* sets you apart in this village of zombies." He reached for the scotch but Anders pulled it back. "You can't go halfway; you can't be you *and* stay in favor. You can't worry about what other people, stupid people, think."

"Yeah," said Anders.

"Now give me some scotch."

"Actually," said Anders, thinking of Sophie as a bridesmaid in Hawaii in a flower-print skirt. "You wouldn't happen to have anything stronger?"

Charlie broke into a grin.

Outside, a mist had rolled in that made concentric circles emanate from the moon and turned the streetlamps into floating yellow orbs. Charlie directed him to the town beach, where they came to a stop on the frozen gravel of the marina between two rows of trailered boats whose big still hulls were wrapped in plastic for the winter. At the end of a row of day sailers and ski boats was a motor cruiser whose brawny hull, out of the water, looked like the nose of a space capsule. Charlie hoisted himself onto the lower deck, where he unlocked the cabin door with a key and disappeared inside. The boat was called *Sophie's Choice*.

Someone had strung Christmas lights from the cabin's low ceiling and rigged a space heater to the galley counter. The rest was leather cushions and chrome trim and the sort of lacquered wood grain that looked as if it were made of poured marbles. Even in winter, it smelled of salt and sand and little splashes of spilled gin, and he didn't have to close his eyes to hear the roar of summer nights, all those people in bathing suits and sunblock, their voices carrying across the sound all the way to shore. It was an ingenious clubhouse.

Charlie came out of the bathroom holding a glass pipe and a lighter and several pieces of vaguely scientific equipment.

"I meant to tell you I figured it out," he said, strolling past Anders and easing himself into a chair. "It was the other reason I came by and I totally forgot."

He began setting the different pieces on a table, placing them in some sort of order, then he dropped a crumpled ball of tinfoil beside them.

"So, Oleg, the old scientist? He hears the dog's heartbeat out in space, right?"

"What is all this stuff?"

"Hang on—so he goes to Moscow and tries to convince them they have to go get her. But of course there's no space program anymore and anyway nobody cares about a dog that symbolized the triumph of a country that no longer exists, right? So they laugh at him. Have a seat." Charlie gestured to a leather chair.

"So Oleg says screw you and starts building his *own* rocket, you know, out of whatever he can. But it's basically a suicide mission because there's no way he'll be able to reenter the atmosphere—which, by the way, was what they knew would happen with *Laika's* mission. She wasn't supposed to make it back."

Charlie opened the crumpled aluminum and sprinkled a pinch of what looked like sea salt into the big bulbous end of his glass pipe.

"So here he is," he said, "crazy old Oleg and his junk rocket—and he *does* it, he *shoots himself into space.*" Charlie examined the stuff in the bulb, shook it. "And it's not until he gets out there that he hears it."

"Hears what?"

Charlie grinned. "The sound everything makes in orbit." He

raised his eyebrows. "You know what sound that is? Buh-*bum*, buh-*bum*, buh-*bum*. Like a heartbeat." Charlie struck the trigger on a butane lighter and a blue flame appeared. "*That's actual science.*"

"Wait, I don't get it."

"There was no Laika out there after all. He was just hearing his conscience. His broken heart or whatever. And without knowing it, he gave himself the exact same end as that beautiful animal. It's *irony*. Or something. But I think how I draw it, you'll know he also felt closer to her out there, or like released from his guilt."

He ran the flame along the bottom of the bulb.

"You don't like it?"

"I think it's really sad."

"I thought it was pretty good."

"Charlie," Anders said. "What is that?"

"This? We call it Peruvian salt, but that's just because the kid I know who makes it is from Peru."

"But what *is* it?"

"Oh," he said. The bulb had begun to sizzle, filling the boat with a terrible chemical smell along with the aroma of something sweet, like Glade. "I have no idea."

He leaned forward and inhaled from the end of the pipe, sucking the smoke in and holding it for what felt like an hour. The fumes were already making Anders woozy.

"All right," Charlie said when he exhaled. "It won't take much. Usually one hit will do it. Also, I recommend removing your shoes."

"Why?"

"Because the carpet will basically feel like the greatest thing in the history of the world. Like kinda orgasmy."

175

"I'll keep them on."

"Suit yourself," said Charlie. "When this thing starts sizzling, put your mouth to the spout."

This one, it turned out, was a lot harsher than the last. At first it felt like sniffing the fumes from a bottle of bleach, but as soon as he tasted it, it permeated the roof of his mouth, passed through the gray folds of his brain, and exited directly through the top of his head.

"Also," said Charlie, already with that absent stoner's glow, "I should warn you that it makes you really horny."

"What?"

"Yeah. That can be weird. But if you just surrender to it, it's actually kinda nice."

Anders sat for a while in a state of joyful paralysis while Charlie talked, briefly holding forth on disjointed topics—wind farms, open-source code, a kind of lizard that could run on its hind legs across the surface of the water—until, exhausted, he fell back on the banquette and squinted up at the Christmas lights as though they were stars.

"Helene's tits are kind of weird," said Anders.

"Dude."

"But I mean I like them. They're big now. And have these scars. A lot of scars."

"Seriously."

"And sometimes they're all I can think about. Like for hours."

"Jesus. Stop it."

"It's unusual."

"My mom has these veiny yoga arms," said Charlie, as if finding a corollary. "Something about them totally makes me want to cry."

"I wish my son would call me," said Anders. "I call him.

Even though he never picks up. I don't know. Maybe I just like hearing his voice on the message."

"Have you ever wondered what would happen if you disappeared?" said Charlie. "Not like died, where everyone cries at your funeral, but like an alien abduction or whatever—just poof? Gone?"

"No."

"Like, what would change, you know?"

"Probably more than you think."

"Like sometimes I have this vision of my life as this web, just this giant network of needs and wants and desires and dependence connecting me to other people, right? And I always thought the more threads I had coming to me and from me, the more, like, important I would be in the world. The harder it was to replace me. The people with like a million threads—you know, like a teacher who teaches a whole bunch of people to read or, I don't know, maybe a minister who gives comfort to sick kids or whatever—they were the ones who mattered. They had like a million threads coming off them. It wasn't about influence or power or any of that—it was about the web, you know?"

"I think so."

"But the truth is that's not really the case. The web is being remade every second of every day—it's like constantly revising itself. It's not this static thing. If you vanished, it's just like other parts of it get stronger. The threads just remake the hole you left. Because the web is always there—it's the *threads*, not the people, that are important."

"My feet feel incredibly weird."

"Dude," said Charlie, looking back at him. "I'm telling you—take off your shoes."

Anders did as he was told, and the carpet became intensely interesting. He sat for a moment clenching and unclenching his toes with the sudden awareness of his own body. It felt tiny and fragile. It felt like a shell that he could discard. He thought about how nice it would be to just step out of it and leave it all behind, and as soon as he thought about that, he was overcome with sadness for himself and for his family and for all the people he would leave with it. He thought about his wife and his grandkids and the day his emaciated son had resurfaced on his doorstep in a tie, a Giacometti in a cheap suit, buzzcut and loafered with his hands clasped before him like a church person with bad news, and how all he wanted to do in that moment was hold him and tell him it was okay, how all of the anger and worry was nothing compared to his need to take him back in, and how this was always the great mystery, how his need to reject was surpassed only by his capacity to forgive.

"Come on," Anders said, putting his shoes back on. "I'm taking you home."

Charlie squinted at him. "You serious? Like, to my *parents?*"

"Yeah, get your things."

"Dude, you're blazed out of your mind right now." Charlie reached into his sweatshirt pocket and tossed a prescription bottle at him. "Take the edge off."

"I'm not kidding. Come with me or I'll call the police to come get you."

Charlie held up his hands. "Relax, all right? Just let me clean this crap up."

He started gathering his things, almost none of which they had used. "What was that for?" said Anders, pointing at the orange plastic barrel of what looked like a flare gun.

"Oh," said Charlie. "It was a stupid idea. I just thought we might want to shoot it off."

Anders shook his head. "I'll be in the car."

Across the marina a halyard was pinging against its flagpole, a distant lonely music. The mist had passed and in its place was a clear, biting cold. He started his car and cranked the heat, feeling the texture of his steering wheel with newfound appreciation. Eventually, he beeped the horn; Charlie was taking his time. He was probably running his hand along the cabinets and marveling at the many tiny cracks of its wood grain.

Anders got out of the car and went back to the boat. It was dark in there, the air still burned with the medicinal smell from the pipe.

"Charlie?" he said. He knocked on the bathroom door.

He should have known there would be nobody there. When he opened the door, the hatch on the ceiling was popped open, and all that remained of Charlie was his turtle, sitting alone on the closed lid of the toilet.

Anders ran out to the deck and shouted Charlie's name, squinting into the dark, but there was nothing. He listened to the breeze, looking at the silhouetted eaves of silent homes, an entire town asleep, early risers and their productive rest, offspring tucked into warm beds, grandfather clocks and the hiss of radiators and dreams of security and comfort, until high above the rooftops, at the edge of the horizon, a magnificent orange streak flared across the sky.

5

Preston Simms Hill had debated, at nearly every stage of his life, getting in his car, pointing it west, and disappearing completely from the big judgmental eye of society. At first this was normal adolescent stuff—he'd grown up in a world so fiercely dedicated to maintaining its own privilege that it practically begged any thinking creature to disrupt it (or, in the case of his former best friend Addy, to torch the gymnasium of their country day school). But as his twenties had become his thirties and the injustices of prep school had receded into the background hum of the rest of childhood, he began to suspect that his desire to vanish from every situation that had expectations of him might be rooted in something other than rebellion. And now that he'd been booted, at thirty-three, from even his childhood home, he could finally understand what all those recovery speakers had been going on about: namely, that waking up for the third morning in a row in the igloo of your own uninsured car probably meant it was time to make a change.

He'd been parked at the back of a gravel carpool lot off exit 18 with a handful of other rusted station cars that had been there since the nineties. He had told his mother, when she'd called to extend her guilt-assuaging invitation to Christmas

Eve dinner, that he was crashing with a friend, a lie that was one hundred percent pride. The truth was that the last of his friends had left town after college, making the great migration to Brooklyn or Boulder, and he couldn't bear to show up on Tommy's doorstep and give his brother another reason to congratulate himself on his extraordinary responsibility. So that left him here, on a sort of road trip without a road, in a hometown without a home, ninety bucks to his name and no winter coat and the troubling sense that he had run out of people to blame.

He sat up in his sleeping bag and felt the creak of his old car's suspension. His breath had frosted the windows, bathing the car in blank white light. He cleared a patch with his palm and looked out at the train tracks and the dead marsh grass of the estuary beyond, where a flock of geese were waddling around, preening. His skin was hot with sleep. Three days without a shower was about the time you began to notice it. He pushed his sleeping bag into the foot well and stumbled into the harsh low light of the morning.

Leaning against his front bumper, shivering in the cold, he Purelled his hands and forearms and brushed his teeth with what was left in his water bottle, trying not to concentrate on the fact that he was once again living out of his car. He could mark each incongruous section of his life with a period in which he had woken up in this car, on this backseat, one bare leg sticking out of his sleeping bag and a bruise on his ribs from the seat-belt buckle. Early on, all his unannounced nights away from home were a reaction to his parents' insistence on squash and Latin and schools that required him to wear a navy blazer with big brass buttons, but by the time he disappeared from his first semester at BU (a school his father had to practically beg to get him into), his little tantrums of independence (his father's words) had grown into something a bit more significant. What that was, at least at first, was a girl named Lizzie Greenleaf—the only good thing to come out of his stay at the expensive rehab in the Arizona desert—who was always going on about road-tripping and troubadouring and the wild freedoms underlying our national mythology. She was the smartest girl he had ever met and after rehab she had made it through only a week at Reed College before she shoved her belongings in a backpack and caught a lift to the Gorge, a field at the edge of a cliff in Washington State, where she camped alone until the Phish tour showed up and swept her down the West Coast to Santa Barbara. Which was when she called Preston from a pay phone and told him he should join her.

Actually, what she had done was ask him about college, and when he said it was pretty cool, that he had a class about *Heart of Darkness* that traced the journeying-upriver theme from Dante all the way to that super eighties Robert Downey Jr. movie about strung-out rich kids in LA, she had seemed bored and quiet until he asked how she was doing and she went off about how she had realized that the greatest education was already living and breathing all around her and that the greatest teacher was already beating inside her ribs. "We happen to have been born at the most peaceful and prosperous time in the history of the world," she said. "Do you really think the payoff for all that sacrifice is the privilege of choosing what cubicle to sit in? Preston, we're beneficiaries of something that until now has only been a fantasy: *We can do whatever we want.*"

It wasn't like her arguments were particularly new, but they were passionate and peppered with references to writers he had never read, and, perhaps most persuasive, they were coming from her. They lived out of the back of his car and ran a small baked-goods business—shroom blondies and hash muffins and, when no oven was available (which turned out to be most of the time), uncooked lumps of dough and stems she carried around the parking lot on sheets of wax paper. Lizzie was from Indian Hill, Ohio, an enclave of Procter and Gamble executives that was a lot like his hometown except everyone there had gotten rich off toothpaste instead of something incomprehensible with stocks, and she was beautiful. She had a boyfriend back in Indian Hill to whom she was disappointingly loyal, which meant she referred to Preston as her friend or her best friend and often held his hand and draped her arm across his chest while they were sleeping, a position that made him feel safer than any seat belt in the world and that meant he frequently had to wait for his boner to chill before he climbed out of his sleeping bag in the morning. She had fine brown hair she had to re-dread every couple of weeks with surfboard wax and a stadium-light smile and a pair of cruelly perfect breasts that were perpetually braless and remained suspended by some miraculous force beneath the gossamer cotton of a vintage T-shirt. All this, no doubt, gave her a tremendous advantage in the baked-goods market, particularly with the backward-hat boys, and they were still to this day his go-to jack-off image, which was weird because he had never actually seen them, and also because she was dead.

Looking back on it all, while it had lasted only a month and a half, it was still the most formative time of his life, despite being an easy joke for pretty much everyone else. Even now, when it came up, his older brother would swirl his hands in the air above his head in a caricature of a moronic noodle dance that Preston wished weren't so accurate and say, "How's the too-ur, bro?" in a sort of developmentally disabled Santa Barbara drawl, to which Preston would nod—*Yes, yes, some people sounded like that*—while his brother kept twirling and tucking his imaginary hair behind his ears. "It's pretty sweet," Preston would have to say eventually to get him to stop.

Lizzie had died in a field. It was a bad dose that did it, which was ironic because she was always harping on about organics, how if it didn't come from the earth, it didn't go into her body, and she basically lived on these steel-cut-oat bars that you could find only at absurdly high-end health-food stores, but that's what happened. And it's not like what followed was a logical progression—he hated that "if this, then that" shit, how it oversimplified everything. The one psychologist his mom had forced him to see had been obsessed with Lizzie—Why did he think he skipped her funeral? Why didn't he go home? Why did he think he never told his parents? Why couldn't he talk about what happened?—on and on, and it's not like he had answers for her. It's not like what happened answered anything. It was the third night at Alpine Valley and it was mid-October in Wisconsin, a little too chilly to be camping but people did anyway, so the grounds had swollen to the size of a medieval city. He and Lizzie had only one ticket that night, which they flipped for because the band had a reputation for playing insane, historically significant sets on the third night at Alpine, and she said he'd won, though Lizzie would never show the flip. She would keep the coin tight in her fist and look at it with one eye as though peering into a microscope, and she would come back with this huge smile, a smile that said *You're never going to believe this*, which was basically her look all the time, like something enormous and wonderful had happened and she was about to share the news. This time she said he won so he went in alone, and the amazing thing was that it *was* a historically significant show. His ticket was for the lawn but he was able to push his way to the front so he was leaning against the guardrail and was close enough to the soles of Trey's Pumas that he could have licked them, and though he was sober as a newborn he was directly under the storm of the band's lights, which gave every movement of the set a kind of full-body experience, one that was topped only by the second set, which he spent on the back of the lawn under the green sky of an actual storm that had gathered and electrified everything down to the hair on his toes. He felt the dense warships of clouds collect above him, and during the soaring end of a song that had started some twenty minutes before, the sky opened into fat sheets of rain and thunder while people on the lawn went bananas dancing, and he lay there, sinking into the mud and having a semimystical experience that he could never find the words to explain.

He liked to think that Lizzie was also lying in the storm, though he didn't really know that for sure. He didn't really know anything, considering that by the time he reached her at the end of the show, it was all emergency vehicles and gawking lot rats and a whole host of stupid rumors. He tried not to listen to any of them, though the weird thing, besides the fact that she had put straight chemicals into her body, was that people kept saying she was with this guy Kendal, who was famous for cheap tabs and methy coke and who was like forty years old and wore SoCal skate shorts and flat-brimmed hats and socks pulled up to his knees—a guy who was pretty much the definition of sketchy. People were saying all kinds of crap, about how he'd killed her, about how she had gone to him asking for an adventure and he had given it to her—but it didn't matter. Once, years later, on a bad night at Northwestern, he had

Googled the guy but there was nothing and it occurred to him that of course Kendal wasn't the guy's real name, and anyway, if he had found him, what could he do?

He couldn't go back to school because it was bullshit and also because the attendance policy wouldn't allow it, and he didn't know what else to do, so he stayed on tour selling Lizzie's goo balls and sleeping in her bag, and, when the tour was over, he kept on with other bands, bands with terrible names but respectable followings, like the Disco Biscuits and Leftover Salmon and the String Cheese Incident, whose music Preston didn't much like but who were great for business, particularly when selling baked goods gave way to selling plain drugs, at which point he began forgoing the shows altogether. When everyone had gone inside, he would lean his seat back in the 4Runner and close his eyes and listen to one of Lizzie's many books on tape—Ginsberg and Bukowski and Hunter S. Thompson and, when those were exhausted, Paul Bowles, Philip K. Dick, even Carl Sagan's lectures on the universe—all of which helped to justify the newly lowered expectations of his life.

Time, in its way, became liquid. At some point he gave up on the jam bands and discovered the trance kids, who had warehouse parties nearly every night on the outskirts of places like Topeka and Spokane and who bought the chemical stuff by the fistful. At another point he decided it was time to get straight so he buzzed his dreads and talked his parents into writing him a check for culinary school, which it turned out was highly demanding and full of stupid people, so he talked them into writing another check for an organic-farming program in New Zealand—*Get away,* he remembered thinking, *far, far away*—but that was also demanding, even though he was paying *them,* so he skipped out of that and hitchhiked to the very bottom of the South Island, where there were penguins and rocks and nothing but water until Antarctica. Also, there was speed. After several months, he made it back to Auckland, twenty-five pounds lighter and dead broke, so he hopped his return flight to LA and crashed with a girl he had known from the trance scene who was kind enough to introduce him to the many pleasures of West Coast opiates.

Addiction narratives are dreadfully repetitive, which was another reason why he disliked recovery, but suffice it to say that at some point after LA he found himself marooned without friends in the exurbs of Phoenix, unclear on exactly how he had gotten there, and for a period, owing to what he could describe only as temporary insanity, he had shared a trailer with three skateboarders who were cooking meth in the same kitchen where he was sleeping. He had awoken one evening with the desert sun coming through the one curtained window over the sink setting the whole place ablaze. The other guys were off videotaping one another skinning their faces on public handrails, and as he looked around their long tin box, with its tubes and pots, its terrible chemical air, a couch and a PlayStation and one shitty watercolor of the desert nailed to the wall, he knew he had made it about as far from home as he could.

To say that he arrived at Northwestern a changed man was an understatement. He didn't so much as drink a beer the whole three years he was in school, spending his evenings consuming books and volunteering at two different crisis centers, where he was mostly asked to help stuff envelopes and laminate signs about their many stringent policies. He finished with a somewhat absurd GPA (which for once correlated with his standardized test scores) but after graduation, once he had papered the city with his scattershot résumé, the downtime grew and grew until he picked up a few shifts, just to make rent, with another old friend's pot-delivery service. This meant he rode around town on a borrowed Vespa with a big bulbous helmet and the many pockets of his backpack lined with neat baggies of weed, which he would deliver, it seemed, exclusively to lawyers, who wouldn't look at him as he stood in the doorways of their high, glass apartments. He couldn't blame them—during this period, he couldn't look at himself either—and as another month ground by and his very old friend offered him many more shifts, he did the only thing he knew to do. He called his mother.

It wasn't like living again in his childhood bedroom was all that bad. On the first night he had actually felt, even with the room repainted a neutral beige and the shelves lined with reproduction antiques, that he had been graced with the gift of returning to the same place he was when he was twelve, which was to say, protected from the cruelties of the world with only opportunities in front of him. He told his mom as much over Chinese take-out that first week, and even though it sounded like the same old bullshit, when he watched her face light up as she twirled her fork with lo mein, he felt as close to her as he had to anyone in years.

The part that he didn't get then was why he had ended up at the jai alai fronton betting money he didn't have on a game he didn't really understand and why, on top of that, he would take the money of a man he was teaching to read and sabotage everything good he had left in his life to gamble it. That was the mystery, and that, he supposed, watching a bar of light break across the sound, was also an indication that, as his father had shouted at him more than once, it was probably time to grow the hell up.

It only took ten minutes to get across town in his rumbling, geriatric 4Runner, and as he turned down Main Street, whose shops were just now opening for the day's onslaught, he kept the clutch in and coasted the road's length so as not to emit any unpleasant fumes in its gleaming aisle of commerce. In a sign of how early it was, he had no problem finding a spot and managed, without punching the gas or setting the timing belt squealing, to guide his car into it with inches to spare at both bumpers.

Gil was open—he could tell by the neon sign in the window that read, simply, LIQUOR and by the long phone cord stretched from the wall near the register all the way down the store to the stockroom. An electronic bell chimed when he opened the door and he could hear Gil's voice in the back explaining to someone the relative merits of the malbec he had in stock versus the one the customer usually ordered. "Not fruity, not fruity," he was saying. "*Earthy.* You know what I mean by that? Not like dirt; like earth. Look, you're going to like it." The place smelled the same as always—some combination of dust and cork and corrugated cardboard, which was everywhere, floor to ceiling; the room was a tunnel of cardboard, which was why, Preston had assumed when he was a kid, his mother called it a package store. Gil's displays were nothing more than boxes cut in half so you could see rows of bottles and their labels, an index card with the price taped to each box. Everything in there was old and solid—the register, the handwritten receipts, the knuckle-buster he used for credit cards. There were big metal shears at the register and a weighted tape dispenser, and the whole shop, even in the middle of a bright morning, was cast in the dim, warm light of a library.

"Help you find something?"

Gil came from the back, gathering the phone cord into a growing tumbleweed, and Preston waited until he looked up. "Well, good God," Gil said. "Look who got a haircut."

Other than his mother, Gil had been his only legitimate-business employer in thirty-three years. Gil had hired him, Preston knew, as a favor to his parents, in the time after he had been expelled from St. Paul's and before his parents had found a third-tier institution that they could pay enough to take him. You couldn't legally sell liquor until you were eighteen, but Gil had found a loophole that said pretty much anyone could transport it, so his job had been to drive around town when the 4Runner was new with cases of wine and magnums of vodka tinking in back, tape blaring from the stereo and the windows down even in winter, racking cases of chablis in people's wine cellars and, for at least one customer, leaving a daily bottle of gin on the back porch. At a time when he professed to dislike everything, he liked this, and so he showed up on time and billed for the right hours and never once felt like a disappointment.

Gil put down the phone, took his glasses from the top of his head, and held Preston by the shoulders at arm's length, squinting at him as though absorbing all the time that had passed. "Your mother told me about Northwestern," he said, and he took a deep, whistling breath through his nose. "Heckuva school."

Preston nodded. The receiver had started to beep from the box where Gil had set it.

"Okay, okay," Gil said and brought the phone back to the wall. The moment he set it down, it rang again, a loud clattering sound. "It's like this till January," he said and picked it up.

Preston wandered down the aisles, tapping his finger on a

bottle here or there, the same way he had as a child while his mother chatted endlessly with Gil—with utter ambivalence for the substances inside.

"That," said Gil when he hung up the phone, "is a fantastic single malt."

Preston realized he had made it down to the stuff behind glass, the only merchandise in the store important enough to be unpacked from the box it was shipped in.

"Oh," said Preston. "I don't drink anymore."

Gil nodded and let his glasses fall to the chain around his neck.

"So what can I do for you?"

"I was actually wondering," said Preston, feeling suddenly dirty and out of place, "if you needed any help." The sentence came out sounding more cryptic than he'd intended.

"You mean work?" Gil said. "You know it's only ever been me and Wayne, and he's just here on Saturdays."

"I was thinking about deliveries."

"Deliveries?"

"Yeah," he said. "I have an SUV."

Gil looked at him. "Are things that bad out there?"

Employers, Preston knew, were always looking for a clear shape to your life (something that resembled the skyward arrow of a stock rally); his looked more like a de Kooning painting—little squiggles everywhere that didn't quite connect. He wasn't just assuaging his conscience when he told himself this was actually how everyone's life looked. Things happened, some of them intentional, most of them not, and the successful people were those who were best at pretending the marks all connected.

The phone rang again.

"I'll sweep up," he said. "Break down boxes."

Gil held up a finger. "Wineshop," he said, and then he covered the mouthpiece. "You said you have an SUV?"

He made three quick deliveries right out of the gate, all garage drop-offs, but already in his pocket he had forty bucks. He rolled down the windows in spite of the cold, cranked up the radio, and cruised along the back roads, which were a blur of old stone walls and sticks, punching it on the straights and kicking up a swirl of dead leaves behind him. He had forgotten how pleasing it was to earn a paycheck, and as he worked through his next three deliveries, he felt like he could go and go through the night if he wanted, that at this rate he could earn enough to pay back Mr. Baptiste and his brother and his mother and all those old roommates who had stopped talking to him. Eventually he had only one more delivery on his run, three cases of wine to a house by the beach, and it wasn't until he tapped the address into his phone and watched its pin fall onto the map that he recognized it.

He had heard enough about the fiasco of the Ashbys' holiday party to know that it had already happened, but judging by their order, he thought they might be gearing up for another. Part of him hoped they would be out now so he could leave their cases anonymously on the back deck and avoid the long, smiley conversation with Sophie Ashby that would be recounted in near-scientific detail to his mother. That was the way with Sophie—she looked at him as though she'd just been looking at his baby picture and was disgusted by the adult she now saw—but at least if she was there he would be able to walk away with a tip.

The Ashbys' house was always catalog-photo clean, especially the exterior, whose still-green lawn and fresh-painted yellow front would have seemed out of season were it not for the miles of garlands that framed the doors and windows. As a child, he had felt that his family was engaged in a domestic competition with the Ashbys that his side was perpetually losing, though he thought then the same thing he did now about the Ashbys' level of meticulousness—namely, that it was intimidating and also kind of sad. It made sense to him that their son was putting on grand displays of independence and Samantha had disappeared to the other coast. Preston had actually seen her out in Seattle. She had had a shaved head and a clipboard under her arm and was asking tourists if they had a moment for the environment. He still wasn't sure why he didn't stop and talk to her—there were photographs of them bathing in a sink together—but he had only watched her for a while as she asked her question again and again, undeterred when people streamed around her without answering. Eventually, he walked another way.

No one answered the front door. He cupped his hands around his eyes at the window but saw only a dark family room, the sort of room in which the cushions were plumped daily and sat on twice a year, so he headed around to the back deck. When he had lugged all three cases to the door, he stopped and rested on the step to the hot tub. He could hear the marsh birds behind him and the hum of the tub. He would be lying if he said he wasn't a little disappointed. He liked the idea of his mother hearing about his gainful employment secondhand, and as he hesitated before leaving, looking at his ghostly reflection in the sliding glass door, a lamp clicked on and Sophie Ashby was sitting there in its glow, staring at him.

She was in a club chair with her narrow legs crossed and, he could see from the lamplight, a cigarette burning in her fingers. She was still, concentrating on something so intently that Preston wondered if she could even see him. She brought the cigarette to her mouth and back to the arm of the chair, and by the time he thought he should maybe get going, he had waited there too long for his leaving without saying something not to be awkward. He went to the glass and knocked gently.

"Sophie," he said, waving. "Hi."

Given the way she shot out of her chair, Preston wasn't sure if she was about to tackle him or hug him, but as soon as she was up, she stopped.

"Didn't mean to startle you," he called, and he gestured to the wine. "I come bearing gifts!"

It was only then he could see she was crying.

◆

Little Charlie, it turned out, had decided to up his game. Or, as his mother put it as she levered open the cork of a warm bottle of white without bothering to remove the foil, he had evaporated. She had tucked him into bed, a boy just out of the hospital, still frail, the night before he was to go to a facility to get well, and when she came to wake him, he was gone. His clothes were still there, and his medicine, so when Preston had shown up at the back door, she had gotten her hopes up. "I know it sounds crazy," she said, pouring the wine with an unsteady hand, "but when I saw you standing out there, I was looking at my son."

She was wearing yoga clothes and had her mat rolled on the table, which made the second cigarette and the 11:00

194

a.m. glass of wine seem especially incongruous. The way Preston saw it, most of parenting, particularly the kind practiced around here, was regulated by fear, so the more time you spent worked up in a cloud of anxiety, the better you were at being a mom. The truth was, on the nights he used to pull a similar disappearing act, it was precisely his parents' outsize reactions that made the whole thing worth it, so as he watched her dial her son's number for the third time, he wanted to tell her Charlie was fine and that all she was doing in alternating between stern and desperate on his voice mail was ensuring he would do it again.

She punched off the phone and sat down at the kitchen island.

"I hate his little guts," she said.

"He'll come back."

"Tell me something," she said. "Are you living out of your car?"

Preston looked down at the front of his sweater. It'd pilled a little but he didn't think it was that bad.

"I only ask," she said, "because your mother said she thought you were living out of your car and I thought that was preposterous, but now that I see you, it sort of looks like you're living out of your car."

"It's only temporary," he said.

She broke into a grin. "Really?"

"I'm working on it." He pointed to the boxes of wine.

"Well, Jesus, that's stupid. Do you want a shower? A sandwich?"

"I'm okay."

"You're homeless," she said.

Her frankness was new for him, and, with it, he could finally

195

see what his mother so liked about her. She pulled two slices of pizza from the fridge and threw them in the microwave. "How much is Gil paying you?"

"The money's really in tips."

"Cheap bastard," said Sophie, shaking her head. She lit another cigarette and the microwave beeped. She slid the slices in front of him. "Eat."

Preston did as he was told.

"It's good you're home," she said. "I know your mother seems pissed, but the holidays are about mothers and children if they're about anything." She gulped the last of her wine. "So she's still insisting on a big Christmas Eve and I guarantee that has something to do with the fact that you're here."

He noticed then that Sophie was wearing skateboarding sneakers, an odd choice that made him think of his own mother's interest, toward the end of his teens, in Adam Sandler comedies and the record of the Houston Rockets.

"He's fucking with me," Sophie said, as if she were just now permitting herself to consider the possibility. "Isn't he? He's pissed off that we're insisting on rehab, so he's throwing a tantrum. That's it, isn't it?"

Preston shrugged. "I don't know."

"But when you used to pull this crap, that was it, wasn't it?"

"Yeah, pretty much."

Whether it was because of the wine or the chain of cigarettes she had sucked down, after hearing this, she seemed to relax. "Okay," she said and dialed the phone again. "Hey, buddy," she said to his voice mail. "Listen, I know I'm bothering you, but ignore those previous messages. Here's the truth: Your father and I have decided to give away the turtle." She looked at Preston and raised her eyebrows. "He's just so old and smelly and a pain in the ass. So you don't want to keep him, do you? Any-way, give me a ring. Love you!

"I give him twenty-five minutes," she said when she hung up. "Now go take a shower. You smell."

When Preston came down from his shower, fruity and floral, his hair nothing but fluff, Sophie was lotused on her mat in front of the television. "Your tip's on the counter," she said without looking up.

"Thanks."

"And your mother's on her way."

Preston stopped on the stairs. "What?"

She stood up and bent her body in half.

"You're homeless," she said by way of explanation.

He went into the kitchen and took the envelope, then stopped by the door. Sophie was on her back, legs up, her body in a perfect L, the flats of her feet facing the ceiling.

"Thank you for the shower," he said.

"Oh, don't run away."

"I'm working, Sophie."

"She was so concerned on the phone."

Preston paused. "I don't doubt that."

She crossed one foot over the other. "Cut her some slack," she said. "She's your mother. She just wants the best for you."

Preston let himself out.

◆

Gil had a line of customers at the register, so he just pointed to the stacks of cases by the back door, each tagged with a pink sales receipt.

"Even these?" Preston called, pointing at two wooden cases, each seared with the crest of a champagne vineyard.

"Yes, sir," said Gil. "That's the real stuff."

The cases were long and awkward, the size of children's coffins, and when he tried to lift them, he realized they each held a single, enormous bottle.

"Who's celebrating?" said Preston.

Gil shook his head. "Everyone."

Preston hit the road. He racked two cases of wine in two different wine cellars, brought a case of Prosecco to a hair salon on the Post Road, and was on his way to a drop-off at an address on Beachside when he decided to open the envelope from Sophie and pulled over. It was, as he had suspected, fat with cash. She had filled it with twenties, but in the back she had also included a photograph, slightly curled with age and tinted with the authentic orangey light of the late seventies. In it, Sophie and his mother were locked arm in arm, sitting at a pea-green counter with fat, bewildered babies in their laps. The ladies were beaming, their eyes alight with the ineluctable pride of new parents. On the back she had written, *Call your mother*, and then, under it, she had added, *(Or I'll find you)*.

The baby in the photo was actually Tommy, not him, and, technically, Preston hadn't left, his mother had tossed him from her home, but he understood Sophie's point. No matter how he felt about his mother's new life or her judgmental sighs or even her big, hairy hydro-fracking boyfriend (who, despite the fact that he happened to represent everything in the world that was evil, wasn't actually such a bad guy), he had fucked up with Mr. Baptiste, there was no way around that, and now it was up to him, for once, to be the bigger person.

He left a message at his mother's office, telling her he was okay, not to worry, he had found a job, and, after a moment of listening to the clacking of his emergency blinkers, he told her he was sorry.

He hung up, amazed at how simple it had been and how good it made him feel. He wanted to call her back and tell her about the wad of cash in his hand, and about how relieved Sophie had seemed to be in talking to him—how, for once, all his screwing up seemed to offer comfort to someone and how he kind of wished she had been there to see it—but the sun had crossed over into its afternoon glare and he could hear the many bottles clinking in the back, so he tapped the address of his next delivery into his phone and realized he was already there.

The trustees of his former country day school, a Vanderbilt summer home whose dormer windows, from where he sat, were peeking over its high stone wall, must have been having some sort of alumni event, which would explain the six cases of wine and the vague instructions to "deliver to the library." He took the long, curving drive around to the front, where the estate was meant to be seen, and the grandeur of it nearly made him drive onto the lawn. It had all the trappings of a museum, down to the walled gardens and courtyards that opened onto still-green playing fields. He idled there in the drive, feeling his car shake in the otherwise serene campus, and he wondered at the pride he must have had to reject this, the arrogance, but in the same moment he remembered that even as a boy, he had sensed something rotten about the place, had had a kind of early awareness of the insidiousness of class, and that, combined with a deep disdain for tucking in his shirt, had produced in him the makings of a private-school anarchist.

His trouble began with a habit of unknotting his tie during

school hours, a tiny rebellion that racked up so many demerits he was asked to re-sign the school's hallowed honor-code book, a task that took him to the dean's office and required his pledging an oath in front of his parents. It was a ceremony that was so offensive to him, such an affront to his self-sovereignty, that he retaliated by breaking into the school a week later and stealing the thing. This was an expellable offense that prompted wild speculation by both staff and students as to who had done it. Several years later, while home on some sort of endless boarding-school recess, he had gone into the crawl space behind his bedroom and found the book sitting there, clear as day, on top of the patio cushions.

Nonetheless, contrary to very popular belief, when the gymnasium went up in flames later that year, Preston had had nothing to do with it. Or almost nothing. It was his best friend who had done it, a small, quiet kid who seemed, at least to the faculty, to be under Preston's influence to a near-hypnotic degree. But the truth was Preston wouldn't have dreamed of something so violent—he was about subversion, not clumsy destruction—and perhaps his only crime in the ordeal was not believing Addy when he told him he was going to do it. Addy was the sort of kid who drew elaborate things on his arm and then said he'd had them tattooed. He was also tiny for the eighth grade, and once his braces came off, he seemed to have the sort of teeth you kept waiting for his head to grow into. For one reason or another, Addy was forever trying to impress him, so when Addy actually did it—torched the place midday while Preston and the rest of the school watched in terrible wonder—somehow everyone, including his parents, had secretly deemed him responsible. And while it wasn't enough to get him expelled, during the unanticipated week off that followed, in which the school proclaimed that everyone should do some "soul-searching," it was enough that his parents quietly shipped him up to St. Paul's.

The day the school burned, he realized, was the last day he'd been here, so it was no wonder the place had accrued so much power in his imagination. At first, he had assumed its continuing influence was due to the grand injustice of it all (he could still hear the pubescent honk of his voice repeating, "I didn't *do* anything!"), but now he understood it to be much simpler: he just hadn't been ready to leave. This place, with its absurd rules, had sent him away, but seeing it now, he had almost no contempt for it. All he felt, other than appreciation for its beauty, was shame in the fact that he'd had to leave it.

There were a few cars, he noticed, parked in the headmaster's lot, a private courtyard at the very front, so he pulled his car in there, rumbling over the cobblestones and barely squeaking by the chrome bumper of a vintage Mercedes. He parked at the most advantageous angle for unloading and propped up the back hatch with a ski pole. By the time he had a case in his hands, Dean Yates was staring at him from the doorway.

"Which one are you?" he said with the same broad, vague smile he'd used to tell Preston he had to re-sign the honor-code book. "Food or drink?"

"Wine," said Preston, waiting to be recognized.

"Wine!" said Dean Yates, holding his arms out for a box. "The most important of all. Come with me."

Though he'd been there since before Preston arrived, which was at least twenty years ago, Dean Yates had the sort of boyish face with deep-set creases that never seemed to age. Combined with the bow tie he wore every day and the rolled sleeves of his oxford shirt and the suede saddle shoes and the aforementioned inscrutable grin, he seemed the embodiment of the school's spirit and ideals. While headmasters came and went, Dean Yates was always there, making announcements about changes in the schedule or new parking regulations, clapping from the bleachers at volleyball games, and upholding the seemingly arbitrary rules and traditions of the place with a protectiveness that was usually reserved for one's family.

"We're just around this corner," he said, leading him into the library, which had been cleared except for a few tables draped in starched cloth. There were a few other faculty members in there, none of whom Preston recognized, and he was relieved Dean Yates was distracted so that he could slip out alone for the rest of the load.

The smell of institutions was remarkable. People cycled in and out, always changing, but the particular odor of cleaning agents and old wood floors and loafer leather and textbook glue and ancient chalkboards that never wiped clean and construction paper stapled to bulletin strips and the mechanical waft of Xerox toner and the sweet-and-sour scent of the lost and found—it was all identical, as though the true soul of the place actually lingered in its air. The permanence of it was comforting—not all that much time had passed—and yet, in his unwashed clothes and unshaven face, Preston felt the enormous distance between the school's expectations and what he'd become.

When he had the whole delivery stacked neatly under a table and sorted by reds and whites, he brought the invoice to Dean Yates, who was rearranging some garlands that had been improperly draped.

"Have something for me?" he said with his back turned.

"Just need a signature."

"I think I can give you one of those," he said and when he turned around he paused, his head cocked slightly to the side, as if he had just now realized he hadn't been talking to himself.

"I didn't recognize you," he said, for once not brandishing his smile. He walked up to him, his face still worried with something, and just before they would have collided, he stopped and pointed. "Preston," he said, and the smile reappeared. Dean Yates held out a hand. "Welcome back."

His ambassadorial sincerity was so finely honed that for a moment Preston forgot why he was there. It was as though he had been invited and had shown up, against all odds, to surprise them. But when he put the dean's words in context he could feel their potential for irony, for mocking, and though Dean Yates's face never broke from its good-naturedness, there was something about *that* that confirmed his suspicion. What Preston mostly felt, trying to squeeze Dean Yates's surprisingly little hand, was underdressed and in need of combing his hair.

"And how are *you?*"

Dean Yates enunciated the *you* as though there had been a recent conversation among the members of the administration about the ones they had lost over the years, the worst cases, and Preston could tell, by the strained width of Dean Yates's grin, that he had a special place in their canon. Preston tried to remember the truest piece of social psychology he had learned in school, which was that no matter how potent one's own shame was in any social interaction—and in this town, every person he spoke with seemed to be smiling at him while simultaneously seeing the shriveled inadequacy of his heart—people were only ever thinking about themselves.

"I'm good," he said, trying to maintain eye contact.

"You look it," said Dean Yates, though there again was a statement that could mean anything. "I saw your mother— gosh, when was it, must have been a year ago now. She told me you'd graduated from Northwestern." Preston nodded. "Fantastic school," he said. "Good for you. Okay, where do I sign?"

Preston handed him the folded invoice and Dean Yates scribbled on it with a pen from his breast pocket.

"There you go," he said and paused with that troubled expression. "Am I supposed to tip you?" And before Preston could respond, he waved his hand. "Don't answer that. Of course I am. Follow me."

They left the library and headed back toward the front of the building, where they wound through the entryway and into the dimmer, mahogany-paneled studies of the school's top brass. He'd been inside Dean Yates's office only once, a terrifying thing as a student, and that was to repledge himself to the codes of the school while his mother and father watched, and as soon as he stepped in there now he remembered why he'd been so distracted the first time. The walls behind the dean's desk were lined with glass display cases filled with decorative eggs, ostrich-sized, with impossible gold-leaf details and the sort of minute patterns he associated with museum china. They were lit from above with pinpoint halogens that cast dramatic shadows all around the room.

"Those yours?" Preston asked while Dean Yates rummaged around in an unlocked drawer.

"Just a hobby," he said. He stopped and looked up. "Here you go." Dean Yates held out three crisp twenties.

"Oh," he said. "Really?"

Dean Yates looked him directly in the eye. "Preston." He had a commanding way of speaking, a kind of elder confidence that even now made Preston go still. "This may be kind of a weird thing to ask," he began, his eyes falling to the desktop. For a moment it seemed as though he might sit down. "It's all ancient history at this point, but I'd be kicking myself if I didn't—" His eyes came back up. "Did you steal the book?"

Preston understood three things about this question. The first was that for a man like Dean Yates, the theft hadn't been just a retaliatory prank but rather an affront to his very identity and therefore something he'd likely thought about for the last nineteen and a quarter years. The second thing was that it meant Preston's parents had never returned the book, and for a moment he was overcome with love for them. And the last thing was that Preston could never in a million years admit he had done it.

"I'm not sure I know what you mean," he said.

Dean Yates chewed the inside of his lip and as he nodded he seemed to let out a little smile. "Must have been mistaken."

Preston smiled back and took his enormous tip.

Exiting the building, filled with the kind of exhilaration that came from beating the house, he should have known something would happen. The last time he had felt this good while sober he had cracked his ribs on a ski slope. But even after he had gotten in his car and cranked the engine, with its squealy belt and gray fart of emission, and heard a clunk from somewhere under the hood and watched all the dials go flat, he still believed the 4Runner was invincible. So he cranked it again, but there was nothing, and again, but nothing. It was silent, a death. Dean Yates was standing with his hands in his pockets, watching him calmly from the doorway.

Gil wasn't happy when Preston reported the situation (he responded with a long, inscrutable pause), and in a moment
of panic Preston promised him he would be back tomorrow,
which, unless he could find a garage that accepted maxed-out
credit cards, seemed highly unlikely. The driver towed it where
he asked, though he warned him that getting caught dumping
a machine that size would cost him easily five grand. Considering what he knew of the Park and Ride, though, Preston wasn't
too concerned. They pushed it into his old spot between the
dead Corolla and the utility van. He gave the tow-truck driver
most of Sophie's money and everything else he had made on
tips, and once he was alone with nothing but the high sounds
of geese somewhere and a phone that was quickly running out
of juice, he propped open the back hatch with the ski pole
and found himself face-to-face with two wooden cases of champagne.

It took three tries with his Leatherman to jimmy the case
open and what he found there, floating in a confetti of high-
end packing peanuts, was the sort of joke-size bottle that
seemed to be used only to pour champagne into the Stanley
Cup. It must have cost a fortune. He lifted it out and hauled it
onto the back bumper.

There were cars idling at the stoplight on the Sherwood con-
nector, and the drivers were gazing at him. All but one had
children in the backseat, and apparently none of them had
seen a jeroboam of champagne before. He heaved it up and
carried it like a toddler against his hip down through the brush
and sticks to the big shale bed of the commuter tracks.

On the marsh side, where the brown matted grass had the
fallow feel of the upper Midwest, he found a seat on a rock. As
a kid, this was his shortcut, a path that bisected town through

backyards and the rear dumpster lots of strip malls, skirting the roofed salt mounds and the recycling center with its giant acrid bins of tin. There was almost zero chance of encountering anyone, and so, like the neutral space on either side of the border, it seemed to render the laws of the land beside it inapplicable. It was where he had coughed through his first cigarette and learned to spit like a major leaguer and where, later, he had lain between the north and south express tracks while monstrous streaks of noise and wind blurred by him in both directions, leaving him shaking and weeping until most of a bag of mushrooms had worked its way out of his system. It was curious that he was still drawn here, that he still bothered to go off in private to do a shameful thing, that he still felt shame at all. He was tired of needing to see himself as a good guy who had merely been sidetracked when the clearest evidence to the contrary was propped between his knees in front of him. He was tired of needing, but more than that, he was tired of pretending he didn't need. The worst part—the exhausting, grueling part that ended up making him feel worse about himself than any credit card number he had stolen from his parents—was the amount of lying it took these days to sustain the general impression that he could take care of himself.

The foil came right off, as did the wire cage. It was cold down there, frozen and gray, and it already felt like the sun was retreating to a tiny white prick through the clouds. Across the mangy marsh grass, the geese were back, his morning buddies, waddling and staring and somehow leaving their oyster shits all over town. He put his thumbs under the lip of the cork and pushed. It squeaked and groaned and eventually came loose with a faint, bassy pop.

All at once, the geese began flapping, taking off together,

and soon they were just specks in the high white sky. He looked down at the mouth of the bottle and was overcome with regret that he had opened it. There was so much champagne, it sickened him—the fumes, the bubbles, the excess of it. He tried to push the cork back in but it had expanded in an impossible way and the foil was torn and the more he tried to rewrap it around the neck, the more it came apart and littered the ground at his feet.

Behind him, the tracks had begun their metallic whinny and the overhead wires swayed. It was a local, hurtling up the coast from Norwalk, and it had a good head of steam. He wasn't so desperate he would do anything stupid, but he couldn't spend any time on a subway platform without falling into a gruesome daydream of every story he had heard about decapitation by train, which caused him to stand a full ten feet back from the yellow strip, and still he flinched when the train blew by him into the station. Something about it fascinated and disturbed him, which was probably why he had gone there as a teenager in the trance of those mushrooms and why he was backing away from the gravel bed now with the jeroboam sloshing down the front of his sweater.

Which was when he had an idea. He hauled the bottle back up to the track and set it down as gingerly as he could on a railroad tie. The train curled around the bend. Its lights were on and it was hauling ass, so Preston retreated to the safety of the frozen marsh. The bottle was so still, almost obedient, that for a moment he felt bad, until an inexorable force blew past in an explosion of glass and foam and gold leaf, a magnificent spray that made him jump up and down and whoop with laughter as the rest of the train galloped by.

The wreckage was exhilarating. There were shards of glass

everywhere, puddles of champagne still fizzing, and down in the trees, he found what was left of the bottleneck, balanced on a felled trunk. He reached for it, a trophy to hang from his rearview, when he noticed a sneaker. It was off the track a ways, on the border of the gravel and the woods, and through the sparse trees and reeds, it seemed to be just another piece of detritus that collected along these tracks. It was here that he had found his first nudie mag, a neon-pink overture into the world of the forbidden, which had made this swath seem sordid and magical. The sneaker had probably been hurled over the power lines by its laces, but as he looked closer, he could see it was attached to a foot, and the foot to a leg, and the leg to a person.

It wasn't clear if he was sleeping—he looked like someone who was sobering up—until Preston was close enough to see his skin. He was gray, his lips the faint blue of snow at dawn, and his mass of dark hair frozen to the leaves. Preston turned and began to run before he stopped himself and went back. He was young, the kid. Preston thought of Sophie and he thought of those two women smiling at him from the photograph. He gagged, pulled his shirt up over his nose, and bent down to check the name on the boy's hospital band.

PART THREE

There's a moment right after the great box stores lock their doors on Christmas Eve, after the frenetic shopping has crescendoed and the long train of headlights on the Post Road has slowed and even the radio stations sound unmanned, a quiet moment when all of the stuff in the backs of the SUVs suddenly feels real and all the money seems as though it were spent in a dream. There's a meal to prepare and presents to wrap, and the songs have yet to be sung, but already there's a new kind of worry—about the food and the gift count, about the wine that seems suddenly too heavy for fish. Everyone will be there and that's what matters, the rest will be forgotten, but still this is it, the ritual of coming together. It's time for all the preparation to pay off.

For Helene this year wasn't so simple. She had spent the better part of the night, her first away from Sophie in nearly a week, debating whether to have Christmas Eve dinner at all. It felt inconvenient and insensitive, an intrusion into everyone's grief. It had been less than a month since Sophie's son had hi-jacked their lives, and what could be worse than "The Most Wonderful Time of the Year" in the wake of your own child's funeral? And yet, wasn't that, in a way, what these occasions were about—bringing people together and affirming their need for one another? Wasn't that the underlying point of all this fuss? And it wasn't just her own hopes coloring things—the months she had looked forward to this, the vision that she had allowed herself of her new family gathered around the table—no, in light of everything, it seemed to her the holiday ritual was more necessary than ever.

She mentioned the dinner to Mitchell and Sophie, who had mumbled from under their mound of comforters that sure, it might be a good way to get out of the house, and she had spent most of the night padding along the halls in her slippers, taking down the garland and putting it back, de-lighting and relighting and worrying over how to reconcile Christmas with death. Eventually, she had woken up on the stiff upholstery in the living room, the sky outside still dark, and decided to leave everything in place. To turn the house into a mausoleum would be no comfort to anyone.

Getting Mitchell and Sophie into the room and making them comfortable would be her top priority. She could install Tommy beside them to keep the conversation pleasant and moving, and most important, she would keep the wine corked in the kitchen. They had enough pharmaceuticals floating in them already—it was the only thing, in those terrible first days, that kept Sophie from wailing like an injured animal. Mitchell, during the final day Helene had spent at their house, had begun to speak, and it was clear from his first quiet sentence that the shock of his grief had settled into something harder to assuage, something closer to a desire for vengeance. And who could blame him? The problem for her was where he was directing it. "The thing

I don't understand," he had said in the lamplight of their blacked-out room, "is what your son was doing there in the first place."

She didn't have an answer for him, or at least not the sort that Mitchell was looking for, though after Preston had shown up at home, shivering and sniffling at their door, and Donny had taken him in, she had learned that he'd been living at the Park and Ride and (if true, this detail destroyed her) was going for a walk along the tracks to try to stay warm. What it didn't explain, though, was why he had called the police but disappeared before the medics and officers arrived or where he had gone for those twenty-four hours, and what it really didn't explain was why, despite the other recreational narcotics that were stuffed in his backpack, Charlie Ashby had decided to swallow half a bottle of his mother's sleeping pills. That, of course, was a matter for the police, who seemed to be in no hurry to resolve any of it, and it was a question that, at least in the dim, still room, while stroking Sophie's head on her pillow, she had opted to keep to herself.

She smelled a waft of coffee from the kitchen and heard the tinkle of cereal in a bowl. It was 4:00 a.m.

"Did I wake you up?" Preston was standing at the cutting board, chopping walnuts. In front of him was a tray of hollowed-out orange halves that he was going to fill with yams.

"Are you *cooking?*"

Preston glanced down at a recipe. "Figured you might need help."

He was fully dressed in a clean button-down, sleeves rolled up, a lone tattoo tentacle (or was it a typographic flourish?) visible on his arm. Donny had told her that Preston seemed different, that he was getting up early and going to meetings, that he was *jogging,* and while she had seen his radical transformations before, she had never seen them involve the general consideration of other people.

"There's coffee," he said.

She sat down with her mug and watched him stir a pot on the stove. "Can I do anything?"

"I think I got it."

His insomnia was of the antsy and restless school, and watching him chop walnuts with unusual urgency, Helene found the behavior all too familiar; it made her want to apologize to him for his cowlicks and his flat feet and his untannable skin, all of which he came by quite naturally.

"Press," she said. "I have to ask you something."

"I was with Dad," he said without looking up.

She put her mug down. "What?"

"That's where I went. When I disappeared. That's what you were asking, right?"

"Yes, actually."

"I called Dad." Preston turned off the stove. "He came and got me."

"Oh," she said. Helene hadn't heard a word from Anders— total radio silence—during any of these rushed, strange days. She swirled her spoon in her coffee.

"You know he's moving."

"He's what?"

"His condo's for sale."

"He's *moving?* Where?"

Preston shrugged. "He said Maine."

"*Maine?*"

"That's what he said."

She stood up. "I'm sorry, that's such a middle-aged male fantasy I can't really even take it seriously. What, is he going to drive a lobster boat and make his own rope?"

Preston scraped a spoonful of yam into a hollowed-out orange. "People make their own rope?"

"Did you know your father was on drugs?"

Preston looked at her. "What?"

"He smoked angel dust with Charlie Ashby."

"That doesn't mean he was on drugs."

"Your father has *lost* his *mind*," said Helene. "That's what it means. He's *moving?*" she said again.

"I think he's already done it."

She looked at him. "He's gone?" she said.

"That's what he told me. He just kind of left."

She sat back down.

"I need to know something," she said. "What were you doing on the tracks in the first place?"

Preston's face changed. His eyes went glassy and distant and for a moment she thought he might begin to yell. "I was living at the Park and Ride," he said, "because I was kicked out. And my car was broken, so I had no heat, so I was trying to stay warm. Is that okay?"

"Oh, honey," she said. "I'm sorry all of that happened."

Preston looked back at the yams, his fingers caked in orange mush.

"And it's not just a middle-aged fantasy," he said. "It's also what I would've done."

◆

What he had actually done was wander the tracks in the dying twilight, hoping another train would come by, and when one hadn't and he had made it all the way to the Southport station, its New Haven–bound platform empty and spotted with yellow light, he had pulled himself onto that cement slab and wept. Then he used the last two percent of his phone battery to call his father.

Despite what Preston knew his mother believed, his extended silence with his father—what, since moving home, had become a childish game of avoidance—wasn't caused by disgust or offense at his father's newfound selfishness; it was caused by absolute fury at it. His reaction to their divorce was so intense, so unexpectedly harsh, that it embarrassed him, and whenever the subject came up with his brother or on one of the weepy calls he received in the aftermath from his mother, it was all he could do to stay silent until the whole topic had passed. He understood the irrationality of his reaction—that he, the family runaway, the family addict, the serial abuser of trust and goodwill, would become outraged at anyone else's impropriety—so he buried it.

And yet, he *was* outraged. He didn't know why, though he suspected it had something to do with the accumulated years of shouting matches with his father, all on the recurrent theme of good-versus-bad decisions, with good decisions, according to his sweaty, purple-faced father, meaning considering the effects of actions on people other than yourself. Which was *funny*, given the last conversation he had had with his father was on the sidewalk outside his graduation dinner, the graduation dinner his father had ruined by choosing to inform his mother he was going to divorce her in the taxi on the way there and then had tried to un-ruin by ordering excessively for the table, a gesture that made his friends uncomfortable and Preston even more uncomfortable, especially when his father made a show of putting the whole thing, more than a grand in wine and un-eaten tapas, on his American Express.

All of which would have been easily forgotten in the high drama of the moment if his father, looking for some kind of praise, hadn't followed him when he slipped outside to smoke and, when Preston wouldn't look at him, hadn't put a hand on his shoulder and told Preston he was being un-grateful.

He couldn't remember what he replied, though he did re-member his father continuing on about *money*, of all things, making the whole moment—his one chance to explain himself—about numbers: the amount he had spent on Pres-ton's schools and rehabs and unfinished programs, the amount he had wasted on his son's extended adolescence. That was the phrase that set Preston off, *extended adolescence*, coming from a man who, hours before, had nuked his family because he didn't feel like dealing with them anymore. A man who, like the rest of his fat, rich, self-absorbed generation, a generation that had spent and drilled and bickered away the largest surplus of wealth and resources anyone had ever inherited, believed that the mark of a good life could be found in the quantity you consumed. Of the stream of hurtful obscenity that followed, Preston remembered spitting something about the fact that his father had written some lovely checks over the course of his fa-therhood, that he should be real proud, and if he felt like he was owed some debt of gratitude, he should just tally them all up and send Preston a goddamn bill.

That was the last thing he had said to his father, *Send me a bill*, and the astonishing thing was that his father actually did. It arrived a week later, an itemized list scribbled on four full pages of yellow legal paper, that was surprisingly detailed—he

219

had clearly taken the time to go through old files—and in the end totaled, including a quarter of the mortgage, two unrefunded expulsions, and a fistful of lost orthodontics, an impressive $2.4 million.

There it was: the price of privilege at the end of the previous century, an imposing figure to contemplate—his cost—and yet somehow relieving. He knew the boundaries of what he owed. And so, newly degreed and highly unemployed, he sat down one night in his shared Evanston living room and wrote out a check for the total. It felt good to spell out the full sum in words, to specify at the end with that strange little fraction that there were no pennies involved, this was it, nothing more, and then to sign his full name in black. And though he may have been a tad blazed when he did it, he addressed the envelope in neat block letters, stuck a ridiculous Bart Simpson stamp on the top, and dropped it in the big mouth of the mailbox at the end of his block. On the memo line he had written, simply, *Freedom.*

His father was at the Southport platform to retrieve him within minutes of Preston's call, stepping out of his ancient orange station car and wrapping his son in a noisy nylon hug. He told him again and again how happy he was to see him, how wonderful it was that he was home, how much he had missed him. "How are you? What are you doing here? I want to hear everything," his father had said as they drove in the rattling wind machine of his car. Preston told him. "You've been living out of your *car?*" His father began to laugh. "Jesus, what took you so long to call?"

"I don't know," Preston said as he watched the commuter tracks disappear behind him.

Seeing his father's condo, Preston understood why his

brother kept talking to him about it, how *interesting* it all was, their father's new home, which he now understood was his brother's way of saying "tacky and somewhat heartbreaking." Trying to crawl inside the bizarre private logic that had led their father here was one of the few things he and Tommy had to talk about, with Tommy eventually dismissing his own anger with one of their mother's pleasantries—"As long as he's happy…"—to which Preston would think but never say, *Of course he's not happy, he's never been happy*, which wasn't actually true, but what he meant was that, like everything else in the grand stoical chess match between fathers and sons, they were never shown it.

"Well, here it is," his dad had said with a smile that seemed, in its own way, proud. They were standing in a living room that was higher than it was wide. It was vacuumed and spotless in a vacation-rental sort of way, with all of the furniture and adornments to demonstrate that somebody lived there and no evidence otherwise of human existence.

"It's great," said Preston.

"We have wi-fi," said his dad. "And the master tub has jets if you want to soak."

Under his coat, his father was skinny, which Preston noticed mostly in his narrow neck and the deepened wrinkles on his face, as if someone had let a bit of air out of a balloon. On the shelf behind him was a replica lobster trap, its wood aged to seem as though it had been brined by the sea. He had heard his friends talk about the moment—in a hospital, say—that their parents all of a sudden became old to them. In their stories, it was often physical frailty—the way the IV tubes were taped to the inside of the arm with little white Xs—that did away with their lifelong fights to surpass them, but for Preston, it was the mental image of

221

his father browsing the shelves of a reproduction-antiques store, picking up a vase or a decoy duck, finding a little jar to put on the back of his toilet for the matches, and trying to figure out, in his own dislocation, how to make a home.

"It's not quite done," said his dad, looking around. "But it's getting there. The guest room's all ready for you. Tommy's never stayed to use it so it's all brand-new—new pillows, new mattress. I even put a globe in there," he said. "You still like those, right?"

Preston nodded.

His father put his hands in his pockets. "God, it is terrific to see you."

"Yeah."

"You know I was starting to worry that something had happened or that maybe you were back on drugs."

"No," said Preston, shaking his head. "Nope, none of that."

"Well, good," said his father, nodding, and a strange silence settled over them. "Hey, want to see something kind of crazy?" his dad said and took him into the bathroom. He pulled aside the shower curtain and there was a turtle in the bathtub, gnawing on a piece of lettuce.

"Recognize him?" his father said.

"Not really."

"C'mon, think back. *Way* back. I'll give you a hint: thing scared the crap out of your mom."

Preston looked up.

"That can't be the same one."

"Crazy, right? Here, hold him." His father picked up the creature and plunked it in his hands. "Don't worry—he's sweet. I've been letting him crawl around. Takes the thing all day to make it to the kitchen."

"Dad," Preston said. "Why the hell do you have this?"

"Sophie and Mitchell's kid brought him by. He needed a turtle-sitter."

The reason he hadn't yet told his father had less to do with his desire to protect him than with his need to pretend the whole thing had never happened. Which was obviously impossible. But during the first few minutes in his father's warm condominium, he had almost been able to forget the image of Charlie lying in those frozen leaves, and the fact that he was so young, and the eerie parallels to his own stunted life.

"Press?" his father said. "You okay?"

And, as if answering for him, the telephone rang.

Listening to his father register the news—a series of questions and *Gods* and a long, grieving silence—Preston was tempted to slip back out into the freezing night and hoof it to his mom's. He found his father sitting on a stool in his narrow kitchen. "Everything okay?" he said. His father didn't look up. In the morning, his father's bags were packed.

Now there was a realty sign out front and the dark, sad windows of an abandoned home. He knew his father wasn't so rash as to leave without the turtle, he knew that, and yet the thought had occurred to him, so here he was, at seven o'clock in the morning, trying to crack the key code on the garage just to be sure.

It was surprisingly easy to get inside—his father had used the same password for the past twenty-five years—and he found a cardboard box in the garage. He punched some holes in the top with a screwdriver, which was the entirety of what he knew about transporting animals, and slowly opened the door inside.

For a man who claimed to be moving, his father had been strangely even that morning, as though there was nothing to it, which he supposed there wasn't when you left all your belongings behind. The furniture was there and there were dishes in the sink; the cupboard was full of food. On the refrigerator was his address in Maine, which he'd left for the real estate agent. But there was no turtle. He checked the bathtub and the guest room, pressed his cheek to the carpet to look under the sofa. Of course his father had taken the creature with him, but for a brief moment, he had thought—he didn't know, it wasn't totally thought through—but he had thought that maybe it would be there, stranded, and maybe there would be some way for him to save it and bring it north, to his father's grateful hands. When he had checked everything and there was still no turtle, he opened the door to his father's bedroom.

It was striking how much it reminded him of the one he had sneaked into as a child, musky and dry with a hint of cedar shoe trees and the dust that collected, along with his pocket change and little rolls of breath mints, on the surface of the dresser. It was the same in this sparse, carpeted room, which was really nothing but an unmade bed and a wall of mirrors. The closet was full of shirts and chinos, starched jeans folded over the cardboard dowels of dry-cleaning hangers, and the floor was strewn with loafers and running shoes soiled with the stains of yard work. Behind the next panel, packed in the grid of a closet organizer, were all the gifts it appeared he'd purchased on some kind of holiday-shopping bender. There were drab Amazon boxes and high-gloss toy boxes, the deckled edges of books and sweaters wrapped in tissue paper and sealed with department-store stickers. Each had been tagged with a sticky note, a name scrawled on it—Emma, Tommy, Emma, Ryan, Helene.

All this shopping made a certain sense to Preston. Some

of his heroic daydreams had him showing up on his mother's doorstep with keys to a new Lexus and Bruins tickets for Donny. As it was, if he sold the 4Runner for scrap, he could pay Gil what he owed him for the jeroboam, and that left him with exactly zero, another year of giving poems as gifts, handwritten sentiments on leftover résumé paper that everyone cheerfully pretended to admire. He found an old gym bag amid the footwear and chose carefully—one per person. What harm could there be? It was all small stuff that would otherwise sit here until the place sold, then get hauled out to the curb in contractor bags. He found a guidebook for Hawaii that was tagged for Donny, a rated-M video game for Ryan, and a microplane zester for Tommy. But for his mother he could find only one gift, a large envelope closed with wire brads. In it, there was paperwork of that awkward legal length that had to be folded at the bottom and typeset in a font that was best read on a microfiche machine. One document was yellow and official-looking, and from what he could make out, Preston realized it was the original mortgage, signed in 1976 and updated ten years ago, and underneath, on regular computer paper, was the deed to the house.

In the weeks Preston had been back home, Tommy had exhibited a near obsession with the story of Franklin Matthiesen, the father of a high-school classmate who had been a trader at Lehman and, after the crash, had lost most of his retirement and all of his pride, and so, according to Tommy, he had found a product on the Internet you could swallow and it would kill you painlessly, which he had taken while his wife was with her book group discussing *Eat, Pray, Love*—a tragedy, no doubt, but one that Tommy wouldn't shut up about whenever anyone mentioned his and Preston's father, who had walked away from his job under totally different circumstances and who would never troll the Internet for suicide products (a phenomenon that Preston couldn't help but find darkly hilarious—that somebody would *market* a product like that, and that an important trader, one of the billions of essential bacteria in the belly of national commerce, had even found a consumerist way to do himself in—a point that he'd brought up the last time they were bickering over the nature of their father's psyche, like didn't Tommy think it was at least a *little* funny, in a sad, ironic, isn't-the-culture-inherently-fucked kind of way, a statement that, as soon as he said it, he knew confirmed his brother's silent suspicion that he was, at his core, somewhat of a dick).

But holding that heavy document and seeing in front of him all of his father's earthly possessions, Preston found himself deeply uncomfortable. He put the gifts back exactly where he'd found them, with the Post-its facing out, and got out of that room and down the hallway in a hurry.

What was his father thinking? Was he up in Maine because he had finally lost himself in the way Tommy had been implying? Was he seriously in the realm of pulling a Franklin Matthiesen? Had they misread all of the signs? And how was it Preston's job to figure that out? His job, at the moment, was to get to the grocery store, where he was supposed to have been an hour ago, and buy some mini-marshmallows and lactose-free half-and-half, an assignment that was pretty much the most he could be expected to handle. His job was to get the hell away from this condo and tell Tommy all that he had found and let the responsibles handle it. His job was to get back in Donny's shiny SUV and feel its huge, smooth engine take him away.

He turned the ignition and felt the Cadillac rumble to life. One gauge rose to *F* and another to *0*; the black expanse of its hood was ready to carry him wherever he pointed it when he realized the envelope was still in his hand. He sighed. His father was angry and lost and isolated. His father was transparent in his pride and in his need for others, and in his inability to reconcile the two. His father, in other words, was more than a little familiar to him.

Preston pulled the car out of the driveway and floored it to I-95, heading north.

◆

The room he had wanted at the Longfellow Inn was no longer available because, it turned out, the Longfellow Inn was no longer an inn at all. It had changed hands so many times with such little upkeep that he was shocked it was still standing. According to his real estate agent, it had retained everything except its name from the days he had worked there, down to its crumbling stone foundation, which was why it had sat on the market for so long and why its new owners were finally going to tear it down and build a home on the property that was worthy of its view.

The place that was available instead was a drafty unit in a row of summer rentals with a sleeping loft and a high-angled roof and a stovepipe that ran up its center like a support beam. It was situated at the end of a forested point, a sea-kayak paddle from the open Atlantic, with a trampled path that led through dense evergreens to the silver glint of the inlet, and, most important, to a view across the water of the Longfellow Inn.

In the five days he had been here, he had made a habit of waking before dawn, walking down that path to a small clearing, setting up a camping chair, and, as the first slice of sunrise caught the old building's eaves across the water, concentrating on all the ways life up here was better. It was peaceful, for one thing, even now, on Christmas Eve day, when he was used to the throngs at the mall and the cart-clogged aisles of the super-market; it was rare up here to hear more than the distant cry of gulls or the occasional pickup along the peninsula road. It was relieving, this silence. People said hello to each other, for another thing, and they dressed in clothes that were functional and drove cars that were functional and knew the importance of good wool socks. Nobody seemed to care how you had made a living or how much money you had or what in your past life you might have done.

Not that he had done anything. Not that a boy's preposterous decision to swallow a handful of sleeping pills had much to do with him. It incensed him when people inflated their own im-portance in the life of a person who had recently died, when they romanticized their final interactions and twisted the story until somehow it had to do with them. And, oh, the twisting they would do. Oh, the righteousness disguised as sympathy, oh, the headshakes and the silence and the gathering demand for blame. Give them their sanctimony, he didn't care; let them have their shaking heads. Charlie Ashby was gone, a fact he re-peated to himself on the hour, and while he longed to stand before the rest of them and howl, he knew it wouldn't do a thing to bring the boy back.

On the opposite shore, through the faint blue wash of dawn, the building looked exactly the same—three Federalist stories skirted by a wraparound porch and topped with a hip roof and twin stone chimneys. It was a treasure, this building, an arti-fact of history, and anyone who couldn't see that, anyone who believed his *view* was more important, was unworthy of it. He had rage for the negligent bums who had allowed it to fall so far into disrepair and he had rage for the greedy offspring of his former bosses who had sold the place to the first bidder, but it was nothing—*nothing*—compared to how he felt for the new owners as he sat on the opposite shore and waited for them to show themselves.

He had started to wonder if they would ever come. It had been five days of staring at an empty building, of watching the gulls swoop and the gray sky get heavy but never snow. Maybe the new owners were waiting until the new house was finished. Maybe they would send bulldozers first, a troubling thought; he was picturing himself chained to the porch with a protest sign around his neck, picturing Christmas alone in jail, when, from the opposite shore, a light came on. It was warm and bright and, in these dark moments before daybreak, looked like a star hovering at the tree line. Anders leaned back in his chair. They had arrived.

When he had gone to the county clerk, the public record of the sale had turned up only one un-Googleable name: Emily Adams of New York, New York. And while there was no information to narrow that down, he had found, in the bowels of the image results, a society-page photograph of a woman in pearl earrings who was sandwiched between two tuxedoed gentlemen at a private-school fund-raiser, all with the affluent glow of winter tans, and he suspected he had found the culprit. Emily S. Adams, treasurer of the capital campaign at Brearley School; annual donor to the Manhattan Theatre Club; gun-control advocate; bike-lane advocate; proponent of spaying and neutering; resident of the West Seventies; resident, also, of Rhinebeck, New York; mother of two; employer of two; employee to none; and, most interesting, according to the items unearthed from the digital landfill of the Internet, at least, wife to no one. There was no divorce he could find, no change of name, no shots of the kids with their dad. It was as though the kids were conjured from the same mysterious source as her endless supply of money.

He waited until a decent hour to knock on the door. The woman who answered had a guarded, tentative look and a child koalaed to her front. She was shorter and wider than any of the people he had seen grinning at him in formal wear from the screen, and in her sweats and with her bullfrog frown, she had the air of a boxing coach.

"Hi," he said. "I'm looking for Emily Adams?"

The woman held his eyes.

"I'm a neighbor," he added, as though that explained everything.

"Just a second."

Through the door, he could see that almost nothing had changed. There were the same old sandy rugs; there was the same huge, drafty fireplace (which someone had gotten crackling quite nicely) and the same swinging door to an ancient industrial kitchen, and, behind the desk, which had been repurposed as a jumbo credenza, was the same old chart of the ragged Maine coast.

"She's in the shower," the woman said when she came back, and it occurred to him all at once that they were a couple. She shook his hand, introduced herself. "Is there anything I can do for you?"

Anders had come armed with a page of talking points, most of them focusing on the value of the building, in terms of both money and the community, whose scenic-calendar-ready New England charm was the engine of both its tourism and its identity. "I understand you have children," he said. "And a young family certainly has needs, but I wondered if you were aware of the historical significance of this building."

"The significance."

"Yes. Supposedly Joshua Chamberlain, the Civil War general, lived here for a while. Did you know that?"

"No."

"Also, for many years, the governor would hold a Fourth of July party here."

"Seems like a good place for one."

"I guess what I'm wondering is if you've considered the larger impact of destroying a building like this."

"I'm sorry," she said, taking a step onto the porch and letting the storm door close behind her, "but who are you?"

She had said her name when she shook his hand and he could have sworn it was Karen, or Sharon. Her eyes narrowed on him in a manner that showed she was comfortable with confrontation—she controlled the silences in the way of someone who was used to being in charge—and it was clear to him where all their money came from.

"All I'm saying is that renovation is cost-effective *and* would maintain the property value."

"I understand what you're saying. What I want to know is how you know about our plans."

"It's public record."

"You looked them up."

Anders could see how this appeared. "I did."

"I'll tell you what," she said. "When you do something to your place, I'll be sure to do you the favor of stopping by and telling you what I think." She flashed him a bland smile and turned toward the house.

"Listen to me," he said to her back. "It's a piece of living history, it's a *landmark*, it's not—"

The storm door, it turned out, still slammed with quite a bang.

When he knocked again after a few hours had passed, he brought everything he had—newspaper clippings with photos of the porch full of men in hats and waiters in ties, of cigars and lobster bibs and bunting along the railing, all from the hundredth anniversary of the place, in 1934, as well as a study on the environmental impact of building something new so close to the shore, the delicate ecosystems that were destroyed and never regenerated, not to mention the economic impact. It was everything he had failed to communicate, just the facts, so they could at least engender a productive dialogue.

Karen answered, still in sweats. "Yes," she said.

"I brought this for you."

She sighed and took the folder. Behind her, they had decorated a tree in blue and white lights.

"You collected all this?" she said, flipping through it.

"I'm a visual person."

She flipped past the photos of lobstermen and sailors, past a stump speech by a now-long-dead governor, and stopped at a chart about the impact of erosion on the Acadian hermit crab.

"The hermit crab."

"I know it seems silly, but the hermit crab is a part of the lobster diet, and if you get rid of the hermit crab, you very well could get rid of the lobster. And if you get rid of the lobster—"

"My family is not going to get rid of the lobster."

"Well, maybe not, but if you consider the aggregate effects—"

"Are you from an environmental group or something?"

"Not really."

"A homeowners' association?"

"No."

"But you do own a home around here."

Anders looked across the inlet. It was all trees and rocks.

"Listen to me," he said. "I don't care how much money you have, you can't just show up here and start tearing apart history. You can't *do* that."

"I'll tell you what." She handed the packet back to him. "I'll give you a minute to get off my property before I call the cops."

Beside the inn, a patch of pines had been ripped out of the ground, to clear room for the equipment, he figured. There were holes where the big fists of roots had been and tread marks striating the frozen dirt.

"I'll buy it," he said.

"I'm sorry?"

"I'll buy it," he said again, this time feeling out the sound of it. Larry's check was still sitting uncashed on the kitchen counter across the inlet.

"It's not for sale."

"You can keep the property. I just want the building."

She squinted at him with her exacting eyes.

"The foundation's cracked," she said. "Crumbling. We didn't want to tear it down either, but the whole thing's sitting on a drying sand castle."

"Look, I'm basically offering to *give* you the waterfront."

"Are you serious?"

Behind her, across the inlet, a car had pulled into his driveway. Someone was getting out. The car door slammed. "I just want the building. You can build what you want on the rest of it."

233

The woman thought about this. "Let me see if Emily's available."

◆

Of all the news that could derail her preparations for the evening—preparations that had gone from a manageable list of beans to boil and silver to polish to an all-out scramble when she realized that once again her son had disappeared—none was as dramatic as the phone call from Sophie that announced she was baking. This was nothing new—Helene couldn't remember a dinner party that hadn't ended in everyone moaning politely as they chewed a square of one sort or another—but this time Sophie was "baking!," a proclamation that indicated she was out of bed and bopping around the kitchen in flour-dusted yoga gear.

"I'm making éclairs," she had said.

"You are?"

"They smell amazing, Helene. I wish you could be here right now to smell them with me, they smell like chocolate and bread and—oh, what's that word, it's on the tip of my—doughnuts, I guess. It smells like doughnuts."

"Sophie, are you okay?"

"I'm great, I am *great*. I love you so much, you know that? Sometimes I think you worry too much. You take on too much but you are *such a good person*."

Compared to Sophie's catatonia of the last week, this was troubling. There was nothing quite as unsettling as seeing someone comatose with grief—unless, of course, it was hearing someone jabbering on about the loveliness of everything while baking a tray of pastries.

It turned out to be three trays, platters piled high and wrapped in foil, one of which, Helene was fairly certain, was a cake. The Ashbys came in with all the familiar hoopla—hugs and kisses and coats and drinks—and they were not only exactingly punctual (they even beat Tommy and the kids) but also, seemingly, remarkably stable. Their clothes had the pristine neatness of dry cleaning just out of the plastic, and although Mitchell's floral tie and his fresh shaving nicks made it seem that Sophie had forced him out of the house, he carried it all with a convincing air of normalcy—a loyal soldier in their joint front of propriety.

"You *guys*," Helene said, looking from one to the other. "You look wonderful."

She brought them into the living room, where they sat on separate ends of the sofa and looked at her as if waiting to be told what to do.

Donny had put Bing Crosby on the stereo, a bounce of schmaltz from the ceiling speakers, and they stared forward at the long string of Christmas cards swagged along three walls—caps and gowns and beach homes, the occasional uncomfortably religious illustration, and one architectural rendering of someone's planned addition. Mostly, though, it was kids—a semicircle of tooth-fairy grins and grandkids in Harry Potter costumes and adorable soccer players with jerseys that fit like dashikis.

"You know what," Helene said, watching them scan the cards, "why don't we go into the dining room?"

Neither of them moved.

"Listen," she said in her softest voice. "You guys don't have to stay. At any point, if you feel uncomfortable, just get up and go, okay?"

It was then that Sophie seemed to register Helene's presence, and she leaned forward to speak as if she were about to reveal something urgent and private. "Is Preston," she said and stopped herself. "Is he okay?"

"He's fine."

"Are you sure?"

"All riiight!" said Donny, charging in with three full goblets of wine. "Who wants red?" There was a long pause in which no one gave any indication of having heard him.

"No one asked for wine, Donny."

"I'll take red," said Mitchell.

Sophie had reverted to the same mannequin stare she had had over the past seven days.

"You know what, Soph?" said Helene. "I'm not going to be drinking tonight, so there's no need to—"

"I'll have red," Sophie said.

"Donny," Helene said. "Can I see you in the kitchen?"

"What we want to know," said Mitchell, his voice firm and tight, "is, Where is your son?"

For a moment her impulse was to lie. It was a reflex whenever anyone asked about Preston, but this time, perhaps the first time in thirty years, she didn't think he'd done anything wrong.

"We don't know where he is," she said. "Actually."

"I thought he lived here."

"He's staying here, yes," she said. "But whatever it is you think he did—"

"*Helene*," said Sophie and before she'd spoke another word, Helene could see that something in her friend had shifted. It was something she couldn't quite place, but it reminded her of the way Sophie had behaved when, not eighteen months after they had both given birth, Preston had come along and suddenly Helene was doing it all again. And what a weird thing! To feel resentment from your best friend for the distance your newborn baby placed between the two of you, an unspeakable undercurrent that came out in tipsy asides about how the only closeness with a child you could ever really trust was when it was living inside you, that everything after that was a total crapshoot, all said with a smile and punctuated by the commiserative clink of wineglasses.

But how was this for unspeakable: When Charlie had been willed into the world at a maternal age that Helene had privately found unethical, Sophie had refused a box of Preston's baby blankets that Helene had been saving for her own grandkids, as though there were a germ of imperfection in it that her miracle baby might catch. And now that it was clear he had caught it anyway, Helene felt an irrational need for vengeance radiating from her friend, as though Sophie believed that since she had lost her second child, it was only fair that Helene should lose hers too.

"Knock-knock!"

Tommy arrived with a pre-dressed turkey on a silver platter (something he had brought her every Christmas Eve since his migration back home), a pair of hyperactive children, and a wife hauling their overnight bags. Lisa was a small, bony woman who refused to take Tommy's last name and seemed to look down at Helene for taking Anders's almost forty years before, even though Helene had maintained a career while raising her kids and Lisa had used her advanced degree to become a Pilates instructor, which was fine, although it seemed mostly like an excuse to wear elastic clothes and be passive-aggressive about things like processed sugar.

"Ho-ho-ho," said Tommy as he led in the rest of the gang. "Hope you guys are hungry!"

As he passed her, Tommy leaned over and whispered, "You should answer your phone once in a while." Before Helene had a chance to ask why, she noticed the two figures on the landing beside Lisa who, judging by their diminutive statures and blank masks of greeting, must have been Lisa's very Lithuanian grandparents, up for a surprise from Teaneck, New Jersey.

"Welcome!" Helene said, muscling her way through the single-kiss, double-cheek dance and taking a pile of coats up to her bed, where she dropped them onto the mattress and had the sudden urge to curl into a ball underneath them. She went back downstairs and poured into glasses the remains of their meager supply of wine—a supply she had thought would be sufficient for a room of nondrinkers and Tommy, who tended to sip a single glass all night, as though he were chaperoning. Now she needed to send Donny to pick up reserves for Lisa, who, it turned out, happily drank when her discomfiting grandparents were around, and for the grandparents themselves, whose background and cultural norms she knew nothing of but who seemed to greatly enjoy petite syrah.

She cranked up the Bing Crosby to drown out their small talk and, before heading back into the living room, took a satisfying pull from their one remaining bottle.

"I have *cheese*," she said, setting out the two wedges of manchego she had prepared for hors d'oeuvres. Mitchell and Sophie had wound up at the end of the sofa across from Lisa's grandparents, a pairing that left all four locked in silence — which, now that Helene thought about it, wasn't actually the worst thing.

"Tommy, can you help me for a second?" she said, and she was back in the incandescence of the kitchen with the only person she felt comfortable with.

She pointed out at the living room. "When?"

"Today," he said. "I tried to call."

Helene shook her head for a while. "In case you haven't noticed, we're having a somewhat different kind of event."

Tommy closed his eyes. "I know. They look terrible."

"They *are* terrible," she said. "They are understandably terrible. But, listen, I need you to tell me where your brother is."

Tommy stared at her blankly.

"He didn't call?" Helene asked.

"He doesn't call me mid-fuckup, Mom, that's you he calls."

Helene shook her head.

"Mitchell and Sophie are convinced," she said, "they're somehow convinced he was with Charlie."

"Preston?"

"It's ludicrous."

"Well, was he?"

Helene looked at him. "Jesus, Tommy, are you serious?"

"I mean, it's not so out of the question, is it?"

"He doesn't even *know* Charlie. He's almost twice his age—what would they even have to talk about?"

Tommy looked at her.

"I don't want to think about that. I just need to be sure he stays away from here. Will you call him and tell him that?"

"That he can't come home? On Christmas Eve?"

Helene stared at him expectantly. Tommy had tied an apron over his shirt and rolled up his sleeves in preparation for his kitchen duties, and for the first time in a while she saw in him the kid who had gamely pretended to be a horse along with Samantha Ashby and her bossy friends, trotting in circles around the backyard and neighing, because it was easier than saying no. "Okay," he said.

It wasn't until she looked away that she noticed someone was listening in the doorway.

"Sophie," she said.

"Mitchell says we need more wine."

◆

His father's rental was wide open and no one was there. It was furnished with the sort of run-down camp furniture that was unexpectedly light, and a sandy linoleum floor that hadn't been cleaned since the previous summer. He sat down on a love seat and listened to the wind whip through the seams around the windows. His father had yet to get the turtle a tank, a fact he figured out by watching the creature in the middle of the living room work his way across the linoleum to the kitchen.

When his father came home, it seemed almost as though he had expected Preston to be there. Despite his father's semivagrant appearance (Preston knew the look of someone who had been sleeping in his clothes), he was happy and light in a way Preston couldn't remember him—jazzed about something and going on and on about it in bewildering detail, as though Preston had been present for the debate that had been raging over the past thirty-six hours in his father's brain.

"Not to mention the tax incentives, which essentially offset the restoration cost if it's amortized over fifteen years. Fifteen years! That's *nothing*. The government's *giving* money away so people will take on projects like this. And I told them that. I told them it doesn't matter if the foundation's crumbling, it'll be cost-effective no matter how you cut it. It's not like this takes much expertise in finance. It's just practical—and it's the right thing to do!"

"Dad."

His father looked up.

"What are you talking about?"

His father took him outside to a trail and down to a clearing. He pointed at a dilapidated old building across the water. "I'm talking about that."

"You *bought* that?"

"They were going to destroy it, Preston. *Destroy* it. These assholes don't know the first thing about history."

"With what money?"

His father glared at him.

"It's not an unreasonable question, Dad."

"Don't worry about it."

"Well, I do. We all do."

"The house in Connecticut is your mother's problem. She can deal with that money hole. It's her rich boyfriend's problem."

"Do they know that?"

"Yes," said his father. "Yes," he repeated, a little less sure.

Preston held up the envelope. "Is that what this is?"

Anders took it. He looked over the documents inside. "Yes," he said, refastening the brads and handing it back to him. "This needs to go to your mother."

"Dad," said Preston. "What're you doing up here?"

"I already told you but clearly you weren't listening."

"Come back with me. Give this to Mom yourself."

"Did you not hear me?" He gestured across to the inn. "I've got things to do."

"It's Christmas Eve. You're up here alone."

"I have permits to get, I need to talk to an architect—"

"What is *wrong* with you?" said Preston. "You always do this. You get lost in these private battles that no one else can see and then you wonder why no one understands you. Do you really think this inn *matters*? Do you really think if you preserve that building *anyone* will care?"

"Of course they'll care! They'll all care! It's a living piece of history and I saved it, goddamn it. I *saved* it!"

Preston took a deep breath. When his father started yelling, it was usually the end of the conversation.

"Well," he said, seeing his father's flushed face. "As long as it makes you feel better."

He was halfway up the trail when his father stopped him. "Wait," he said. He had run up behind him and was catching his breath. "You drove all the way up here for that?"

"I was worried about you."

His father looked him in the eye.

"I can't go back there."

"Just give them their gifts."

"It's my fault," his father said. That boy is gone and it's all my fault."

◆

It never snowed in southern Connecticut on Christmas Eve, though sometimes it rained, and now, looking through the windshield, they saw sleet had started to fall. Compared to the white dusting on the lawns of Maine, this was gray and grim, and it made the high windows on their kitchen seem like a warm beacon of light.

"Only an hour and a half late," his son said.

"There are a lot of cars here. Aren't there a lot of cars?"

"Don't worry," said Preston, climbing out of the Escalade. "You know all these people."

"I thought you said it was family only," he said.

Preston closed the car door behind him.

"Hey," Anders called. "What am I supposed to do?"

"Bring the stuff," said his son, heading to the house.

On the way down, Preston had promised him a quiet family affair, with gifts under the tree and the grandkids watching Claymation specials on TV and a turkey that Tommy had spent the week brining. They would all exchange gifts, he said, a simple ritual, nothing more to it, and spend the evening together as they always had, sipping wine beneath a sound track of carols. They had stopped at the drugstore and bought what wrapping paper was left and then spent a frantic half hour at Anders's condo wrapping the presents, and now, in Anders's lap, there was a laundry basket filled with objects that were wrapped in shiny unseasonable paper. It was quite a pile, and maybe a tad embarrassing—a concern he had raised repeatedly with his son and that Preston had assured him was unfounded and overthought. "It's Christmas," he had said. "This is what you're supposed to do."

He was right, of course, and under normal circumstances Anders would have taken great pleasure in this display of generosity, might even have hauled them over in a laundry sack and ho-ho-ho'd his way through distributing them, a pleasant thought that vanished along with his confidence as soon as the front door opened. Tommy's wife, Lisa, was standing there.

243

"Anders?" she said. "What are you doing here?"

"I was—did Preston go in this way?"

"Preston's not here," she said and looked at the laundry basket. "What *is* all that?" Lisa had always looked down on Anders, particularly after the divorce, but her usual polite condescension turned, with a stifled laugh, to something much more sinister.

"Ho-ho-ho," he said.

"Oh, those are—oh! Hang on," she said, and she went back into the house.

A few moments later Tommy came out in a tie and an apron, his hair frozen with the tracks of his comb.

"Dad?" he said. "What're you doing here?" He was holding a long narrow carving knife.

"Preston brought me. I mean, Jesus, Tom, he said it was just *family*—"

"Shh," said Tommy, stepping toward him. "Keep your voice down." Anders's arms were getting tired. Tommy looked at the basket and sighed. "Okay, follow me."

They walked past the dining room, where he could hear more than a few voices mumbling their way through a conversation, and into the bright modern lights of the kitchen.

"You've got to be kidding me," said Helene, looking at Anders. "You have got to be fucking kidding me."

"Merry Christmas," said Preston.

She had sequestered him on a stool on the other side of the room, her arms crossed in front of her, and she appeared to have been lecturing him quietly.

"He can't be here," she said to Tommy.

"Mom, just hang on a second," said Preston.

"*You*," she said, turning around, "don't get a say. *You* can't be here either."

Anders looked at Preston. "What the hell happened?"

"I didn't know," he said. "I thought—"

"What is all that?" said Helene.

Anders looked down at the pile of things in the basket. They seemed suddenly cheap, a mound of Mylar sutured with tape.

"They're gifts," said Anders. "I thought we were going to exchange."

Helene let out a tiny amused huff.

"But you know what, forget it," he said. "I just wanted to give you this."

He had fixed an adhesive bow to the envelope.

"What is this?"

"It's a gift, I guess. Or not really. You can open it later."

Helene unfastened the brads and tore open the envelope. "Is this—" She looked up. Her face had softened.

Anders shrugged. "Tell Donny he has a deal."

For a moment he thought she might run over and hug him, either that or fling it back at him in disgust—it was often hard to tell the two moods apart. And before he could decipher which one it was, the door to the dining room swung open.

Donny was standing there with two empty wine bottles, the table of people beyond him sitting in silence. "Oh," he said, and the door swung shut behind him.

"I need some fucking *help* in there." He held up the two bottles. "It's like a silent drinking contest."

"Tell them we're out of wine."

"We *are* out of wine," said Donny.

"Actually," said Anders. He held up one of his gifts, a jumbo cabernet wrapped in a reflective bag. Helene began to laugh.

"No," she said. "Please. Put it away."

"Come on, it's for you."

"Should I just serve it?" said Donny, taking the bottle.

"No, Donny, put it down."

"*Wow*," said someone behind them.

Mitchell Ashby was standing in the doorway with an unlit cigar in his mouth. His face was a faint purple, as though the wine had filled his skull and been dyeing it from the inside out. He took the crinkly-bagged bottle and put his arm around Donny. "I had a feeling you might be hiding some people back here," he said and pointed across the room at Preston. "Look who it is. The guy who disappeared."

"They're on their way out," said Helene.

"Oh, I hope not," said Mitchell, his wavering gaze finding Anders. "*You'll* stay for a drink, at least."

"You know," Anders said, "we were actually just leaving."

"Oh, bullshit," said Mitchell. "It's *Christmas*. Come here." He went to Anders and wrapped him in a lengthy, tight hug. Anders stood there for a while, unsure of what to do, and when Mitchell pulled away, Anders could see his eyes had welled up with tears.

"Of course," said Anders. "Of course we have time for a drink."

Whether or not his son had known that the Ashbys would be there was now beside the point. In Maine, on that freezing trail, Preston had repeated the polite refrain of *Nobody blames you* until Anders had agreed to come down with him, a phrase that his son must have truly believed, since he would never have knowingly brought him into the belly of the beast. And when Mitchell led Anders by the arm into the dining room, pulled out a chair for him, poured him some wine, and told him again and again how truly great it was to see him—as though the years of quietly competitive shit-shooting and the recent months of disapproval had all been washed away by their tragedy—it seemed, surprisingly, that his son had been right.

"Look who I found," said Mitchell to the others at the table. "Hiding back there in the kitchen."

While Anders didn't recognize the elderly man who was sitting in his former seat, or the man's diminutive wife, or even the new pieces of modernist art, washes of color and squiggles that were hanging on the walls, it was hard to miss Sophie Ashby, who was sitting at the head of the table and staring at him like a tranquilized animal.

"What happened to the boy?" said Mitchell, looking at Helene, who was hovering in the doorway like a security guard. "He was just here."

"He stepped out," said Helene.

"Ah, well," said Mitchell, lighting his cigar with a match and taking a few puffs to get it rolling. "He'll be back. Always is. For now I want to hear about this guy."

A haze of gray smoke settled over the table and Anders realized that Mitchell was making chitchat, an impulse he supposed he understood: make things normal. "Well," he said. "I'm moving."

"Again?" said Mitchell. "What is it with you, you miss the boxes or something?"

"No, um, this time it's to Maine."

Mitchell nodded. "Like for the summers?"

"No," said Anders. "Like for good."

"What do you mean," said Mitchell. "You're leaving us here?"

"I guess I am," said Anders. "I'm—" It all felt so inappropriate, explaining his plans for a new life. "Figuring it out."

Mitchell nodded, but his eyes had drifted somewhere else. "Where do you think he goes?" he said.

"I'm sorry?"

"Ours went to my boat," he said. "Which is pretty good." He smiled, almost proud. "He would hide out in my boat in the middle of winter with his punk friends. It's clever, right? You're invisible."

Anders looked down at the table. There it was, the subtext of everything.

"Mitchell," he said. "Sophie. I'm so sorry. He was an exceptional kid. He was—" He couldn't think of what else to say. There were no words for these moments, only platitudes, only the interiors of greeting cards. This was why people cooked, he thought. This was why they brought casseroles. He remembered then about the graphic novel, the animal in space. It was still in his condo somewhere, those beautiful stark drawings. He would wrap it up and send it to them. He would summarize the ending as Charlie had explained it to him, that scientist floating out there, hearing the heartbeat of his own vessel in orbit and feeling, finally, released from his guilt.

The table had fallen into silence and he couldn't think of anything that would ease them until Sophie finally spoke. "He admired you," she said, still looking at Anders.

"That's nice of you to say."

"I could never figure it out," she added and Anders chuckled. It seemed like a joke, an honest joke, but she wasn't smiling.

"I mean, why you? What's so much more *acceptable* about you?" She took a sip of wine. "And then I realized," she said. "You're the fucked-up one." She shook her head. "You're the one who threw everything away."

Mitchell drained the rest of his wine. "Sophie, leave the guy alone."

"No," she said. "Mitchell. I won't. I want to know some things. I have some *questions*. How could it be that our child looked up to him and hated us, and his child is still alive?"

Anders looked down at his empty plate and the place card in front of it that Helene had made for Preston. Wherever his son had gone, it was starting to feel like a very wise decision.

"I'm asking you a question," said Sophie. "Tell me. Please. How does that make any sense?"

◆

Outside, the sleet had turned to rain, big wet drops he could feel on his scalp, and Preston, of course, was still without a coat. He did have the keys to the Escalade, a dry escape pod with the plush leather seats and clean neutral carpet of an executive suite. He turned on the car, listened to the smooth purr of its engine, and appreciated the distance it put between him and Mitchell Ashby's scattershot rage.

He waited in the dark SUV long enough to get it good and toasty, and he was wondering when his dad would emerge when he noticed the smell. It was uric and vaguely maritime and coming from the foot well in the backseat. He could not believe, when he punched on the overhead light, that their forgetting the turtle in the freezing car had been the sole cause of its death. According to his father, it hadn't been eating recently, or moving around much, for that matter, and he wondered if it had been afflicted by some sort of illness before they had even gotten it. But still, the little guy looked so sad on the carpeted floor, all limp arms and closed eyes, that he picked it up and held it in his lap.

Still his father didn't come, and soon the smell from the turtle was overpowering. He could feel it clinging to the interior of the car and to his clothes and skin, so he opened the door and brought it with him into the rain. The disposal of a turtle body in the cover of night should have been no big deal. Preston took it over to the dark edge of the property and got down on his knees to dig a hole in the dirt with his fingers. But it was like trying to claw through concrete. He tried with a stick and with a rock, and when he was good and soaked and shivering from the cold, he carried the turtle around to the back door, where just inside, he knew, there was a closetful of driveway salt and fertilizer and a spade his mother used to plant her begonias. The door, though, was locked and his brief, frustrated rattle was enough for Donny to come over and flip on the floodlights, then squint at him standing in the rain.

"Donny, please."

He opened the door.

"You gotta leave."

"Yeah, well, I kind of have a situation here."

Donny looked down at the turtle.

"The hell is that?"

"It's really cold out here, is what it is, so if you don't mind, Donny."

"Is it *dead?*"

Preston didn't respond. He had started to shiver and his sneakers were soaked through to his socks. "Yes," he said finally. "It is, all right? It's dead."

Donny shook his head. "Goddamn," he said and stepped outside to the landing. "Where the hell did it come from?"

"It's a long story," said Preston.

Donny opened the top of the garbage can. "It stinks. Put it in there."

Preston looked down at the creature. He was still limp and smooth, his little eyes closed.

"I need to talk to my dad."

"Ah, Jesus," said Donny. "Just give it to me."

Preston pushed past him and into the house. It was hot inside and eerily quiet. The CD had ended and no one had bothered to change it. In the kitchen, the turkey was carved and sitting untouched on the counter beside the tray of yams he had made and a squash casserole that had gone cold. He left the turtle on the counter and walked through the swinging door to retrieve his father.

"Dad," he said. It reeked of cigar in there. Everyone was sitting—his brother and his mother and his father beside the Ashbys, all bathed in candlelight at a table set with the family silver and his mother's china and a pitcher of ice water sweating on its trivet—and were it not for the silence, it would have all seemed entirely normal. There were place cards written in his mother's careful cursive and a dessert fork laid horizontally in front of each setting and a felt-lined coaster for the bottle of wine that was inscribed *Un repas sans vin est un jour sans soleil.* "Dad," he said again, and Mitchell Ashby got out of his chair.

"Have a seat!" he said, pulling out his own chair. "Join us." Preston glanced around the table. The old folks and Lisa were looking at their plates. "Don't worry. We won't bite."

Preston sat down as he had been told. Mitchell's seat was warm from the hour he'd been occupying it. A cigar was burning on the charger plate in front of him.

"There," said Mitchell, standing behind him. "Now we're all here. The whole gang."

251

"Mitchell," said Helene.

"What? I don't want him to feel like he has to hide from us."

"He didn't do anything," she said.

"I know," said Mitchell in the high-pitched voice of a good sport. "Nobody said he did."

His mother sighed.

"Though I would like to know," he said, "what you were doing on the railroad tracks. It seems like an odd place to be taking a stroll."

"He was trying to get warm," said Helene.

"Would you let the boy speak for himself?"

"I was trying to get warm," said Preston.

"I'm sorry?" said Mitchell, leaning over. "I couldn't hear you."

It wasn't until he was next to Mitchell's face that Preston understood how drunk the man was. Mitchell smelled of wine, and his whole body swayed slightly as he waited for Preston to repeat himself. He was holding the back of his chair, Preston realized, for balance.

"I was trying to get warm," he said again.

"See," said Mitchell, straightening up, "I don't believe that. Why would you walk along the frozen gravel with the wind whipping off the water when you could just—I dunno—go to a diner?"

"I was trying to clear my head."

"Ah," said Mitchell. "So the story changes."

"Leave him alone," said Helene.

"No, this is interesting. Now the story is changing. Were you getting warm or were you clearing your head?"

"Both, I guess."

"Both!" said Mitchell. "Were you doing anything else?"

"No," said Preston.

"I'm sorry, young man, I couldn't hear you."

"No," said Preston, louder.

"The trouble with that," said Mitchell, "is that you have a bit of a history of playing loose with the truth, don't you?"

Preston didn't answer.

"Don't you?"

"I was drinking," said Preston. "Champagne. I had stolen champagne."

Mitchell smiled. "*There* you go," he said. "Now we're getting somewhere."

"Mitchell," said his mother. "That's enough."

"Now, why would that be enough when we're just getting to the truth?"

"Because I was with him," said his father. "I was with Charlie." He was so calm. "Isn't that what you wanted to know?"

"You were with him?"

"Yes."

Mitchell shook his head. "Now how am I supposed to believe that?"

"Because he came over to my house in the middle of the night. With his turtle. Relic. He wanted me to watch Relic."

At this, Mitchell was quiet.

"Did you wonder where the turtle went?"

Mitchell looked at Sophie.

"Did you even notice it was gone? Well, I have him," Anders said.

Across the table, Sophie was shaking her head.

"No," she said. "He wouldn't bring you that. He wouldn't bring you his turtle. He wouldn't have done that."

"Um," said Anders. "I can show you, if you want."

253

"Why would he do that?" she said. "He's crazy about that turtle. Why would he do that?"

"I don't really know," said Anders. "I think he was worried about him."

Sophie's eyes went glassy, and immediately Anders regretted saying anything.

"Look," he said. "I'm trying to tell you: you didn't do anything wrong."

"He was with *you?*" she said.

"Yes and—"

"Why didn't you *call* us?"

It was a good question and one that he had been dreading. "I was going to," he began. "I had the phone in my hand."

Sophie shook her head. "It doesn't matter," she said.

"No," said Anders. "It does. It matters a great deal. I should have done more. I should have called you."

"It doesn't matter," said Sophie again. "It doesn't matter."

"I'm responsible," said Anders. "*I'm* responsible."

Sophie kept shaking her head.

"Look, I did drugs with the kid."

She looked up.

"When?"

"That night." He sighed. "That same night."

"You know what," said Helene, taking Sophie by the elbow. "Why don't we get some air."

Sophie wrenched her arm away. "No," she said and she looked up at Anders. "You want to tell me about my son? You know nothing. The things I could tell you about *your* life. The things *I* know."

"Sophie," said Helene. "Let's not do this."

"Your wife was screwing Fred Flintstone." She pointed down

the table at Donny, who was standing in the doorway. "Him," she said. "You know that? For years."

The tone of the whole thing, all that petulance combined with the ridiculous nickname, was almost enough to make him laugh, but as he glanced around the table at all those averted eyes, at Donny's empty face and Helene's ashen one, he could see that no one else had found it amusing.

"What?" he said and focused on Helene. He smiled. "Is she serious?" But still no one at the table would meet his eye.

"Dad," said Preston. He had stood and was trying to get Anders to do the same. "Come on." Anders let his son lead him out of the room, which was suddenly terribly hot, and into the glare of the kitchen.

"Was she serious?" Anders said, but Preston was looking for something.

"Where did it—" he said and then he was charging out the back door to the garbage cans.

Anders followed. "Preston, please," he said as his son opened both cans. "Was that true?"

His son sighed. "I'm sorry we came here."

"What does that mean?" he said. "Yes? Are you saying *yes?*"

His son reached into one of the garbage cans and pulled out the limp body of a turtle.

Anders examined the creature for a brief, sad second. "What," he said, running his hand along its shell.

"It was like this, Dad. We didn't do anything, I mean, clearly it was sick—"

Anders carried the creature by its shell back into the kitchen and through the swinging door. Everyone was still sitting in a stunned sort of quiet when he dropped it onto Sophie Ashby's plate. "There you go," he said.

Even before she yelped and jumped out of her seat and the whole room went to pieces, Anders knew that it would seem as though he had finally come completely undone. He put his arms in the air to try to quiet them, to take control of the room and tell them, especially his wife, whom he had failed, and the Ashbys, whose grief he could never ease, that he was sorry, but before he could speak a heavy object fell from the ceiling and landed on the back of his head.

In moments of crisis, it's important to recognize how much your body knows, considering how little your mind does. The weave of the dining-room rug was rough as burlap against his cheek, and someone somewhere was yelling—shrieking, really—and his neck was wet. When he opened his eyes it seemed as though a hundred cameras had just snapped a hundred pictures, their halos blooming, and when he managed to roll himself over, what came into focus above him was Mitchell Ashby holding a candlestick like a billy club.

The candlestick fell to the floor with a clatter and Mitchell was kneeling over him, his fat cigar burning in his mouth, holding Anders's wrists to the floor with all of his body weight. Someone was still shouting, going apeshit, really, but Mitchell had the same tender look on his face that he'd had when he found Anders alone on the porch at his party, a concerned little grimace that made Anders feel both pitied and loved.

Mitchell burned him directly on the forehead, searing a wound so round and deep, it extinguished the cigar completely.

To hear Anders howl must have been disturbing to the others, but for Helene it was a relief. There was a moment, a terrible moment right after the sound of candlestick-on-head—a high, muted *tink* she'd never forget—when Anders had

256

dropped to the floor so hard and fast she could only conclude he'd been murdered. Which was probably why she had started yelling, and it was definitely why she now found herself pushing Donny's arms out of her way and running to her ex-husband, who was clutching his head, and explaining to him at a regrettable volume that he was okay, that everything was okay, that she was there.

He had a concussion; that much was clear, because he was confused and kept asking questions—"Where am I? *Your* house? Why did you say *your* house? Moved? Where would I move? Why?"—and then, after nodding and going quiet, apparently satisfied with the answers, he'd start asking again, the same questions over and over: "Where am I?"

She got him out of the room and up the stairs, where she helped him out of his bloody clothes and into the bathtub. She was able to pick through his hair and find the source of the bleeding, a wound that had swollen into a bump and could be tended with a washrag. The bath was warm and Anders seemed comfortable, which was a good start, and after a while, his questions faded away, and he just sat there like a little kid, leaning forward so she could wash his neck.

"You really want to get married to him?" he said. His voice was unexpectedly lucid.

"I don't want to talk about this now."

"But you love him?"

Helene thought about it.

"I do," she said, and he nodded.

"That's good."

Running the washcloth along his back, she had the sudden urge to hurt him, to turn the diamond on her finger around and start in on his pink skin, to show him all the odious things that had grown inside her, the depths of resentment and fury and hatred that took root when you were promised a life and then abandoned.

"I'm sorry," he said, his head still bowed. "I'm so, so sorry."

"I know," she said.

And he stayed like that while she cleaned the rest of him.

◆

In later years, from time to time, as a customer was checking in, Anders would see him pause for a second, caught off guard by the scar on his forehead. Most would avoid the subject—it wasn't so pronounced; more like a spot someone might try to rub away with a wet thumb—but occasionally a person would ask and he would have to come up with an easy way to explain it. He told people he had walked into a steam pipe or sometimes that it was from surgery long ago; the easiest way was to call it a birthmark and be done with it, though once he'd tried out the truth. "I was burned by the end of a cigar," he told the young woman who had asked. She giggled at his playful answer and rolled her bag to her room.

To explain the real truth, of course, would have taken some time. Occasionally he mentioned to guests, often a few of the white-hairs sitting on the porch admiring the sunset, that he had worked at this same inn in college, a fact that never failed to please them as they stared off at the water. It was exceedingly rare, he knew, to circle back like that, to give cohesion to the unceasing march of adulthood, and he enjoyed watching them light up at the fact that someone had done it. *Here*, he seemed to say, *was where I was happiest. Here was the prime of my life. So I returned to it.*

It was a nice thought, though inevitably there was a pause after he had said it, an unspoken moment when he could tell they knew it was just that—a thought. Inside his story was the enormous doughnut hole of family and marriage and work, all the things that tied you to other people, and this part, at the end, was something else.

"A gift," an elderly guest had called it. "A time for you." He had a full head of soft white hair that he had parted, Anders supposed, the same way for his entire life, and a cotton sweater tied around his shoulders like a cape. It was September and getting cool already and the man had come out to the porch early. It turned out he had lived in Fairfield and commuted to Morgan Stanley until his hip gave out. "I can't tell you," he said, "how many times I dreamed of doing something like this."

"Well," said Anders. "It wasn't all that planned out." He was once again mortgaged up to his eye sockets and he spent his days fixing boiler valves and chipped baseboards, stacking wood under the back portico, and reminding Preston to fix the loose brick on the inn's front path. It was one project after another that seemed to leave him happily exhausted and with even less time than his days riding the train had.

"No," the man said. "I suppose not. It's just that sometimes you feel as if you could spend all your time trying to take care of what's in front of you and never—" He paused. "Well, clearly you understand."

Soon the other guests made their way down from their rooms and gathered on the front porch, strangers chatting and laughing in the held-over light of summer, enjoying the glasses of wine his son had poured them, and the man got up to go to bed.

"Anyway," he had said, putting a hand on Anders's shoulder as he went inside and pausing to add a phrase that Anders would repeat to himself as the water went from blue to copper to black. "Seems to me you played it right," the man said. "Seems to me you played everything exactly right."

◆

The people who went on to buy the house, a young couple who, Helene was relieved to find, seemed to have decent taste, lived there eight months before breaking ground on a new addition—a giant glass box that came off the back of their colonial like an unfilled tank at SeaWorld. Whenever she was in town, Helene took long, complicated detours just to avoid it. "You just can't trust people," she had said to Donny. "They seem perfectly nice and then they go and do something like this." By then, retirement had started among her friends, which meant the exodus was under way, all of them yielding their homes and the property taxes that came with them to the pregnants and the junior executives and the pregnant junior executives, who, if they were anything like the couple who had bought Helene's house, were not all that young and also unusually nervous. They called her about the clicking sound the boiler made in the basement and the precise kind of fiberglass she had used to insulate the attic and, once, about the population of ticks in the backyard, as though this, too, were something she had installed.

"I just don't get it," she said to Donny, looking out from the kitchen window of their town house as the ambient lights of Bridgeport shimmered across the water. "There's *bug spray*. I told her just to get bug spray."

Even Tommy had been priced out of the area by then, had disappeared into the sticks of Dutchess County with her only grandchildren as hostages, and Preston had finally found something approximating employment, working on a crew of two to maintain an antique New England inn (a building that, at least according to the photos his father had sent, had been gorgeously restored), so she had started to feel like the last of a breed, a maple after all the leaves had scattered. She didn't understand why everyone was always expected to leave, why the whole thing was like one of those models of the Big Bang, a nucleus that was designed to fly apart, a whole country of people hurtling away from the place where they came from, and for what? The promise of landing someplace better, someplace permanent? This one, this affluent dot along the Metro North train, was like one of those beaches where sea tortoises drop off their eggs—no one was from here, and they stayed only as long as it took the little ones to hatch. It had stone walls and old wells and access to a sea that was always mild, and in the summer, the leaves on the trees waved at you like the bright green palms of youth itself, but, as with everything else, at some point you had to concede it was no longer yours.

The new family finished the addition the following spring. Half of the yard had been stripped to mud and needed reseeding, but the other half was an explosion of perennials that it was clear the new owners had no idea what to do with. So Helene went by on a warm June evening to explain, one by one, what they needed. She talked them through the black-eyed Susans and the Shasta daisies and the daylilies that should've stopped blooming a decade ago, and soon they were out along the far edge of the property where there were bellflowers that predated even her and hardwoods as old as the Puritans. From there, the house looked like a simple shape in the high, green canopy of leaves. If she had been alone, she might have allowed herself to linger, to wonder at the magnificent illusion of property, at the things we owned and the ones that owned us. But of course, she wasn't alone. And while she would have loved to stay in the shade of those trees, planted among the roots of those hardwoods, she could see by the look on her hosts' faces that it was time for her to go home.

ACKNOWLEDGMENTS

Thank you to the Elizabeth George Foundation, the Truman Capote Trust, and the Iowa Writers' Workshop for their generous support; to Brush Creek Foundation for the Arts and Writers Omi at Ledig House for the space and time; to the Bread Loaf Writers' Conference for the early encouragement and the lasting community; to Lan Samantha Chang, James Alan McPherson, Ethan Canin, Charles D'Ambrosio, Robert Boswell, Darin Strauss, and Charles Baxter: teachers, mentors, and heroes all; and to the trusted friends and brilliant readers who saw earlier drafts of this novel: Andrew Milward, Zach Falcon, and Stuart Nadler (who also helped find its title).

Thank you also to Kate Sachs, Nate and Thea Brown, Craig Eley, Alexis Stevens, Tim O'Keefe, Laurence Lowe, Megan Conway, Scott Seeley, Wayne Lavender, Merrill Feitell (for the early push), Laura van den Berg, Nina McConigley (and my whole back-office family); to Kathy Sova, Leigh Zona, Terry Nemeth, Sarah Vowell, Julia Fierro, and the Sackett Street Writers' Workshop; to Andrea Walker and Laura Tisdel, whose editorial comments made this book immeasurably better; to PJ Mark, the best agent I could ever have asked for, Cecile Barendsma, and everyone at Janklow and Nesbit; and to my editor, Reagan Arthur, who has the patience of a saint and whose scalpel-sharp notes improved pretty much everything about this book.

Thanks especially to my family: Reid Thompson, John Sellers, Pam and Joe McClean, and, of course, Mom and Dad, in whose barn I drafted the first pass of this novel and whose unflinching support gave me the strength to finish it. I love you all.

Finally, to Carrie, without whom this book would never have been completed—I love you.

ABOUT THE AUTHOR

Ted Thompson is a recent graduate of the Iowa Writers' Workshop, where he was awarded a Truman Capote Fellowship. His work has appeared in *Tin House*, *American Short Fiction*, and *Best New American Voices*, among other publications. He was born in Connecticut and now lives in Brooklyn with his wife.